KENNY ROGER
THE GAMBLER

KENNY ROGERS SINGS THE GAMBLER

Grant Stewart

Flamingo
An Imprint of HarperCollins*Publishers*

Flamingo
An Imprint of HarperCollins*Publishers*
77–85 Fulham Palace Road,
Hammersmith, London w6 8jb

Published by Flamingo 1998
1 3 5 7 9 8 6 4 2

Copyright © Grant Stewart 1998

Grant Stewart asserts the moral right to
be identified as the author of this work

This novel is entirely a work of fiction.
The names, characters and indcidents portrayed in it
are the work of the author's imagination.
Any resemblance to actual persons, living or dead,
events or localities, is entirely coincidental.

Photograph of Grant Stewart by
Neil Guegan

ISBN 0 00 225776 9

Set in Ehrhardt by
Rowland Phototypesetting Ltd,
Bury St Edmunds, Suffolk

Printed in England by Clays Ltd, St Ives plc

All rights reserved. No part of this publication may be
reproduced, stored in a retrieval system, or transmitted,
in any form or by any means, electronic, mechanical,
photocopying, recording or otherwise, without the prior
permission of the publishers.

Mary and Dennis

You've got to
Know when to hold 'em, know when to fold 'em,
know when to walk away and know when to run.
Never count your money when you're
Sitting at the table.
There'll be time enough for countin'
When the dealin's done.

Kenny Rogers sings The Gambler

When they said REPENT
I wonder what they meant

Leonard Cohen sings The Future

PART ONE

1

Rob said: 'What is your problem? Give me one good reason why I shouldn't do it.'

I said: 'Because you could die?'

Rob smiled sicky-sweetly and said: 'That's not a good reason, Natasha, dear. That's just being emotional.'

I gritted my emotional teeth and replied: 'It's being brutally logical, you twat. Your heart stops: you die. That's generally the pattern.'

Rich said: 'It sounds like a pretty good reason to me, Rob.'

And so it went on.

Rob: 'Look, Graeme's doing it, and he's not stupid.'

I gave him a look.

Rob shrugged and reddened. 'You know what I mean.'

Me: 'I know you've lost your page.'

Rich slitted his eyes at Rob and leaned low and slow across the kitchen table. 'You've been scoring whizz and not giving us any, that's what it is, isn't it? That's not very friendly. You jack little bastard. You've been doing sly whizz and it's sent your greedy little mind off to fantasy island.'

But, alas, it wasn't that simple.

What Rob was trying, quite seriously and soberly, to sell to me and my better half – Rich had been my boyfriend since the doomed days of college – was his mate Graeme the Steak's latest career move. Graeme the Steak worked for various drug companies as a career guinea pig. He'd started out at the bottom, popping aspirins under test conditions at thirty quid a time, but had soon impressed his lab-coated employers sufficiently to be offered a try at the flu jab programme. The flu jab programme was big time.

The deal was they simply injected you with flu germs, observed your progress through one long dark night of the soul, then sent you toddling off home with five hundred quid in your pyjama pocket. Hey Presto, money. The Steak was, of course, a natural: born to cultivate germs. He caught flu beautifully. His projectile vomiting and glassy perspiring won him handshakes and bonuses. Those monthly flu traumas paid for The Steak's third year at the LSE.

But if the flu jab programme was the big time, The Steak's next promotion was no comparison: operations. A simple faux appendectomy or a bit of splicing and rib-spreading netted The Steak a cool two grand minimum. Which was, of course, how he got his nickname – for what is so beautifully carved as a truly fine steak? Not that I could remember, at the time we were having the argument with Rob, the first thing about a truly fine steak.

But this time Graeme had, according to me and Rich, really crossed the line. Get this: The Steak was willing to have his heart stopped – under supervised medical conditions, of course – for ten seconds, for a pay off of ten grand. Can you believe it? He was going to let them stop his heart. I mean okay, you'd think about it, wouldn't you? For that kind of money you'd think about it. And in the end that's all you'd do. Now, if Graeme wanted to go through with it that was fine, the pincushion-head could do whatever he liked – to himself. But now he was trying to involve our mate, our loyal homeboy, our third musketeer, our mouthy twerp, Rob. And that wouldn't do.

In the end Rob didn't argue his case for long: he was never hard to persuade about anything involving basic style and subtlety – of which he freely admitted he had almost none.

4

(Clothes would have been a classic example if we'd ever had money to buy any. You couldn't have let him loose unchaperoned even in decent shops: he'd have managed to find something that cut cheese.)

But those were my boys. Those were the days.

'Honestly, there's no risk. It's a BMA-approved scheme,' Rob was saying, sounding significantly less convinced now than a few minutes earlier. Yep, we had him. No Risk, he said.

But I don't believe in No Risk, not any more. No. They don't pay you ten grand to suck Rennies. They pay you ten grand to dice with Dave Death.

But that wasn't the point any more. Rob had been swayed, but I'd been pretty hard on the poor lad, and the trick now would be to get him back on side, convince him we still loved his stupid arse before he started to sulk. You have not seen the true face of misery in all its patheticness until you have seen Robin sulking.

A change of tactics. 'Okay,' I said.

'Okay what?'

'Okay, you can do it.'

'I don't need your approval, thanks.'

'I mean I won't make a fuss – on one condition.'

'Go on.'

Rich coughed, looked down, and bit on his sleeve.

Straight face. 'Well,' I said. 'We'll have to test your heart. See if it's up to the strain.'

'Hmm.' Rob stroked his chinny chin chin. 'Is that right. Now what, pray, might that involve?'

'Waaaarrgg!!!'

It involved a loud synchronised scream and me and Rich leaping from our chairs, knocking Rob out of his, and pinning him to the lino floor. Now, like a lot of people who aren't necessarily the sharpest knives in the drawer, Rob compensates with brute strength; if we hadn't gone straight for his ribs we'd

5

have been hamburger. But we got him good and held him down for at least a minute. We tickled, he squealed like a pig. Then the bastards turned on me.

Rob: 'Rich! Truce?'

Rich: 'Why?'

'So I won't kill you!'

Rich, thinks: 'Deal!'

'Waaaarrgg!!!'

And then they're on top of me. Hang on, that's not my ribs. 'That's not my ribs! THAT'S NOT MY RIBS! What are you doing?' I'm pinned to the floor, helpless.

Rob: 'I'm about to demonstrate to Richard here the chest massage technique which will be required to restart my heart. It's okay, he knows the risks.'

'Rich, stop him, he's holding my tits!'

'One of them, dear – I've got the other. And it's in the interests of medical science. Carry on, Dr Robert.'

'Thank you, Sir Richard.'

'Waaaarrgg!!!'

So a potentially sullen and sulky encounter turned out well – for everyone but my pinched and pummelled breasts, that is. And this latest of our sorry money-making schemes went the way of most of its predecessors.

And we went on with planning a party.

2

It's a good story, isn't it? A funny story. I hadn't planned on starting in a light-hearted vein. But I just read in *The Advertiser* about Graeme the Steak's death last week on the operating table. I don't know what bit of him they were paying and displaying – I stopped reading before I got that far. But reading the little bit I did, just as I was about to start telling this story, it seemed to make a strange kind of sense. And then a few other things started to make a little more sense. Remembering Graeme and those times made me sad, but it made me smile too.

The argument with Rob was over six years ago. Like I said, it makes a funny story. But not everything back then was a joke, not by a long way. And unless you're a particularly cold-hearted capitalist this story doesn't contain too many laughs.

Our domestic arrangements, for one, were far from amusing when we had to rely on one-off pieces of luck like how we'd come by the flat we were living in – I'll come back to the flat, but suffice to say for now that we thought of it as our big break. So big that we were set on hosting a party in it that we couldn't afford. Hence the row with Rob about heart-stopping operations and our ongoing financial plight. So although the flat put one worry temporarily out of the way we were still absolutely skint. And, short of signing up for permanent flu or having our hearts stopped, we couldn't see how it was going to change. So these were serious times.

During which we did a lot of things both serious and stupid.

7

First off, we applied for jobs for which we knew we were qualified, and at which we were prepared to work hard (which, in hindsight, really was stupid); we thought up hare-brained get-rich schemes (some plausible, some insane); we begged, stole, and borrowed. We worried. We sweated. We fought. We talked.

Which brings me to the point.

It is time I talked again.

Now, they've got all sorts of places for you to talk these days, all kinds of groups and ready-made confessionals. Places for drunks, junkies, lesbians, husband-beaters, gamblers, trans-sexuals, ex-cons – all kinds of big talkers who need places to go. But I doubt if they've got a place for me. No, not for me and my kind – if there are any others like me, that is. Nope, not slotting nicely in with any of the above, there wouldn't be a state-funded hug-group where I could share my recovery. Which, when you think about it, is just as well.

But I do need to talk, and I need to stop making jokes. There are things I need to confess. Which brings me to you.

Hello.

Strictly speaking I'd fall in with those gamblers, but only very strictly speaking. Gambling is only one part of my story, and the very least of my confessions. My trouble – addiction, you could call it – was very specific. Very, very specific. I promise you, you couldn't muster a roomful of recovering thieves, drunks, and losers the world over who've done what I did. And you certainly couldn't find even one who'd be willing to stand up before said roomful of thieves, drunks, and losers and admit to it.

So I guess it's just us. My trust meets your judgement, whoever you are. Which is fine by me. I am not seeking absolution, just an ear. To be fair, though, if you're reading this, if you've made it this far, I like to think you are not unsympathetic. I imagine I know something about you, and your concerns, and vice versa: something has brought us together. We are neither of us really as unique as we think. No one who knows trouble, however strange the trouble, is ever alone: it just feels that way. That's the beauty of trouble: the terrible, tedious, comical justice of it.

Maybe this is a funny story after all.

Well, like I said, it's you and me. My trust, your judgement on me, a bargain – a bet, if you like. Yes, we have to take a gamble on trusting each other. For my part I already trust your verdict on what I did. I mean, it can't be more damning than what I've put myself through.

And your part of the bargain?

Just believe me. That's all. It would just mean everything to have someone know the truth. I don't care what you think of me after that. I know this story is crazy. But I really feel that if you can put yourself in that roomful of drunks and listen the way one of them would listen, then you'll see your way into what I did.

Try it. Take a seat. They are steel and plastic seats like the ones in your school assembly hall. On a folding table to your right are plain digestives and nothing stronger than coffee. The men and women seated around you, apparently gazing at the floor, do not look like men and women you want to be in a room with. Except you are one of them now. Yes, people like you and me. Sit down, smell the smells, look into the stares, hear the coughs and the sighs, imagine the hopes. Imagine the unimaginable. It's not such a big leap.

Imagine me getting to my feet and saying my name ('Hi, I'm Natasha. Although back then I was nearly always just plain Trash'), and nervously beginning my story, which begins six years ago in a borrowed flat.

3

Six years ago with the suspiciously pretty gatecrasher.

Our party was peaking, noise and sweat-wise when, during an attempted escape to the kitchen, I noticed her. There were two reasons why she had to be a gatecrasher. First, I didn't know her from Adam. And second, she was very pretty. Worryingly pretty. It didn't fit, and I was still sober enough to notice that it didn't fit.

It didn't fit because gatecrashers are not pretty – pretty people get invited. But she even smelled pretty. The air in every room was striped with grey smoke that stung the nose and eyes, and the back-to-basics, four-trackesque grind of Lou Reed's *Strawman* was flooding every sense that was still aware.

Strawman, going straight to the devil
Strawman, going straight to hell.

But everyone was noticing Madeleine – that was the gatecrasher's foxy name – and everyone wanted to breathe in a bit of this vision by the fridge. I looked around for Richard, but he was safely in the other room, for now. I would be keeping an eye on Ms Madeleine.

Strawman . . . does anyone need a sixty thousand dollar car?
So, the party.

The flat belonged to another of Robin's dodgy playmates, this one an amphetamine wholesaler and retailer known, without any irony, as blond Bob. That his name described him accurately is about all I can say in favour of blond Bob, which you could construe as ungrateful. But, no apologies, I just couldn't bring myself to like him. And it wasn't that I actively disliked him – he didn't give me the creeps or anything – there was just nothing to put in his plus column as far as I could see. Certainly nothing for Rob to get pally with. Bob was Bob. He sold drugs. And he was blond. And beyond that he might have been a robot. He gave away absolutely nothing about what made him tick. But he did have quite a nice flat.

And we did owe him. Oh yes, we owed him big, big time for the loan of his quite nice flat. And he was grateful to us, too.

The story went thus: the speed business was getting a little too fast for blond Bob lately. So, considering it politic to be out of the country for an indefinite period, he approached his old mucker Rob for a flatsitting favour.

I give Rob many shameless kisses and cuddles and iron both his shirts, Rich spends the last of his giro on two tins of stuffed vine leaves and seven cans of Sainsbury's strong, and Rob says yes, yes, YES – provided me and Rich can come along and share the shifts – and here we are celebrating our new home by way of this gentle soirée.

Strawman . . . when you spit in the wind
It comes right back at you.

All this despite my minor objections concerning Bob's prosperity being founded on dope and quick profit, insubstantial things which, it seemed to me then, apart from being scarily illegal, were likely to disappear in a puff of smoke at a moment's notice. Not like a real career, or real ideas, with a real future. How little I knew.

Had things panned out differently, the flat could have been good for us for a while. Getting in there certainly bailed us out in the short term, and all kinds of things were ripe to crumble without it. You see, by the time blond Bob made his offer, everything between the three of us was just about pissed away and ready to evaporate and stink. The stink of old relationships. Things, principally money and frustration and the lack of self-esteem that comes with such worries, were starting to grate at our cozy triangle. Cracks were showing.

And then what happens is some luck comes along out of nowhere and you just say okay. You just grab the luck and hold on. That's the way you have to look at it, I think – by not thinking about it too much. Luck isn't rationed fairly. It's nobody's fault.

Just think about it happening to you. You have a flat. For nothing.

For us it meant everything.

Me and Rich came to the end of our temp contracts at the Department of Employment in late July. We had no work, and without work we couldn't stay in the stately home – that was what we called our 'comfortable & spacious dbl rm in friendly shrd hse nr Leyton tube. £35pw inc. 1 mth dep.' We'd taken it despite the ad in *Loot* being a masterpiece of hyperbole concealing at least four lies. Well, it was cheap and it was ours, and we could kid ourselves it gave us independence. We told ourselves it would give us time and space to look for proper jobs. But if you've ever sojourned in bedsitland you'll know the kind of places where you want to have as little time and space as possible. So we inevitably ended up going out just to avoid going crazy. Which meant drinking, which meant spending, which meant not saving the money we'd need to get a half-decent place. Maybe not a fullblown unavoidable vicious circle, but a jolly grumpy one. And accepting the offer of moving in with my folks, the teacher and the diplomat (I say diplomat, but strictly lower echelon: admin, single-breasted, no pope-kissing or feathery hats – wrong accent and university), was way beneath us. I don't think I even thanked them for the offer. I certainly didn't appreciate the significance of their making it. I was young.

12

So when blond Bob's virtual penthouse beckoned, me and Lord Rich vacated our estate without giving notice, owing three weeks' rent and foregoing our deposit – SOP for moving on in London, leaving the landlord a week's money better off, and us without the harrowing departure interview/inspection with its implicit risk of losing your deposit *and* having to stump up for back rent. Rob sacked the knickers bar job he'd had since graduating with honours, and everything looked set for a new start in hippest of the hip Crouch End.

Bob's flat, our latest home, was one Lego block of one of those gorgeous big terraced houses built long ago for upstairs-downstairs families, and now fragmented to accommodate singles or nests of strangers such as ourselves. Never many marrieds or families, though. Which is no surprise. It takes money and security to think about getting married. Okay, the money might come along for a while, but it's a trap to think that just because it's there now it will always be there. Prosperity is the modern illusion. Your money is an illusion. It's not secure. You know it in the back of your mind. A good job is a good job until some terrified number cruncher with a pie-chart, whose continued employment depends on the termination of yours, decides your department could use a bit of downsizing; a successful industry is only that until it relocates to Matabeleland or becomes obsolete overnight. And it happens. It happens more every year. The speed of change alone is more than people can keep pace with, so who can settle? Who can think about getting married? I'm getting off the point a bit, but it all connects. No, I don't think I am getting off the point, and it does all connect.

Oh, boy. We're going to have to invent a new unit of calendar time. Something with the duration of a month and the significance of a year. We need to downsize time to keep up with

13

how events are speeding up within it. And then the new unit will have to keep on being downsized to keep up with accelerating acceleration. We'll wake up in the year 3000 and only be ten years older. Because one year means nothing when it contains the accumulated panic of twenty or thirty. I mean it, watch the news on New Year's eve. You'll wonder where you've been. I know people who've moved flats or changed jobs – or both – three times in one year. And no, I can't say I notice many of my friends exuding settled coziness all over the place and thinking about a future with 2.2 kids and a Volvo. Not then and not now.

After so long in the stately home, blond Bob's place was a bit frightening, probably too spacious and homely. We weren't used to homely. But it had something. Okay, the paint was peeling, walls were visibly fracturing at the corners from decades of subsidence, but there was love in those cracks.

Yes, this home was bloody beautiful. Everything about it looked and smelled as mortal and downright condemned as most of the city we thought we knew and loved, but like the rest of the city its mere survival this far suggested a certain resilience, a faint suggestion of hope, perhaps.

Hope. I'm afraid I wince at that word.

Wincing aside, Rich and me shared what we called the master bedroom, which, along with the kitchen, was on the top attic floor. It was really the wide living room of the one-bedroom flat into which the diplomat – my saintlike dad – helped shift my three-quarter-size bed from home. I remember he hardly said anything all day, just drove the van. Then after the lifting bit was done he stood for a long while by the big front window, not really doing anything, or looking like he wanted to go anywhere. We had to shift stuff around him. I remember he'd asked once on the way over how we'd come by the flat, and

14

I'd told him not to worry, and he hadn't said anything else. So I'd assumed he wasn't worrying.

I wish I'd listened more to my dad's silences, the way it seems he heard things in mine. But that's hindsight.

Now he was just standing, opening and shutting the heavy dark curtains – I think they were velvet, I remember feeling something velvet – alternately letting in, then shutting out the light. I didn't feel like asking what was on his mind.

Rob's room was the actual bedroom. Now, to me, a real bedroom is a room which is supposed to make you feel at home. But after student halls and the stately home it somehow didn't feel right. I know I sound obsessed, but it was and is true – I just couldn't relax. I didn't know when what we had would be taken away, I just knew it was inevitable. Something in me resisted being lured into settling in somewhere. And not just blond Bob's, but anywhere, because I was programmed now into accepting that everywhere was temporary. You know the deal: why bother getting comfortable, you'll be bugging out in six months. The homely furniture – bits like bedside dressers, and lamps and suchlike, blond Bob surprised me there – invited us to relax and contemplate actually living there, as if it were ours. I'm glad it wasn't my room.

Moving on up, in the deep eaves adjacent to the m.b. and directly above Rob's room was an outrageous old attic kitchen. I liked to think there wasn't a lovelier room in the whole building. Guilty as charged on all stereotypes, but if there was one bit of that flat that I played house in, it was the kitchen. Two porthole skylights peeked down through the sloping ceiling, onto an ancient white stainless steel sink unit and a massive pine table. Perfect. Old. As if to emphasise the room's credentials, a modern fridge freezer and gas oven cowered in the corners.

This was the room where we would make our decisions, discoveries, and mistakes, over black coffee, lousy Bulgarian red and recycled roll-ups, under the rare threads of sun that made it through the skylights.

The bathroom, by contrast, had been designed to save space in a submarine.

Once in: first things first. We signed on en masse, getting the worst job out of the way. I hate dealing with the system. I don't like to think about it. I'd rather work almost anywhere than go through the misery and humiliation of signing on again. Which I suppose is the idea.

Second things second: Rob took on the daytime cleaning shift at the truly tacky Barbarossa Diner because he knew that was when he could steal the most food, and because it was cash in hand. Our freezer ranneth over. We lived on ribs and prawns, and scanned the local free sheets in vain for real jobs, or any jobs. And in the few good weeks before Madeleine and the party we squeezed every grain of pleasure out of having our own decent place. Rob effectively kept us all and never once complained.

Right.

Strawman.

But one thing I did know was that us living in Bob's flat wasn't permanent, wasn't even reliably temporary. But what else were we going to do? Finding a place is hard enough when you have money; when you don't, and we certainly didn't, you do things like flat-sit for drug dealers, and like it. And anyway it was space, in two senses of the word: it was a place where we were free to pretend for a while, and it was time to plan and to relax.

The party was going well. All the pukers had made it to the toilet, and nothing more sacred than blond Bob's No Drugs rule had got broken. Yes, a No Drugs rule: our absentee landlord took a professional's view of other people mixing business and pleasure in his home. Whatever. We were all good drunks.

We'd invited mostly old student friends I was glad to see and to talk to again. I hadn't realised how much I needed to talk about some things. It had been a while. So, I communed with my peers, compared stories, discovered everyone's were pretty much the same as mine and the boys', and that a few were even worse. It was all more or less as I'd suspected. Read on.

A year after graduation and not a single one of our old circle had what you'd call a real job. And I don't think of my friends as slackers. And now most were barely getting by – sleeping on friends' floors, waiting on week to week temp work, pulling pints, or burning dogburgers at Mickey D's. But all seemingly reluctant to make a decision which would lead them in any specific direction.

Which is not strictly fair.

Specific direction? That's a good one – as much of a joke as applying for a proper job. Any one of us would have gone in any direction which meant we could settle down and shut off our crisis radar for six months. But not a chance. Anywhere. It was sad to see my friends like that. It was sad and it was a waste, all that talent and potential and hard work. People who'd once been so cocky and so awesome, and who were now absolutely cowed, shellshocked. I suppose I must have looked the same – although at least, for now, I had this flat.

Yes, I suppose I must have looked like a different person too. I mean, you don't necessarily notice these changes in yourself, but I'd made the mistake of quizzing Paul the Hippy, the first guest to turn up, about his somewhat haggard demeanour. After what he said I didn't like to question anyone else.

'God, look at the state of you. Heavy night, hippy?'

Kisses. Bottle of Thunderbird in the fridge – as if that would help it.

'Heavy week.'

'Been hitting the shandy, flower?'

Hippy shook his head. 'Staying in.'

'Okay. Lady friend?'

Hippy laughed. 'You're joking. I couldn't pull a cracker.' He held out a shaky right hand with a huge callous on the middle finger. 'Nope. Application Form Fatigue.'

I got him a drink.

Application Form Fatigue didn't just mean fatigue from writing application forms. It meant from lying.

Telling lies is a draining business, but SOP now – Standard Operating Procedure.

See, companies don't advertise jobs any more, they advertise Application Forms. You send off for one and you can spend a week doing it properly, honing your lies against theirs, tailoring your hypothetical skills to fit their hyperbolised requirements: and you send it off, and you wait. And you worry that you've filled it out all wrong and fucked yourself. And you wait. And two months later if you're lucky you get a form reply stating: your application is being held on file. And you think, on file? But I applied for a job, not a file? Just tell me yes or no. And then you think back to the advert and right enough there was never actually any mention of anything as substantial or vacant as an actual job. What you applied for was in fact the privilege of being held on file. Of waiting for something. In a drawer. Provided, that is, they're not lying to you.

Dear Mr Paul the Hippy, congratulations, you got the file!

Hey ho. Doom and gloom apart it was a good feeling to re-establish links with these people. I'd missed some of them a lot. But unlike the parties of two or three years ago people were definitely subdued. The energy now was nervous, the vibe not so much charged as recharging, running on low. It was tempting under the influence of too much Sainsbury's lager and Tesco bourbon – yes, there is such a thing as Tesco bourbon, and it's not half bad either – to follow that thought to its conclusion, to infer that what was not on show was the hidden nine-tenths of some psyche iceberg. That somewhere under the skin of every person in my kitchen was a little whirring motor, each small engine a small part of the collective hum of a generation regenerating. Only I was getting too clever. Trash the analyst. But I can't be accurate. I don't know how much of this is grafted on in hindsight. And I was tired. But it was good to see them.

The hours passed quickly. It was fun and then it was late and they were gone.

Except for the fragrant gatecrasher. But my radar had calmed down a few bleeps now she was – god, it was true, she was with Rob! Wonders, as they say. They looked pleased with themselves, creeping out of his room, modelling that just-fucked look. So Robin got lucky, good for him. Somebody always gets lucky.

But it makes me shiver now, remembering Robin with that girl, and her smiling. And her sweet smell, which I imagine wasn't quite so sweet any more just at that moment. Whatever, it gives me a chill. I still liked her at that point, at the party. So much for instinct – so much for trusting your sense of smell, of all things. Looking back, of all the shabby ex-student parties in all the shabby flats in all the shabby old world, I wish she'd walked into anyone's except mine. That sounds flippant. And I don't mean it flippantly. I don't know. Would I really wish everything else that hadn't happened yet on someone else? Could I be that cold? Sometimes I could, yes.

I wasn't thinking all this back then, of course. I don't remember exactly what was on my mind, just that I snapped out of a boozy reverie in time to hear our gatecrasher telling us how she knew a good party game. I bet she did. And no drugs required, she promised. And no stripping. Although by then who cared?

I didn't know what was going to happen. How could I? No one could have known what was going to happen.

4

I went along with it because I couldn't think of a good reason not to, and because I was curious. It seemed harmless, after all. Rich was one of those selflessly sweet, silly anniversary remembering boyfriends who would always get behind anything he thought would make me happy (he'd made a point all night of telling everyone the party was for me, the sweetheart) and Rob wasn't going to party-poop his most impressive conquest in months and possibly years.

Ah, Robin and Madeleine. I should explain about Rob and women. He doesn't often have girlfriends as such. Most of the time he makes do with Country & Western records. I mean it. It can be a bit of a worry, watching him longing, loving, and losing by proxy, through whining steel guitars and weeping fiddles. Johnny Cash, Hank Williams. I have to admit, some of it's pretty cool. Two years earlier I'd have laughed, said him and Rich should lighten up, get out a bit more, walk in the sun. But some of these songs have real teeth, a way of bypassing extraneous sentiment and cutting to the real business of the heart. They give you a raw memory. I was beginning to fall in with them and their damn country songs.

Anyway, as far as the real world goes, Robin makes the odd raid into enemy territory from time to time, and dates an actual girl. Then it's back to the wogbox and the Kristofferson tapes. Now, I like Kristofferson. That man has lived. I suppose that's what it is. In his and Kristofferson's defence Rob claims it's not possible to understand the opposite sex, only to accommodate them for a period of time. And he'd rather accommodate them for a week or two each at most. I'm not sure that's Rob's real problem, though. There's a lot of bravado about Rob, covering up a lot of uncertainty. In the meantime I think, rather like Kristofferson, you either accept him or you don't.

So there we were. Ready for a new experience. Ready for party games with Madeleine the gatecrasher.

A situation which came together by accident.

A chance meeting.

Some booze, some sexual communion, a new acquaintance.

Nobody planned what happened next. But somewhere deep down under the stagnant Now of our lives, we must have wanted it to happen.

That can be hard to take sometimes, knowing that something like this happened to me – that I actively participated in it. You look around and it seems that stories are always happening to the wrong people. Like what happened to the plan? Where's the script?

Wake up. Where do you think?

I'm not one for secrets, so I'll come clean now. Maddy's party game was a seance. Nothing too bad about that.

But it didn't end there. Me and the boys carried on and, using the methods we learned that night, held more seances of our own.

Still nothing wrong with that.

Until it got weird.

I don't quite know how to say how it got weird. Perhaps I won't, yet. I don't think I feel ready to. But I should explain about the gambling.

You know how some friends form a band together, or find god, or go skiing twice a year every year. Well, we invested in the occasional wager. I don't remember how it first suggested itself as a common recreational interest. Maybe because it was something none of our peers were doing. It seemed like a big adventure, even on our titchy scale. Poker, fixed-odds, football, the dogs – the dogs because it's easy to go along and get involved. There's a good buzz, and it's a good way to feel close to people. I mean it. If you play enough with someone you know, watch the way they bet, you learn about that person very quickly. The way a person gambles can reveal everything about them. It can even tell you if they are fundamentally good and generous, or if they have a petty, malicious streak. It can tell you if they are capable of love and of being in love. It can tell you about what they want from life, and how far they will go to get it. It can show you their soul.

Now, take the dogs. I don't go expecting to win any money, but I rarely lose. I just like being there, with the beers and the hot dogs (no pun) and cigars (acquired taste, but an essential corny prop), and legging it to the tote twenty seconds before the race to put my quid down – that's the way I do it: just watch the odds fall down from the crazy numbers, not a clue about the form or the animals. Just watch the odds settle down. Whichever animal still has a vaguely outlandish price when the race starts gets my money. From a thirteen-race card you're bound to get at least two outsiders a night come in at 6-1 or better. And there you are, a break-even evening with a full tummy, a spinning head, and everything to smile about.

And the boys have their own methods. Rich goes the whole hog. It's his evening out and he's going to enjoy it. Rich risks. All the big combinations, 1,2,3,4 in that order – massive odds. Never wins so much as a turd. But that's never the point. Rich loves seeing his friends' pleasure. So he provides our entertainment. He still only loses two quid a race, but he gives

23

us some big moments. Sometimes he's *this* close, and we have to do the big consolation routine. Group hug. That's ma boy. My Rich can structure the highs and lows of an evening as if he's written the script. He is my star in this story.

Rob, on the other hand, performs for nobody. It is not a game to Rob. He makes no concessions to mere recreation. He even pretends to understand the form, and to be thinking about what he's doing, which has got to be bullshit. What he really does is hang around the private bookies at the edge of the track, the ones who offer the decent odds. He never places with them, just susses the action and comes back to his seat looking focused and determined. And then he loses – never as heavily as Rich, only with a little more planning. And he knows he's been betting; it's a fight to him. He's challenging the mystery of the system, goading it to go one on one with the gloves off. That's Rob. Rob wants to challenge someone, all the time.

Poker's the same, three different styles. But the thing we love which is common to both is the sense of occasion. The pretence of the big time. None of us has ever won or lost more than thirty quid in a game, not even in the mammoth all-nighters we sometimes do with a few fellow masochists – basically because we don't have that kind of money, big money, to lose. But we feed on the whole atmosphere. We don't mind being laughed at when we pass round the cigars and put on the tape. And people always show respect when Kenny comes on, and starts telling us to *know when to hold 'em, know when to fold 'em.*

Yeah.

5

Here's Madeleine in the damn flat.

Tearing sheets of foolscap into small squares.

This is Madeleine making a ouija board.

I couldn't help watching her. I watched her mouth and her hands – she seemed to be talking to herself in time with the movements of her thin arms. Her wrists looked very delicate as she worked with the paper. In fact, concentrating on her now, her only substantial bits were those impressive boobs. Lucky so-and-so, I thought. I mentioned she was pretty. She had a lovely face, very *Just Seventeen*, although I doubt the boys bothered to look that high up. Her mouth was a subtle overbite around very white teeth like milk teeth, which gave her a shy look. Dinky freckles clustered where her nose and cheeks touched her wire glasses. Her hair was short and noth-ingy which, like the rest of her look – very plain, ever-so-unplanned – must have taken some confidence to carry off. And she really did seem confident to the extent that she was unconcerned, even unaware of her own physical form. And she'd slept with one of the boys in the room! If I'd been five years younger I'd have instantly elevated her to Perfect Role Model status and made it my life's work to be just like her. But I wasn't five years younger and, if anything, I felt slightly uneasy.

It was all controlled from the eyes, I decided. Very very pretty, and very very modest, but with something behind them. It was the glasses that made it work. Without those little frames her red–brown eyes would have been too intense, and you might have noticed nothing but eyes and boobs, and she would have risked looking awkward. This way she could tone down her look and use the eyes if she wanted. Cunning. I wondered if I ever inspired such intense scrutiny and analysis. Then I wondered what Rich thought about every little thing about me. Then I looked across at Madeleine's boobs and down at my own, and over at Rich, and decided it was going to be a long night.

She sat cross-legged in the centre of the carpet, tearing paper amid the corks and cans and cigarette butts. Rob lay on his stomach a few feet away, looking about ready for seconds of her body. But he'd have to wait. I was leaning against Rich where he sat with his back to the bed. When I rubbed my cheek across his thick shoulder I could breathe in the flavours of his hair and skin.

Maddy's bits of foolscap were about an inch square and they reminded me uncomfortably of communion wafers. When Madeleine put them aside she seemed to know how many she had. Then she took another sheet and began tearing off longer strips of about one inch by three. She made four of these.

She said: 'Pen.' Rob fetched.

This is all very very silly, thinks Trash. Trash is very mature. But Trash is enjoying it.

She's enjoying watching the fragrant gatecrasher take the Barbarossa ballpoint and begin writing on the scraps of paper in big, clear upper case characters. The letters of the alphabet A–Z and the numbers 0–9 – I was right, exactly thirty-six squares.

She took the four large rectangles of paper and wrote on them. One neat word each: YES. NO. GOOD. BAD.

I was feeling fidgety now and not so drunk. I was paying

attention against my will. I wanted to watch Madeleine but I also wanted to get her out of my home, and to go to bed and to sleep and not to have to think or to know that I'd ever met her. This was a strange thing she was doing in my home. But she was hypnotising me, and I was letting her. Blood was rushing to my legs. When she breathed out and whispered I could hear my heart.

'Flat surface.'

Maddy's voice was barely more than a breath, but we jumped to it as if we'd heard the words inside our heads, and carried in the glass coffee table from Rob's room and set it down. We waited. She looked up and winked and smiled, and we breathed and sat back down.

Why was I so curious?

'One on each side.'

We spaced ourselves around the square table as instructed.

Why was I letting this girl boss me? She was – just about – prettier than me and she was in my house and getting all the attention. I should have been bristling, but instead I felt good and comfortable – *that's* what I didn't like. I could see the boys' reflections in the clean smoked glass to my left and straight ahead, Madeleine's to my right. I whispered, 'What happens now?' (Why did I think I had to whisper?) Maddy didn't answer but began moving the papers from the floor onto the table.

They arranged themselves under her fingers like a big flower, with the alphabet and numbers forming a circle, as wide as the table could hold. Inside this outer ring Maddy placed her four words, GOOD, BAD, YES, NO. YES and NO made the left and right points of a loosely-structured diamond. The high and low points were GOOD and BAD. In the centre of the word diamond was a space. Maddy was waiting for something. She seemed to think we should know what. After a few moments she said, "Glass." Nobody moved.

She said it again in that big little voice.

A real glass. Now, Bob had packed away most of his break-ables, and our stuff consisted strictly of essentials.

There's a thought. I wonder if I could have stopped every-thing there and then, just by saying, no, we don't have any wine glasses.

Anyway I remembered the plastic cups we'd splashed out on for the party, and before I realised I was doing it, I'd suggested using one. To my surprise Maddy said: 'Fine.'

'So what happens next?'

'I need fingers, one each on the bottom of the cup.'

The required digits were duly volunteered.

'Don't press heavily, just rest your finger lightly and relax the whole of your arm. Imagine four little fingers falling asleep together.' She looked into Robin's eyes, and then for longer into mine. 'When the cup starts to move, go with it. Let your arm be led.'

I felt hot.

'Now breathe out and relax.'

Maddy's eyes closed and she began breathing deeply and steadily. We mimicked her automatically. I opened one eye and watched her cheeks change colour, her shoulders and chest rising and falling. I let myself inhale the warm wine smell coming from her mouth, or maybe it was from mine. When she stopped the heavy breathing she was rocking gently back and forth, finally slowing to a stop.

'Is there anybody there?'

That ruined it. Those words broke the spell for me. I was tempted to laugh, but that would have been cruel. But did people really say that? Was she taking the piss out of us?

She carried on.

'Is there anybody there who wants to talk to us? Any of us?'

I was disappointed and I was sobering up and I needed a wee.

'Does anyone have a message for anyone here?'

28

Nope.

'Is there anyone at all?'

After about five minutes of this I was dead fidgety and I really needed that wee. But I also felt sorry for Maddy. I hoped she hadn't picked up any cruel vibes coming off me. I wanted her to get somewhere with this now just so she could save face. But I didn't know what getting somewhere meant.

Maddy didn't look embarrassed, or in the least discouraged. I suppose her composure and confidence were infectious because I let myself fall under her spell again. Her eyes were still closed, and not clenched shut in intense concentration, but heavy and still, as if they had slid shut like perfect little doors. Just the tips of her white teeth were showing under her top lip. And I felt my eyelids slipping and the room becoming fuzzy. And she breathed and her top lip flickered between breaths and words, and when she spoke I shook myself awake, and she licked her lips and closed her eyes tight, like she'd felt a sharp pain.

Then the cup moved.

What am I doing here?

6

The stint at the Department of Employment was my first real job ever, and it showed. I'd been pretty sheltered up till then. I know me and Rich were lucky getting work at the same place – getting any work at all – but it still seemed like a hell of a pointless slog. It was a shock to the system. It was a temp contract – no benefits, no overtime, zip.

And it was nights.

In our case the work itself was easy enough, if dull, just basic data input. Nine hour shifts, lunch at one a.m. No big deal in theory. But – and this is where it becomes difficult to explain – nights are absolutely a whole different perspective. Literally a darker experience. It gets to some people. All those horror movies about crazy blade-wielding nightwatchmen? Totally plausible. I promise you, a few random axe murders seem like reasonable behaviour after a week on the graveyard shift. Just the different thoughts that occur to you, staring out of your cubicle window at the black and orange night, the cold windows and walls; well, I won't go into it. There are black silences at those times which, I am convinced, are the silences you are only meant to sleep through. You are seeing places in the mind you shouldn't see.

No, it's no big deal in theory. But adjusting, so that for five days out of seven, day becomes night, attacks your system in ways that your body clock just won't accept. It is not the way humans are meant to live. Examples: your skin sags; your shit turns some weird colours; your periods stop (for men it seems like they start); sleep feels like concussion, or an overdose of anaesthetic; you have a never-ending head cold. By every Thursday night you want to spit blood and kill children. No prisoners. Come over to the dark side.

The effect of all this on my relationship with Rich isn't hard to imagine. At college we'd been used to our time being our own. You worked hard or you didn't, and the rest of the time you did what you wanted. And if you could cope with the grind of study and a diet of plain pasta, it could be a good life. You could imagine a purpose, a goal. But that job working nights was some sharp taste of my new reality. If before it I had been naïve, now I just felt tired and grey.

On top of that we hardly saved a penny from that job. Apart from needing to get out of the stately home our money trickled away on a succession of little rewards to ourselves for the shit we'd gone through earning it.

It was all waste. Just existing. Any spare energy we had went on fighting which, I'm not proud to say, occasionally got physical. And I don't blame Rich. I can't remember who started it, but I know the hands usually lashed out in both directions. It's hard learning that you're not too good to sink to that level. It's hard but it's part of life; learning that no one is too good to be worse than the worst there is. We shouldn't judge so much. I don't remember much love of any kind during that time. The few times we reached for each other were desperate, like we were making up for something. I felt sorry for Rich, struggling to tell me with his body what we both knew and felt instinctively: I'm sorry that this is our life. And I couldn't help him, because I had no ideas. I couldn't see how anything was going to change. But fighting is the way it always ends up: you turn in on yourselves. An age-old problem. You hit sideways and downward instead of striking up towards the cause of the problem, the hand that drip-feeds you.

And that's just it. Despite everything, I remember how grate-

31

ful I felt every time our contract at that dump was extended – in the end we did a whole year.

And there was Rob, who had his own troubles. I won't pretend I wasn't one of them – we weren't immune to the Three's a Crowd thing, which worked in all sorts of permutations. But poor Rob. Working in a crumby bar, the one thing he'd gone to college to avoid ever having to do again. This was how easy it was to prize friends apart. One day you're the three musketeers, all for one and all that, the next you just care more about yourself in the end than about them, you're learning to look out for number one, although you swore all kinds of allegiances and sacrifice. And when you realise the allegiances might mean nothing it makes you ashamed of yourself. It all goes through your mind, all this stuff, before you see it for what it really means: that you're just sick of struggle.

Yes, there was college, and now there was this. There were three years of excelling at something *absolutely useless*, and now there was working in a pub for three quid an hour.

My head hurts.

Money.

Money becomes the one thing which is important, although you swore blind you'd never crave money in that way, that money isn't everything, it's just a means to an end, blah blah blah. But you can't stand being poor with your friends. You want to look up to them. You want to have time to love someone. You are immature, you don't understand that what you are doing, this very struggle, is itself the strongest kind of love.

Crap. That means nothing. You just want some money. You want out, you see yourself in your mind clawing your way over the rim of the pail, and that's all you aim for.

Madeleine's beaker crawled in slow jerks to the left and settled for a moment by the word YES, then slid back to where it had started from in the centre of the table. Maddy smiled. I bet my face was as white as the boys'. I felt shock, then suspicion, then I don't remember what.

Rich spoke first. 'Who did that?' he whispered. The whispering of a novice.

Rob said: 'I didn't move it.'

Me: 'Me neither.'

'No one moved it.' Maddy's voice was too cocky.

Rob (no longer whispering): 'I swear I didn't move it.'

Rich: 'Well it wasn't me, boyo.'

Me, not convinced: 'Someone did. This is pants, it's a trick. One of you was pushing that cup.'

This routine must happen every time, and I suppose whether you go any further depends on how much you trust the people around the table. Whatever, it's very repetitive, and it gets very boring very quickly. Maddy must have heard it a hundred times, assuming she played this game a lot. Now, she just sighed and left us to argue it out.

Rich again: 'How could we, though? Think about it.'

Yep, we thought about it.

'It would take two people working together to move that cup.'

Good point. Three pairs of eyes scanned the group, looking for clues to possible alliances.

'It can't be done,' Maddy interrupted, apparently unflappable. Then, very slowly, for the benefit of us idiots: 'If any number of us tried to move that cup the others would suss it straight away. Just watch everybody's arms. That's why I told you to relax.' She made circular movements with her hands. 'You would see the tension. The cup falls over with too much pressure, I've seen it happen.' That was that, then. 'Now, do you want to go on?'

7

It sounds simple. Did I want to go on?

Well, the cup had moved, the rules had changed. I don't know what I had expected to happen – probably nothing.

But something had certainly happened to me.

I'm trying to remember if I was scared in those first moments. Was it then or later I thought about the warnings drummed into me all my life from people: teachers, priests, nuns. Warnings to recoil from anything stronger than Sunday supplement astrology. Now I lost faith long ago. But believe me, those warnings come back at you from somewhere. I know that's why I was so reluctant to get into the game at first, and I'm sure it's at least partly why I was so devout when I did come around. I'm a catholic, trained in magic from birth; transubstantiation is in my blood whether I want it there or not, always.

The boys' belief in the game is harder to explain, although simpler to understand in the end.

I wish, though, that I'd listened to those warning voices: *Don't pry here, this is not your place, this is another place.* No, I don't remember being scared, as such. But I do recall knowing how much the teacher and the diplomat would hate what we were doing. Which on its own was enough to make me want to go on, and on. Nope, there ain't nothing like a good sin.

And this was a good sin. It felt cool and different, and I don't want to give the impression that it was – in theory – anything else. But I'll stress what Maddy stressed before we went any further, that if handled carelessly this would very quickly cease to be a bit of a giggle, and would become uncool, pronto. There are real dangers in fiddling with dead people.

Okay, Maddy's list of principle precautions and hazards which, at this stage, we were taking with a big dose of salt.

One: the necessity of a thorough ritual banishing of the spirit at the end of each session so it couldn't remain in the cup and hence the room. This had to be done with absolute care and concentration. You didn't want ghosts in your home. (Was that really possible? She's the boss, I suppose.)

Next: there were mischievous spirits who would tell us lies. We had to watch out for these. (What did she mean? We'll come back to it, you'll see.)

Finally the most important warning: there may be things we didn't really want to know, and that we ought not to ask, however much we were tempted. (Again, mystified, but curious.)

Right, so Maddy very responsibly warned us about all these things. And she was right, they were dangers. Dangers, warnings, consequences. But as I said before, you make your own mistakes.

Our father
who art in heaven,
what happened next served us
bloody well right.
    Amen.

'Is there anybody there?' Maddy began again. This time the cup moved immediately. It crawled to YES and stayed there. 'Go back to the centre of the board,' Maddy ordered. Her voice was soft and the cup obeyed.

Maddy was right, nobody was pushing the cup.

This was a good party game. Yes, doors in our minds were creaking slowly open.

'Do you have a message for anybody here?' Maddy asked. I glanced at the boys in turn, reading their thoughts. (Let it be me, but DON'T let it be me, but let it be me only DON'T let it. And so on.)

The cup said YES. It moved back to the centre and from then on did so after each completed answer.

'Who do you have a message for?' Something in the sound of her words was beautiful to hear.

The cup stuttered away from the centre of the circle. I remember thinking: It seems so easy. Could I do this?

I licked my teeth. Little white teeth.

It picked up speed and left the word diamond, heading toward the outer ring of numbers and letters, then completed a revolution of the board before settling on the letter R. The boys exchanged a look. Rob started to say something but the cup overtook him. *Now* I was getting scared. For the first time it occurred to me that this might be more than just moving objects and Is There Anybody There.

On Maddy's version of the board the letter R lay almost pre-cisely at the 6 o'clock position. The cup moved back on itself, from left to right, past the letter O. That was it. A flash of eye contact around the table and Rich took a deep breath.

Then the cup stopped, doubled back, and arrowed off its course to touch the paper edge of the letter O.

Rich exhaled.

Rob whispered, 'You fucking cheat.'

I stifled a laugh.

The cup made a further stop at B, then insisted on sanding our nerves by crawling slowly in turn to I and N. Then back to the centre.

Maddy looked at Rob. 'Keep going?'

The boy had no choice, we'd have lynched him if he'd

chickened out now. And anyway it was just a bit of fun.

Rob looked up at no one in particular and nodded. '*Vaya co dios, muchachos.*'

Maddy looked bemused.

I said: 'Never mind.'

We waited for her next question. What is the message? That's what she would ask. Ask it, Maddy . . .

'Ask it, Trash?'

'What?'

'Ask it the next question.'

I reddened. 'I'm not doing this,' I said, my voice trembling.

'It's all right, you'll be fine. Just ask the right questions. You don't need me.'

I managed a whisper: 'I don't want to.'

We were talking to each other, no one else. 'It's okay. Go on, I'm not doing all the work. Not all night.' Maddy smiled and her lips opened.

I looked away, not knowing what I wanted to do. 'It's your game,' I said. 'It's not *my* game.'

I heard her speak and couldn't answer. 'It can be your game. It's your party.'

What was I thinking? I looked at Rich for support, got none. He looked perfectly happy for me to take control. He looked like it was the perfectly natural thing to do. He couldn't have known the things that were in my mind. I'm not sure I knew what all of them were myself. Maddy caught my eye, then closed her eyes and nodded, and that was that.

Shifting from my bottom to my knees I took my finger off the cup, did a bit of theatrical hand-stretching, giggled, and replaced my finger. I nodded at Maddy and cleared my throat.

I mumbled something hopeless.

Maddy: 'Try again, Trash.'

'What's your message?'

37

Still nothing.

Rob: 'Try something else.'

'Ask a different question.' It was Rich. He was really into this.

I began to get just a wee bit carried away.

'Who is the message from? Who are you?'

Maddy whispering: '*Good!*'

Nothing. *Nada*, as Rob would say.

'Who are you?' I asked again, louder, the sound of my own voice surprising me. I sounded good, but I didn't sound like Maddy. The only way I can describe what I heard in my voice was that I didn't sound like myself any more. Definitely someone else. But the voice and the face that my subconscious chose to present me with was, for some reason, James T. Kirk. I swear.

Oh, boy. Beam me up.

The cup set off from the centre with quite a pull towards the 9 o'clock position – the number 1 – but continued clockwise without stopping until it reached the letter F at about 2 o'clock. It indicated F and continued clockwise. Next was R. Then the cup backtracked, past F to E. It seemed to stall for a few seconds at E, then limped to D.

Rob started to protest: 'Easy, tiger. Don't pass GO. Don't know any Freds. I don't – oh, shit.' It hadn't finished.

With daunting speed the thing launched itself around the makeshift ouija board, pausing at letters to indicate its choices, moving on, spelling, talking. Finally it made two complete turns without stopping and returned to the centre. Maddy had been writing down the letters as they were indicated. I was wired. I started unscrambling the message in my head. In the end it was easy enough to read.

FREDALOVESOURROBIN.

FREDA LOVES OUR ROBIN.

And no spelling mistakes.

Very touching.

Jesus. Big. Fat. Deal.

I sighed and collapsed on the carpet.

8

Well, that's lesson one in talking to the dead.

I'll spare you the rest of Rob's chat with his granny, you didn't miss much. Don't get me wrong, seeing the process was interesting and we were all reasonably impressed by the whole show. But we'd have preferred a juicier subject. Our encounter with Freda was hardly *The Exorcist*.

But we learned a few important things.

For example, ghosts – if you believe these were ghosts, and we really didn't yet – are just like anyone else in that they mess up when they get tired. It's possible, and quite fascinating, to follow the pattern of their deterioration. First their spelling goes, then the cup slows down to a crawl, and finally their messages get garbled and come out like code, and you have to become an interpreter. Although once that starts happening, Maddy said, it wasn't worth persevering. The ghost is all used up.

She was right about other things, too. Our next contact was with one of those cheeky spirits she'd warned us about. This promised to be more interesting. I was still master of ceremonies. We made the contact straight away. It went like this.

'Can you give us your name?'

YES.

'Spell it, please.'

The cup with four fingers set off around our sad arrangement of scrap paper, moving steadily, not stalling.

RUTH.

'Return to the centre.' It did. 'Anyone know a Ruth?'

A weary sigh from Rob's corner. 'Oops.'

'Relative?' I asked quietly. I was getting more confident, but I was still quite in awe of what I appeared to be doing, and definitely still in awe of our guest. Although the boys seemed to have switched their attention completely to the game. Which was fine by me.

'Great-grandmother.'

'Oh, come on, man,' Rich moaned. 'Don't hog the spooks. Give someone else a go.'

'Fuck off. Get your own ancestors.' Spontaneous giggling all round. 'And anyway.'

We waited.

Rich: 'And anyway what?'

Rob suppressed his giggling fit with a cough. 'And anyway Ruth's a wee bit different.'

'Go on,' Maddy told him.

'Freda's mother.' Robin creased his brow and stretched away from the cup and the table. He pinched the bridge of his nose and squinted theatrically. Then from nowhere he produced his pocket torch and shone it under his chin. He looked great, and we exploded with the giggles again. Okay, it was funny and sharp and deserved the laugh it got, but being nominally in charge I wanted to calm everyone down and take it all a bit more seriously.

But then Rob began doing Christopher Lee, which killed the laughter quicker than anything I could have said. Poor Rob. 'She was quite a colourful character, dear old *Ruuuth*. Caused the family a fair bit of scandal and pain. Theft, lies, affairs, all that kind of thing.'

'Oh, cool!'

'Not necessarily.' In his own voice now. Perhaps this was serious. 'She was a bit of a schemer, by all accounts. Not exactly very trustworthy. Betrayals, hidden money after she died. We

41

could talk to her, but she sounds like the type you were warning us against, Maddy.'

Me: 'Maybe we'll find the money?'

'Sorry. They found it. It wasn't where it was supposed to be and it wasn't nearly as much as they thought. She tricked them all. See what I mean? And that's only one story. She'll enjoy doing it to us, is my guess.'

Maddy shook her head. 'Doesn't necessarily follow. Bad person in life can be a good contact at the table. They often love to show off, but they're not always naughty. They can sometimes just give you a good laugh. But you're right, she could be trouble. We should stay on our toes.'

'Trouble how?' I asked, a smidgen concerned.

Maddy stretched her hands and laid them in her lap. She had nice narrow palms with smooth white fingers and short clean nails. 'Well, like I said. She could lie, or she could refuse to leave – at the very least she could waste a lot of your time.'

'Time we have. Anything else?'

Sip of wine. 'She could turn up again pretending to be someone else – that's something to watch out for every time with one of this type. She could go on all night like that, until she's too tired, that is. And by then the whole session's over.' She nodded to herself and drank again. 'Yep. She could fuck it all up if we let her.'

I said: 'How would we know? About Ruth? Is there any way we could tell if she was lying?'

Maddy drained her drink. She'd drained a few drinks, and she wasn't looking tired. 'It's surprisingly easy. So easy it seems daft.'

Oh, well, if it's daft.

'It seems silly but these are the rules I learned, and I had a good teacher.' She stopped talking and looked thoughtful, then said quietly: 'A very good teacher.' Another pause, then she was herself again. 'One way would be to test her. You can test any spirit just by asking them questions they should know the answers to if they are who they say they are. It's fairly simple, but wastes time and the board's energy.'

'What does "the board's energy" mean?'

'It means there's a limited amount of spiritual fuel, if you like, that a group of people like us can pool before our aura gets tired and it's all just a waste of time.' She looked at me. 'The spell doesn't last if you don't get what you want pretty much right away. But if you want to be sure you're not dealing with trouble, you have to test your spirit.' She looked around her for something – Rob's cigarettes – took one for herself, lit it, and returned to us. 'It's a drain, but you always want to know as accurately as possible who you're dealing with. It may waste time and cost you some gas, but it's better than the alternative.'

Rob took the words out of my mouth. 'That's a bit dramatic isn't it? It's just a game.'

Maddy gave him a look. Never mind the messages from the cup, that look was the most convincing thing I'd seen all evening. It was as if she'd slipped out of her routine to let us in on a secret, or to warn us about something. But it was gone in a second. What she said was: 'Keep asking. Even if you end up getting nothing. Always, *always* ask as many questions as it takes.'

Amen.

Ruth passed with flying colours and gave us a good run for our money. Beyond revealing her identity she refused to answer Rob's questions until we challenged her to prove who she was. And after that it took an actual statement of disbelief from us to get anything solid out of her. And then she went back to lies and insults – but pretty interesting lies and insults. She must have been a colourful lady. I liked this game.

43

And she came back.

Having amused ourselves sufficiently with Ruth we bid the unsavoury crone begone and tried for a third contact, and found ourselves quizzing a long dead relative of Rich's from the eighteenth century. I was really excited about him. But after a few contradictory answers Maddy popped a surprise question: Henry, are you in fact Rob's great-grandma Ruth?

YES.

Who was lying? Henry or Ruth? Was there actually a Henry or a Ruth? All very good questions. Ask all the questions you need to, Maddy had warned. And keep asking them, and keep returning to the answers, I might have added.

For the first time Maddy looked ruffled. There was no point continuing. She couldn't give us a good answer as to why some spirits owned up straight off when challenged as liars. It didn't follow any logic. I didn't like to think there was a limit to her knowledge or her power, but there it was. None of it beyond the fact of the moving cup was very mindblowing. And what did it matter? It was a party game. Plus we were tired. We had, as Maddy described it, a knackered aura. We would get nothing else tonight.

Although I felt inclined to disagree. I could have sat there in that room with those people and gone on a little longer.

This is important.

Starting that night I stopped sleeping.

That's not quite what I mean. How can I put it?

There've been spells in the six years since all this began when I've been kept awake by my guilt about what happened – about what I did. But after the seance it was different. I slept, but I didn't. I closed my eyes and lost consciousness, but it wasn't rest. It wasn't warm and hollow and rejuvenating like sleep is meant to be. In fact, it was utterly exhausting.

44

What do I mean?

Get ready for this.

Dreams. I slept a sleep filled with indecipherable dreams played out at sprint pace against a background of TV snow and white noise. It was weird. And it certainly was not like being asleep, and not even much like being alive. Call me unbalanced, but it felt like the sleep of the dead. Nothing seemed alive.

And that wasn't all. You've heard people say how they've gone to bed so excited by some idea that they sleep restlessly, although soundly – that they are still 'buzzing'. Well, my buzzing noise was loud, as loud and as real as any dream can be, which can be pretty real. The moment sleep came, so did the noises. The buzzing first, then the dreams, the frantic race by inhuman voices and shapes to become a life. And never getting there. Never quite pushing me aside. I sensed a pressure cooker of ghosts in those dreams, trying to burst out. It was my strength they wanted.

My life?

I remember feeling cheated even while it was happening, not only of my sleep – real sleep – but cheated of my own dreams, because these were so obviously someone else's. They had to be. Where were the nights scheduled to be mine? Where was my consciousness while all this was drowning out my peace? These acid cartoon scenes were someone else's nightmare. I wanted none of them.

As for specific dreams, I can't help you there. No. All I seemed able to recall was noise, lights, more noise – and the basic plot. How the point of these dreams was always the same – the struggle of someone or many someones to join the living.

There was one more dream, one I do remember. And I first had it that night. But I didn't think it meant anything beyond the obvious – back then I wouldn't have admitted dreams were

45

anything more than emotional exhaust fumes giving off a stink on their way out into the ether.

This dream did not seem connected to the others or to the buzzing. It was a clear picture. It was of me walking into a bar which was decorated in black and red, but overpoweringly red. And a girl, Madeleine I see, is sitting on a soft stool at the bar drinking a white disposable beaker of thick red wine which sticks to her lips when she drinks. And she turns and smiles when she sees me come into the bar, and she looks pretty. And I sit down beside her and I'm sweating and impatient because there's something I need to ask her. And then the buzzing takes over and the picture goes wrong like a broken TV losing its signal and I'm back into the babel of the other dream. And that's all.

46

9

The morning after the party had slid into midday by the time I padded into the kitchen. The boys were sitting at the table under the dirty skylights, and looking only technically awake. Mugs of black coffee were in front of them. I breathed in its good, bitter smell. Home sweet home.

They'd been laughing about something when I walked in, and now Rich was groaning and holding his head like maybe laughing wasn't such a good idea. I smiled to myself. The two of them sat at opposites, Rob in his *Star Trek* jimjams – LIVE LONG AND PROSPER stitched above the pocket – Rich looking like a big bear in my towelling dressing gown. I think I was in knickers and a yellow football shirt, somebody's away kit. I descended carefully into the seat at the head of the table, assessed my own headache, relieved Rich of his coffee, and began sipping it, elbows on table.

That was a table. It felt good under your elbows. A family table. It and the area around it were so sacred that, tucked away under one corner, a matching pine milking stool piled with a few of blond Bob's odds and ends still sat where it had remained undisturbed since we'd moved in, even through the party. Strange. I must have inventoried the little heap of things on it a hundred times. Let me see: some classical CDs, mostly Wagner; a couple of books on immigration and emigration; a box of floppy disks sealed with duct tape and, at the top of the heap, under a tiny set of scales, a battered French paperback.

Something called *Le Locataire Chimerique*. Why do I remember that? Blond Bob, who are you?

Rich reached over and flicked on the kettle. It was almost lunchtime in the world and the morning traffic hum had died and the streets and the air were waiting for the second rush. Rich's tape of Green On Red's double CD *No Free Lunch/ The Killer Inside Me* was providing the perfect sandpaper and soul soundtrack to our hangovers.

> *There ain't no free lunch, no free lunch today;*
> *I'll buy you a steak but I'll take it outa yer pay.*

And the boys were looking how the song sounded. Even through a blurry head I could make out precisely their tired features: Robin's angular facial lines against his broad fighter's physique, which made him look taller than his modest five nine. Watchful eyes: sentry's eyes, I thought. You'd probably say Rob was handsome, though you wouldn't tell him to his face. You'd set off his insecure brand of vanity and then you'd never hear the end of it. Best just to shut up. Narrow eyes. Yes, soldier's eyes. I only knew him as a fighter in my imagination then, but I was sure that part of him would show itself somehow, sometime. He was waiting for his chance.

By contrast there is no fight at all in Rich's looks, and he's not so much handsome as cute. Rich's aura feels fashioned for absorbing impacts, making peace, spreading laughter. A different kind of man. He is short, and soft in the belly, and his baby blond hair makes him look impossibly angelic whenever he tries to be serious, which he says he hates.

And this morning – afternoon – with the raw lines, the facey film of oil, the deep pores of the day after – no, they hadn't slept well either.

Rob least of all. Madeleine had stayed over, and he wasted no time now in giving me all the gore, which was nothing new from Rob. I hoped Rich didn't talk about us that way. It's some need Robin has, to spread news of his conquests far and wide or else they don't seem to mean anything to him. There'd never be any question of Robin having sex merely to enjoy being with someone he liked. *People had to know*. Rich's stoic expression told me that he was hearing this for at least the second time. But Rich would never say anything. I've asked myself sometimes just what Rich sees in his best mate that's worth being best mates with. And then what goes and happens but Rob does something beautifully human which takes me totally by surprise, like working to support us all in that flat and meaning it, and not grudging us a moment. And then I have to think of him in a different light – until his next display of Neanderthal sensitivity.

Having said that, for once I couldn't help myself, and I giggled and cringed with delight all through Robin's version of the night's exploits. When Rich started to shake his head and gasp in mock distaste I gave in to it completely and just guffawed in a most unladylike manner.

Somehow hearing about Maddy like that temporarily broke a spell, although I wasn't sure exactly what the spell was. And by the time Robin got round to describing their final unnatural act the hypnotic Madeleine was no more to me than a good-looking gatecrasher on whom Rob had got his paws. Or was it the other way around? Whatever.

And then she disappeared while he was asleep. No phone number, no nothing. Just a game to remember her by.

Which left us.

'So what were you laughing about when I came in?'

Rich: 'I was just wondering if that cup of coffee you stole was going to reject my body if I drank it. I decided probably.' He coughed up a bad one. 'Yuck. Get out and walk, you bastard.'

I patted him on the back to help it along. The things you did. 'So I saved your life, pet.'

'You hi-jacked a valid medical experiment.' Rich spat into some loo paper.

'We should call Graeme the Steak. Get his opinion.'

'We couldn't afford his fee.'

The tape was onto *Sorry Naomi*. In the song I think Naomi is a dog.

> *Sorry, Naomi, there ain't no good old days,*
> *Just sixteen hours of hell for one day's pay.*

Ain't that the truth, Naomi.

'We were talking about places we've lived,' Robin said. 'Comparing them to this palatial residence.'

'I think this is pretty damn palatial.' A lorry rattled the windows.

'I'm not trying to be ironic, dear. You don't know the type of bijou residences we were talking about.'

'Poor love. Tell me.'

'You'd be bored.'

I pulled at Rich's – my – dressing gown, and whined: 'Tell me anyway. You were laughing when I came in. Don't leave me out. I want a laugh.'

'All right,' Rob moaned. 'Anything to shut you up. Actually, I'll tell you about the nuclear bunker.'

'Goody. Do tell about the nuclear bunker.'

'Oh, my soul. That was a place.'

'Go on.'

Rob drained his mug and breathed deeply in readiness for his performance.

'The nuclear bunker, named not least for its mysterious patches of radioactive damp, but primarily because we had some serious asbestos doubts about the place–'

'Fuck!'

50

'–some *serious* asbestos doubts, was a basement flat in Brixton.'

Rich: 'Stockwell.'

'Between Brixton and Stockwell. And it hadn't always been a flat. Which is the point. We don't know what it had been before, hence the serious asbestos worries. They could have had anything in there. We'd never know. Nothing smelled right.' Rob wrinkled his nose, remembering something. 'Anyway, once it was converted into a flat it was a seriously bad one. More chicken wire than glass in the windows. I don't even want to think about the wildlife. Ick.' Rob shivered. 'Apart from the bugs, we co-habited with a couple of star characters. They were a couple, but they had a room each while we had to share a big double room called the dorm. Never did work that out.'

'They had more money.'

'Mystery solved. Thanks for that. Let me see. There was Annie, whose only earthly use was that her boyfriend was the biggest Victor Charles dealer south of the Thames. Very generous guy. Remember that coat, Rich?'

Rich shook his head in recognition. 'By George, yes.'

Rob continued. 'Annie's boyfriend slipped us a taste of C from time to time, very lord of the manor. And he also gave Rich this coat. Beautiful wool winter coat. Secondhand, mind, but real quality. Annie's bloke's just too flash to only have one winter coat. What was his name?'

'Nigel.'

'That's right. Honest to god. He was a Nigel. Nigel the dealer. Not much of a ring to it. Anyway, it's February, and the first time Rich is out in freezing weather in his new coat – handout coat because he can't afford his own. He probably can't even afford a pint, if I remember rightly, and he's got dark green army surplus gloves on, and he sticks his hands in his pockets to get warm, and he's got a cold so he takes a hand out of his pocket to wipe his nose and, I'm not kidding, one of his green gloves is just white, just covered in fucking Charlie, just lining the fucking inside of his pocket.'

Unable to control myself any longer I laughed and opened my eyes wide. Then, walking straight into their dramatic pause, I asked, 'So what did you do?'

Rich: 'I sucked my fucking glove, what the fuck would you do?'

Rob began laughing at his set-up, and I joined in with a hearty cackle. Most genteel. I loved all this. It was total pantomime, of course – I knew every one of these stories by heart.

I wanted more. 'Tell me about the lodge.'

'You know about the lodge.'

'I wanna hear it.' Whining again, but still laughing. 'Tell me about queerfella.'

At the mention of queerfella, Rob assumed a pained and exhausted expression, which set off my giggles yet again. And the story and its cast of characters unfolded for what must have been the hundredth time.

The tape had ground its way round to *Mighty Gun* – Rob's favourite on the album. He interrupted his telling of the story every time the chorus came around, and during the shiversome, graveyard harmonica solo.

That's the way the west was really won:
Plenty of cheap labour, and the mighty gun.

The lodge, or Queerfella lodge, to give it its full name, was a rooming house in Finsbury Park which a few years back the boys had reluctantly patronised for almost eighteen months. I couldn't count the viciously funny stories I'd heard concerning that place, all so vile that they had to be true. I suppose in that sense alone it had been good value. 'Tell me about the lodge' was one of my standard antidotes to boredom or arguing.

The lodge had been decorated exclusively in brown, but not in the last thirty years. First and foremost amongst its inhabitants were the landlords, two Greek brothers that the boys had christened Queerfella and Anal Man. I forget their real names. Their dad, who occasionally came round to mow the lawn and give the boys obsolete career advice – 'Be a doctor!' – was Rigsby. Queerfella wasn't gay at all, there was just something 'jolly queer' about him, Uncle Quentin-type queer. He was actually a gentle and harmless retard who spoke in a self-conscious falsetto and tiptoed around the house in a peach-coloured dressing gown. Spying on the tenants, the boys claimed. Poor soul, he was probably just trying to be friends. The boys were cruel about him.

Rob: 'A retard with his pockets stuffed full of my rent money. He wasn't so fucking retarded. I ask you, the guy's a retard. I'm paying rent to a retard. Something's going fucking wrong. What's he gonna do with all my fucking money? Probably buy small boys and keep them locked in the cellar. He wasn't so fucking retarded when it came to divvying up a gas bill.'

Me – laughing, admittedly: 'Don't be so awful.'

Rich: 'Don't knock the cellar idea. We never did see what was in that cellar. I'm telling you, he was sinister.'

And so on, about him and Anal Man. Now, Anal Man was funny. So named because of his obsession with sellotaping IMPORTANT! messages to all the light switches.

'I don't know why he thought people had the urge to read when they turned on a light. PLEASE MOVE QUIETLY AND LIGHTLY ABOUT THE HOUSE AND STAIRS AT ALL TIMES! IMPORTANT! Jesus. PLEASE DO NOT FLUSH SANITARY TOWELS OR TAMPONS IN THIS TOILET! VERY IMPORTANT!!'

Rich: 'Why sanitary towels? There wasn't a single woman living in that house all the time we were there.'

'Probably all buried in the cellar with half the local kids.'

Me: 'Yuck! You sick sod!'

We were all laughing at Rob's revolting imagination now. It's good to remember laughing.

Rich: 'I wonder if he thought that mattered. I mean, I never saw him with a girl, ever. I bet he had stacks of tampons sitting in his room, him wondering what to do with them. Just hoping none of the other men tried to flush any of theirs down one of his bogs, because that's definitely not what you do with them. IMPORTANT!'

I was in tatters, tears were rolling down my cheeks.

Rob: 'There were never likely to be any women in that house, either. My god, you'd have died of shame taking a chick back to that hellhole.'

Me, blowing my nose: 'Just a suggestion, but perhaps if you didn't call us chicks?'

'Birds, whatever.'

I shouldn't have risen to it. Ever.

The cast of characters went on. On the next floor up was IRA Man, a reclusive nightwatchman from Derry with famously stinky feet who probably wasn't reclusive at all but just trying to catch some zeds after work, either that or ashamed of his stinky feet. Or maybe he was an IRA man and the smell was something more sinister. Then there was my favourite, Toilet Boy, a wannabe thrash metal bass player from Switzerland who cared about two things – his Fender, and his hair. His nickname – and this is gross but completely true – stemmed from an inconceivably lousy aim over the bowl, *with the seat down*. In the end the boys decided his urinating antics were a tactic to get one of the house's two loos all to himself by making sure the one he used was in such a state no one else would ever want to go near it. The mind boggles.

Finally, living stooped in the attic room, was Magi, a huge Ghanaian law student with a basketball physique who couldn't keep his hale and hearty voice below about a billion decibels

54

and who definitely didn't MOVE QUIETLY AND LIGHTLY ABOUT THE HOUSE AT ALL TIMES! I quite liked Magi. The boys were there for his first British winter. When it snowed he refused to come down from the attic for days.

Rob: 'When he eventually emerged he looked like death – he'd turned white.'

'Ha ha.'

Rob went all mock-philosophical. 'It was like he'd been cheated or something. He thought the world was one way and then he woke up one morning and found it was a different colour. Weird.'

'Poor bloke.'

'Poor bloke my fucking arse. Noisiest, most inconsiderate sod you've ever met. Jesus, I did cartwheels the day we got out of that place. Sixty quid a week to clean up after the fucking Addams family.'

'I'd like to clean it with a fucking blowtorch.'

From there on the recollections turned bitter, as they sometimes did. Because the funny stories that came out of living in places like that were only funny as a kind of safety valve. My brief stay in the stately home had taught me something about that.

But it stays with you that there are a great many people, people with what should count as okay jobs and salaries, who have to live in these places, maybe because they just don't earn enough to crawl out of the trap, or because they're paying off the debts they built up looking for a job. And all the while the landlords are stuffing it in the wardrobes and under mattresses, and the people are never going to pay back the debt and move on because they're forking out all this rent on a dump. It's treading water, all the time. I don't want to think about it. I don't want to think about when and how it ends.

The tape reached its second title track, *The Killer Inside Me*.

55

There's a light in your eyes
That always finds the darkness
In my soul . . .

So far no one had mentioned the party game.

We forced ourselves back to life and faced the debris. It wasn't too bad. The place was back shipshape in half an hour. Then more coffee.

Then, about two, we warmed up a couple of rusty-looking baguettes and grilled some liberated swordfish. But for some reason we were all still ravenous, so we ate a second meal – I forget what. But something like hunger was still there. It was weird. More coffee didn't fill the void, but just made us wired as well as unsatisfied. The day was strange.

We were fidgety, so Rob's cleaning money bought tickets for the teatime showing of *Jurassic Park* at Turnpike Lane. Popcorn, chocs – still hungry. The flick was forgettable. Something about monsters summoned up by tricks to a second life. Although I seem to remember Jeff Goldblum in leather trousers, which is a plus.

Back at base the food situation was getting embarrassing. They were going to have to roll me from the kitchen to toilet and back if this went on. But we were absolutely starving. We scavenged the party leftovers for anything ingestible, and siphoned the wine dregs, both colours, into a half-gallon jug.

When night came it was me who suggested another seance. I looked outside and it was dark, and the boys nodded yes, and for the first time that day we started to relax.

10

I met the boys at college.

They'd teamed up while working the eateries of Hampstead and the West End, as prep chefs and waiters. Dead-end jobs.

How did they end up in London?

I'm thinking about the boys and about why they came here, but I'm also thinking about everyone who comes here hoping. What do they think will be better? It's hard for me to get into the head of the person who decides that Hickville, Nowhere isn't for them, and heads for the smoke. I've always been just down the road in the suburbs; London is a commuter hop away from my family home. So it's hard for me to imagine a landscape I was anxious to flee – which seems pretty much to hit the nail on the head for most people. That and the small matter of there being no actual jobs in Hicksville, Norfolk and Nowhere. I suppose that would pretty much get you up and on the road to the smoke.

The boys both talked about having been desperate to get out of small towns. Rob had a favourite saying about where he came from. 'The smaller the town, the smaller the mind,' he'd recite. Meaning, I suppose, that he felt constrained, unable to express himself before he came here. Which I only ever found semi-convincing.

I don't know why he needs to hate where he comes from, and to have you know it. Then to constantly draw a line under things, to see everything as black and white. Finished or ongoing. Then and Now. But I suppose it must have taken that kind of strength of will to force yourself away from comfort – even stagnant comfort – into the lottery of sinking or swimming in the big city.

But what brings so many people here? Hasn't the word got back?

There's no gold.

But then we're back at my ignorance of the alternative. I've never been to Runcorn or Blackpool or Hickville. My imagination is anchored here.

And for me there is no imagination and no mind without London. It could never be the scene of failure and familiarity in the way Rich's or Robin's hometowns were, because London will always be the scene of too much collective longing, loving, and losing to be claimed as the exclusive scene of someone's personal drama. That's it's beauty; it holds no memories. You can leave it and come back and it will always forgive you. It's the Lie you Love. No matter how much we buy into it it will always remind us that it will be here, bought and re-bought for what it's worth and more, long after we are gone.

One day there'll be a study, a kind of genetic and behavioural census of the capital. And they'll puzzle over an answer as to why whole generations who have no blood ties to the place, who hail from anywhere and everywhere but within the mystical time zone limits of the M25, have developed physiologically and psychologically into the same race: a genus of teens and twenties who came to London to study or work, and who never left. And now they occupy the capital's spiritual halls of residence. Rent-land. They move flats once a year because the last place was shit. Of course, the next place will be shit as well, but it will be new and different shit for a while.

This species drinks and smokes and doesn't have proper carpets or any furniture of its own. The landlord is usually some soulless staypress bastard. They are overqualified for their jobs – they are overqualified for most jobs, which raises the question of Why Get Qualified? None of them are from London, hence the huge mix of accents and backgrounds and colours. But those old identities are quickly forgotten and absorbed into the fast future that five or ten years of this new life creates.

They bitch about a life they would never give up. And before you know it you're looking at my new race: the London Girls and London Boys, although they're really too old to be called girls and boys, but then again they're not men and women because men and women do things like buy homes and get married and have children, and this species doesn't have the genetic information to execute those functions. It has jettisoned unnecessary information.

They party as routine, acting their era, not their age. They're always seen with their own kind, moving on together towards thirty-five summers of being twenty-one and miles from mummy and daddy, a thirty-five year blaze of glory, a be all and end all, a means to a means and an end to an end. The freedom of the nineties with the prospects of the thirties. The effortlessly unbeautiful people. The girls abandon fashion and chic in favour of looking rough and street and just crazy enough to avoid hassle on the tube from all but the most dedicated psychos. The boys look just chic enough not to be mistaken for the psychos. It's a wonderful life, and they love it, and it's killing them. And it's better than Runcorn.

I digress. It's a fact.

Anyway, the boys met when Robin answered Rich's ad for a flatmate, and they began sharing. They may even have been working at the same place around that time, too. I was always surprised by the stories about what they did for a living, if living is the right word; they were bright boys but then again they didn't have a decent qualification between them. But I knew them, and I knew they were worth more than qualifications, or more than what they did to pay the rent. I suppose they just fell into the trap of getting something – in this case lousy restaurant work – to tide them over, but getting stuck with it. It must have been easy to do. When they first arrived here they were simply up for an adventure, they had no notions of careers and security, or of having to provide for a leaner future.

There were horror stories about those jobs in the same vein as the ones about where they'd lived. Most students have done it for a few terms, but the boys stumbled from job to job for something like five years, sometimes progressing, sometimes having to go back to square one. They alternately earned good money and bad money. Sometimes no money. Times like those they worked for people like blond Bob.

There were spells of relative affluence when they drank what they should have saved, and regretted it, and times when they were enjoying themselves just enough to forget about where they were. And then there were the times when they came down from the high; sobering times when they saw friends and workmates burn out or just give up from drugs, overwork, or just the city's wild appetite for fuel at the bottom end of living. Because the city eats the tired and the troubled. So, a steady stream of the defeated and shell-shocked returned home to the small towns, to distrusting families and suspicious former friends. And, first, to the dole. The long climb back.

There they were: working and living together, sharing their tips, wishes and woes, and what could be generously termed flats, all the time fighting the associated losing battles with damp, cockroaches, flu, mice, ringworm. Spending everything, and *nada* for a rainy day. Not in terms of money or of anything else that might matter. Five years of this. It couldn't go on forever, they decided. No, they would fight it. They would go to university and get in the fast lane before they burned themselves out. Bend before you snap.

I liked them straight away. I think it was simply because they were older. Most boys at university are precisely that – boys. And Trash thought she was a woman. It makes me cringe to think what I was like then. I suppose I must have had some good points.

So by the time I came along they had a history: they were a little wild. Just wild enough, in fact. They led me astray but didn't abandon me there. And at nineteen I was about ready to go a little wild. I had all the A levels and tennis trophies a low-end private education could buy, and I wasn't looking to make more friends like myself. I suppose it was my rebellious phase. The boys were pushing twenty-five, hardly old, but nigh on Leonard Cohen and Johnny Cash in my book. Wizened and weathered gods with willies.

There was something else about them. Something I sensed would come to matter, at least to me personally. It was that they were at university for a reason, not just because mummy and daddy expected it of them. I sensed real motivation in these two. A real determination – no, more, a real *need* – to take away something solid from the situation. There were a lot of wasters around: people taking their apparent freedom for granted, casually burning time.

But the boys had been through that. And on the way they had forged a real connection of work and love and respect, an *earned* tap into each other's story that I couldn't yet claim. Of course I resented that a little.

And yet they accepted me. They saw that I valued them, were grateful in return, and their gratitude was wonderful. They allowed me to stray further between them than most outsiders, especially a girl, would have dared push. They say

61

you can never truly understand someone else's marriage, never hope to get inside it. Well, that also goes for the friendships of men.

I'll get back to the story soon, I promise. But I'm enjoying remembering a lot of this. You have to allow me this part, considering what comes next. Remembering these things keeps me from other thoughts which I'm not ready for yet. Oh, I know their time will have to come. But let's get our fill of pleasantness before all this turns.

Anyway, we studied history. The boys really grafted, in fact. They saw it as their last chance. They had to settle on something and make it work. They didn't want to be waiters and cocktail barmen any more. I suppose they looked into the future and something they saw there frightened them.

The first two years went way too fast. We accompanied each other through the spectrum of academic life from occasional enlightenment to routine oblivion.

I told them we were all mature and cool, and they humoured me.

We did penance for our excesses, worked hard at our studies. No Education Is Ever Wasted, as people keep telling me. People who've never wasted their time getting educated, usually. We took extra courses. Rich acquired pidgin Spanish, boring us to death in the process. Rob concocted boiling polemics on Life and Art for *Campus Cramp*. I organised women's football. We were dreadful, but it seemed to mean something, something about equality and power. They seem like strange words to me now. Empty.

And that summer of the second year, like every other year, there were exams and there was a ball. I loved that ball. It meant so much, although I hadn't planned what was going to happen. I remember dancing with Richard for the first time, slow dances to all the wrong records. But that was how we felt. We danced entwined like that through the night until they

62

killed the music and turfed us all out into the dawn and the birdsong with our plastic champagne glasses and creased ballgowns. Mine was some monstrous shade of maroon, and Margaret from my Great Depression seminar group had pinned up my hair like something out of *Dangerous Liaisons*. I felt a bit of a dweeb, but Rich said I looked lovely. We kissed, and danced to the accelerating music of our emotions, and then we walked, leaning against each other, to my room, and were wonderfully alone until it was undeniably day and we were inescapably sober.

Then everything changed. And I don't mean because of me and Rich – Rob was fine with that. I'd never seen the effect of change coming over someone the way this one came over the boys. They were used to upheaval and nasty surprises, but this must have been like a punch to the gut.

Year three, final year. Reality dawned. Overnight the boys became serious and quiet. They were going to be out in the world again and they were going to need jobs and places to live. I couldn't imagine that yet – didn't want to. Didn't need to. I was okay. I had my family, and my family had money, and I could always lean on them.

Always, that's what I thought. Always.

But anyway, the boys had to be sorted, quickly.

It was the same for a lot of people. Discreet panic simmered tangibly everywhere. There was no more time to be tortured intellectuals, you needed to know where you would stand in this new world. You had to study your options and grab the thickest, heaviest lifeline.

First stop, careers officer. Which is a strange job title, considering. Ms Coffey informed me I was her fifteenth history undergraduate of the week. That set alarm bells ringing right away.

'Jolly nice young people. Jolly interesting subject, history. Jolly *interesting*. But of course, not terribly *vocational*.'

Go on.

Following a short speech (but not short enough) about what she called the 'spiritual rewards of the academic life,' and 'the mobile borders of the shifting employment landscape' (wow), Ms Coffey informed me that I might be adequately qualified to seek employment, in the short term, as a nanny. Although experience would help even in this area. Experience, Ms Coffey emphasised using the rubber end of a pencil, is invaluable. No work experience, she added, is ever wasted. I wondered on what experience of work she had based this wisdom.

'So, any younger brothers and sisters? Any little nephews, nieces?' That woman. My gaze drifted to the aluminium window – it was a new office.

The boys called in on Ms Coffey, too. (Numbers 27 & 28.) No joy. They, apparently, were not really nanny material. I wondered out loud if experience was the problem.

The graffiti on the loo roll dispenser in the Ladies in the Union bar which read: HUMANITIES DEGREES, PLEASE TAKE ONE had, after all, proved undeniably prophetic, if a trifle cruel.

No one had actually promised us a decent life or even just a job at the end of three years but, like everyone else, we'd assumed that was the deal. I was pretty sure that was how my parents had done it. Wasn't that how they'd done it? That's what they'd told me. You work hard at school you get into Uni. You swot at Uni, you get the job of your dreams and marry Jeff Goldblum. A lot must have changed.

A lot had changed, primarily in – to borrow Ms Coffey's phrase – the shifting employment landscape, which had evidently shifted somewhere else, and no one needed that many graduates any more. So why were we still graduating? Why hadn't anybody told us, YOU ARE WASTING YOUR TIME? Middle management, that was the problem, apparently. I mean that there wasn't any any more. An entire stratum of opportunity and security, gone, hacked out of the equation. Jobs at the top and at the bottom: one out of reach, the other out of the question. Welcome to Burger King.

For what it was worth – not much as it turned out – we walked the exams. We'd worked hard, after all. Three Firsts. Our fat defunct dissertations were lauded as model research and then locked away in grey metal drawers. We walked out of the Faculty of Arts & Humanities and into the wide world with, in one respect, a clear view of our future.

Of the tunnel at the end of the light.

And that was right. It was all suddenly backwards. We'd been told to expect everything. And now we had nothing. No job, no home, no hope of either. Nothing that meant anything. Now, none of this is the end of the world – if you are prepared for it: humans are resourceful animals when we can see the whole picture. But it was that sudden reversal which was the shock to the system. Many of us reacted badly, which is what some of this story is about. Here we were, supposedly the elite, the ones with all the opportunities.

But there were no opportunities. That is true. That is the part which is not a story. Our parents had grown up in the fifties and sixties and hadn't had to look much further than the end of the road to find a job for life. Now it was double and quit, double dip recession. Get on your bike and fuck off the figures. Opportunity sucks.

What left us feeling even more high and dry was that we were new to all this. There are plenty of stories of people born into shit and stuck in it their whole lives, and they are terrible and true stories. But we weren't born into shit, we didn't start there. Do you see what I am saying? We were added later. The heap of human waste is growing, and what is left for the lucky few is shrinking fast. Fewer people need fewer people. The boys, and now me, hadn't had the time to wonder about how to get out of the shit because we were still wondering how the hell we'd got in it.

I remember watching telly in Rich's room in halls, the morning we had to vacate. Students' parents were turning up with siblings and missed dogs, and tennis rackets and teddies were doing a reverse time thing back into the boots of cars. There were farewells, tears and laughter.

And there was an advert on the telly. I forget which charity it was for. It went something like this:

Little Abu sweeps the street outside his uncle's café.

(Shot of little Abu, black, gorgeous, ten or eleven. You want to take little Abu home and cuddle him, or at least sponsor him through medical school, which I suppose is the idea.)

Little Abu has the brains to become a doctor . . .

(Here we go. Shot of little Abu's bright eyes behind which, presumably, we are supposed to imagine his impressive brains.)

. . . *if his parents only had money to send him to school.*

(It's that simple is it? I must remember.)

Abu has the strength to be a farmer . . .

(Close up of Abu's skinny arms. This is obviously leading in to something heartbreaking.)

. . . *if his country only had the technology to back his strength.*

(Fair point. Abu's backers are winning me over.)

Abu has the nouse to be a merchant . . .

(Zoom into Abu's ten-year-old expression, a unique semi-starved wisdom.)

. . . *if he only had the capital to start a business.*

(And here alarm bells start to ring.)

Abu has the dedication to be a teacher . . .

(Tricky. How do they film dedication? They obviously aren't sure, because they show a shot of his broom instead.)

. . . *if there was only money to train him.*

66

WAAAH! WAAAH! NE-NA, NEE-NA! Alarm bells are busting my skull at this point. LIARS! FRAUD! I knew plenty of very able people who couldn't get into teacher training in *this* country, because there isn't the money to train them *here*. And then it dawned on me. And I was in deep shock for the rest of the day, even after Rich came to take the telly away.

Abu needs your help. Click. Hang in there, Abu.

It dawned on me that that ad could just as well have been made about little Seamus from Toxteth, or little Meera from Moss Side, or little Dawn from Streatham. And then I'm thinking, you bastards. What about me? Little Abu's in Africa and me and little Seamus and little Meera and little Dawn are *here*. And yes I knew I was being selfish, and yes I knew I was feeling sorry for myself and perhaps being unfair to little Abu and his entire unfortunate nation who were never going to get out of their profoundly deep shit because our banks had been bleeding them for decades. But I also knew that everything I was thinking while feeling sorry for myself was true, and that I had every right to spend a few minutes feeling sorry for myself and wishing terrible things on the likes of little Abu.

11

'Is there anybody there?'

'I've just thought,' Rich said, too quietly. 'I've just thought what wankers we're gonna look if any fucker ever finds out about this.'

I hadn't thought of that. The nightmare scenario. You'd *never* live that down. We had friends who were olympic standard vicious pisstakers. We all blushed bright red in a fit of group panic.

'Oooh Boy,' Rob said, laughing nervously. 'No way I'm looking a wanker. Not when I cover my arse by telling everyone I was just winding you two up all along.' Which he thought was dead, dead funny until I pointed out it could work both ways. Or, it occurred to me, three ways. I didn't like that thought. I had to thump both the boys for making me think it.

'You just watch it, Robin laddy,' I said as menacingly as I could. 'You wanted to do this. You believe this crap just as much as we do.'

'And do you believe it?' He wasn't laughing. Did I believe it?

Before I could answer, Rich said: 'Does it matter?' Good. That would do for now.

Again: 'Is there anybody there at all?' Just about managing not to laugh, we waited in silence for about twenty seconds. I was about to repeat the question again when the cup began to move. A crappy disposable beaker scraping over a piece of Habitat junk. But despite all the jokes, all the ribbing, you could sense the impression the cup moving made.

Why was that – that ridiculous sense of pride and achievement? What was so special about what we were doing? Was there anything about it which wasn't tacky and juvenile, perhaps even irresponsible? Was it really such a great game? But I'm getting ahead of myself.

The cup moved to YES.

'Will you spell out your name for us.'

NO.

Then back to the centre without being asked.

This wasn't supposed to happen. We looked at each other.

'Do you have a name?' I tried again.

YES.

Centre.

'Will you tell us your name?'

NO.

Centre at speed.

'Just dandy.' We were reaching our boredom and frustration threshold.

'What do we do now?' Rob whispered. The whispering was starting to niggle, considering we were getting nowhere.

'Ask it something else,' Rich suggested.

I nodded and took a deep breath. 'Here goes: do you have a message for us?'

YES.

More like it. Centre.

'Will you spell the message for us?'

YES.

Centre.

'Spell it now, please.'

The cup began its dance, pushing to select and nudge letters before racing on. Our movements were from the same comic ballet, arms and faces dragged in sync around the board by the message in the cup. There we sat: a messed up triple yin and yang, intoning the musical accompaniment to the dance. Three

69

voices repeating letters in murmuring monotones. *Ell . . . eee
. . . aay . . . vee*. More ballet. *Eee . . . eye . . . tee*. Humming
and leaning, following the spirit's voice.

My spare hand clumsily jotted each letter as it was revealed.
Two more: *bee . . .* another *eee*. Then the cup stuttered, stalled,
and returned to settle at the centre of the board.

LEAVEITBE.

We all mumbled at once, trying to work it out.

Rich was first. 'Leave it be.'

'Leave it be,' Rob repeated. At least he'd stopped whispering.
'Leave what be?' He looked at me. 'Ask it something else,
Trash. This is Y-fronts.'

'Like what?' Stumped.

'I don't know.' Robin sounded bored and wasn't hiding it.
'Try a different tack. Get something more out of it.'

'I don't think we'll get diddly shit from this guy.'

Rich yawned. 'Ask for another message, love.'

'Okay.' I shrugged and tried again. 'Do you have anything
else to tell us?'

NO.

'Do you have a message for anyone here?'

The cup moved away from the centre, downward this time,
and touched the word BAD.

Which stopped us in our tracks.

12

For about five seconds, anyway.

It was all part of the pantomime. We were still playing. *Behind you . . . dan-dan-daah!*

But the melodrama had a dark edge to it now; something about the strangeness of these messages rang authentic.

Although never mind danger or common sense or being just plain wrong, once you get this far into something it's not BAD, it's exhilarating. It's why you started, and it was why we went on.

'Okay. What does your message mean?'

The cup repeated LEAVE IT BE.

Silence.

Rob said, 'I think we should leave this gringo be.'

And then a thought occurred to me and before I knew it I was thinking the thought out loud: 'It's a warning.'

'What?'

All our hands drew back from the cup. We were taking this seriously.

'No big deal.' I shrugged. 'Just the most basic kind of warning. Someone who doesn't want us to go on with this. LEAVE IT BE. BAD. I think this is someone trying to scare us off.'

'Cool!' Rich's finger left the cup again and he started rubbing his hands in mock glee. 'This is like a film.'

Rob: 'If it's a warning it doesn't seem like it's a very friendly one.'

He was right. 'Point taken.'

Rich, no longer rubbing his hands: 'Is it saying this could be dangerous?'

I let a big smile register on my chops. 'You two are scared aren't you? Big soft lads getting scared.'

'Getting careful,' Rob said, reddening. 'Remember what Maddy said.'

So, was it dangerous? I thought about it and the only thing that made sense was that that was what we were meant to think. That would be consistent with my theory about a warning. I shook my head. 'Nope. I don't reckon it's dangerous.'

Rich leaned closer to listen. 'Go on, Trash.'

'Well, not necessarily dangerous. Perhaps this character just doesn't approve of this kind of thing – a lot of people wouldn't.' Rich nodded.

I said: 'I'm going to try something else.' I took a long drink of the pink concoction and cleared my throat. I wiped the back of my arm across my lips, and tried to think how Maddy would have approached this. I closed my eyes. Then I opened them and replaced my finger. The boys did the same, and I addressed the cup once more.

In a quiet voice: 'Can you tell us when you died?'

'Uh, easy, tiger,' Rob interrupted. 'Where's this leading?' I nearly laughed out loud; Rob looked terrified.

'Just let her do it, Rob.'

The cup ignored Rob and moved.

YES.

Good. 'Spell out the year of your death.'

I hoped this was going somewhere. I admit I was half-bluffing. But I thought I could see the shape of a story.

The cup slid towards the top left of the circle in the direction of the numbers. It moved among them, pausing at 1, 8, 2 and 0, in that order. I looked up at Rich and then back down at my pad. He was concentrating on me.

72

A quick scribble.

'You died in 1820?'

YES.

'Then what happened?'

Rob looked puzzled but Rich held a finger to his lips, hush. The cup spelled two words.

TO GLORY.

'He's a priest.' That was the story I'd seen.

I'd lost them now.

'Don't you see it?'

Blank looks. I don't blame them. I'm not sure what, if anything, I saw in the messages. There wasn't much to go on, just the good buzz of a hunch.

'Listen. The LEAVE IT BE business is clear enough. A warning. But I don't believe in the dangerous bit. The BAD business. I think that's just to scare us off. And who would want to scare us off? Someone with a moral – or religious – objection to this sort of hocus pocus. It's a dead giveaway.'

Rob: 'That doesn't have to mean a priest.'

'Granted, poppet. But TO GLORY. That's got to be somebody religious. Someone like a priest. Come on, help me here. And 1820? Pious times. Hallelujah. People probably spoke like that? Probably?' I wasn't convincing them. 'Beliefs mattered.' I shrugged and looked at them in appeal. 'I think it fits. I'd like to ask him.'

Rich shrugged. 'Why not? *Per que no?*'

Rob: 'Why didn't you ask straightaway if he was a priest?'

'Because you gotta be subtle, chuck' – because I'm making this up as I go along – 'gotta tease the answers out of them. Remember Ruth?'

Rich: 'Ask away. Nothing ventured.'

Rob: 'And how do we know he won't lie?'

73

He wasn't letting go. He was winding my works by being right too often. I ignored the big fuck. It's just a game.

'Fingers back. Any more objections?'

If Rob came up with one more argument I was going to say sod it and sack the whole sorry show. My finger withdrew, and the boys' followed it. I caught Robin's eye and worked myself up for a minor tantrum. I narrowed my eyes at Rob. He leaned back and closed his eyes, then opened them in a wide blink.

He said: 'Fantasma.'

'What?'

'*Fantasma.*'

Then I got it. 'Spanish?'

'For ghost. *Fantasma.*'

'Oh. Cool.'

'Thanks.'

I sighed. Situation defused. We all put fingers back on the cup.

'So, were you a priest when you were alive?'

A short pause.

YES.

Bingo.

'Fuck me!' Rich said. 'Clever girl! Clever fucking girl! Sold!' He laughed loud and hugged me, hammered my back, ouch. Rob shook his head and smiled.

'Bloody hell, Trash,' Rich went on. 'You can keep doing this. Job for life – sorry, death.'

'Oh, ha, ha.' But I was chuffed and glowing.

'Robin, m'boy. Meet our go-between in all future dealings with the next world. Just queue up with your questions. Anything you want to know. Jesus!'

We all laughed and drank. This was a stupid game, but way

74

cool. And we were high as anything. The famous five go med-
dling in the afterlife.

'Anything you want to know,' Rich repeated, not really aware
of what he was saying, not really believing what we'd done.

'Come to think of it –' Rob had stopped laughing quite
suddenly, '– there are a couple of things I'm curious about.'

13

I turned to listen, not sure what I was about to hear.

'For a start, is that priest hombre right, or what?'

'What about?' Rich asked.

'About going to glory. I understand why he said the other stuff, the warnings. But what about TO GLORY?'

'I'm not with you,' Rich said.

But I was.

Rob went on. 'Well, did he really go to glory? And if so, have we just proved the existence of god? Can it really be that simple to do what we've just done? Because if it is,' he lowered his voice, 'we've just got it straight from a priest. And he's not likely to lie.'

This was getting way out of hand.

'Who says?' I said, and laughed. But not for long – the boys didn't get it. C of E, the both of them. Besides which it didn't resolve anything. 'And who says he's a priest anyway?'

'You did – and he did.'

'But it's just a game.' Blank looks. 'Oh, come on. I don't believe you're taking this that seriously.' Pause, nothing. I looked round the table and attempted a laugh. 'Stop it. You're trying to scare me now.' This was where they were supposed to give away the joke and start laughing and jump on me and pin me down and tickle me until I cried. It didn't happen. I picked up the cup and twiddled its empty airiness in my fingers. 'Look, it's a little crappy beaker. A game.'

I might as well have cursed their mothers. Rob jumped two feet in the air. 'Put it back, Trash!'

'What?'

Rich: 'Put it BACK!'

I put it back.

Way, way out of hand.

Then I noticed the noise in my head, the buzzing noise which had been there all the time but which I'd only noticed now as it got louder and, for a long moment as we exchanged looks filled the room. This I knew then: they'd heard it.

A car alarm out in the street broke the spell. The buzzing receded.

Rich breathed in and out, stretched his hands behind his head and frowned. 'Shit. I don't know,' he said slowly. 'I don't know what to think.' I watched his face change as he took in what Rob had been suggesting. The poor lad looked as though at the very least his evening, and maybe a lot more, was in danger of being ruined. Eventually, still trying to appear relaxed, he turned to me. 'You're our resident former papist, Trash. Come on. Have we just proved the existence of god?'

Blank. Pause.

Rich again: 'Please tell me we haven't.' Another pause. 'Please say something to that effect.'

You could safely say that, coming to that morning, furry-tongued, not a little hungover, and farting like a Great Dane, I hadn't anticipated being expected to answer questions of quite that magnitude. The way I'd felt, just name, age, and telephone number would have presented a significant challenge. But, hey. *Que sera*.

Here goes.

Why me?

Because you got yourself into this mess. Trying to be too

clever. Enjoying your power. Making this too convincing.

Being too much like Maddy.

I looked at the two faces in front of me, the ugly, lovely mugs of my boys, flushed with wine and drawn with lack of sleep. They didn't want to deal with any heavy shit – heavy *mierda*, they would have said. Not now, not never. I could relate to that. This was supposed to be a party game for christ's sake. We had to draw some lines.

'Well,' I began, trying to look knowledgeable and sound confident about saying very little. I tried to focus on something, concentrate my thoughts. My eyes fixed on the drying rail in the corner by the bed. It was underwear day. A selection of my knickers, Rob's briefs, Rich's boxers, and a sad array of holes held together by bits of sock. What on earth was I doing?

I cleared my throat. 'I think all we've really done is prove to ourselves that it's possible to communicate with ghosts – and we sort of knew that last night. So really nothing's changed. There's no new revelation here, nothing to worry about.' So far so good. 'Listen, it seems to me we're talking to the living personalities of these ghosts, not their dead spirits. So what they tell us is what they would think when they were alive.' That wasn't bad. 'These aren't haunty ghosts – think of Rob's grannies: Freda's a darling, Ruth's a slag – no offence.'

'Absolutely none taken.'

'They're the same people dead as alive, to us. So it's okay.'

Nodding all round. They looked satisfied.

But was it much of an answer? Should it have been enough for me? Probably not. But I think they just wanted to hear a voice. Just about any answer would have been enough for people way too jaded to waste breath on questions of Life and Theology, and whose collective priorities just then didn't extend beyond Fun and Food. Everything else being too uncertain, too depressing. Yes, it was enough.

'Let's lose the priest,' Rich said. 'He won't tell us anything else. And we are in danger of taking this way too seriously.'

'Amen. Sorry.'

Groans and weary laughter.

Rich again: 'Let's find someone fun. One of the devil's lot.'

'WoooOOO!'

'Good woo, Rob.'

'*Gracias.*'

This was more like it. I poured more pink wine.

'Talking to ghosts. I like that: "My name is Richie and I talk to ghosts."'

'Arse.'

The rhythm was back. The right mood. I loved my boys like this. It made it easy to be a different person, and yet still be myself. I could pretend to be tough.

There was another round of refills.

Rob: 'So, what do we want to know?'

'The kind of stuff people usually ask dead people – if you get my meaning. We haven't done any of that, yet. We've got hardly any answers – any information. For starters we could ask about the future.'

It sounds daft now, but when Rich said that, it actually sounded harmless.

'Will they tell us?'

'What do you think, Trash?'

The expert.

I thought for a second. 'As long as we don't get carried away with the answers I don't see the harm it can do to ask. They either tell us or they don't. It might all be gibberish anyway.' It still felt like a game. 'It's like horoscopes. You don't have to believe any of it.'

Nobody added: but a part of you always does.

'Okay. Rob?'

Rob nodded.

'Okay, let's sack the vicar.'

'Priest, you infidel.'

Off he went back to glory without a struggle, and I put him out of my mind – I'd pretty much forgotten about him until now, in fact. At the time I certainly blanked the questions his presence raised. Although I have done plenty of thinking about them since.

It kicked off again in the usual way.

'Is there anybody there who wants to talk to us?' It brought an immediate YES. Rich was right, somebody stop me, I was too good at this.

Next question. 'Spell your name for us.'

This was the procedure. The questions didn't always have to be the same ones, but they had to be the right type, and in the right order. Once you had the basics you could get brave, like with the priest questions. This time the cup moved out of the circle of letters and began to spell. It took a while. I copied a long message onto the pad.

KNOW MY NAME.

'What does that mean?'

'I'll try it again: we want to know your name. We don't know it now. Spell it for us.'

A longer message.

YOU KNOW MY NAME ALL.

'Oh, Jesus,' Rich said. 'Does he mean we know his name already, or that his name is Al, or All?'

'Or his initials are A.L.L., or what?'

'Or does it mean that we *all* know his name?' Rob added.

'Or all of his name?'

'Once more on the name,' I said.

Same reply.

'I don't think we're going to get anywhere. Better try a different tack.'

'But,' said Rich. 'If this spook means that it knows us it would be a shame to talk to it all night and not know who it is.'

'The name might not matter. We didn't know the priest's name.'

'And got nothing. We want someone we know, or someone who will tell us something cool. Not grannies and vicars. When you look at what we've got so far it's not a lot.'

'Absolute bikini briefs,' was Rob's contribution.

'Look, I'm doing my best, stop picking on me.'

What now? Almost out of desperation I just asked the simplest question I could think of. I asked it what the boys wanted, no tricks.

'Will you tell us the answer to anything we ask you?'

YES.

Woah.

'Anything we want to know?'

YES.

Implications.

'Are you lying to us?'

NO.

I looked up at the boys. Rob's blank mug was saying: Jesus, where did all this come from?

What was my next question? What would Maddy say? But by then we were beyond anything Maddy would ever say. We knew in that moment that we'd moved onto a different level of the game altogether.

'Will you tell us about the future?'

YES.

For the hundredth time that night I looked into the faces of the two men with whom I shared the place I lived. And what I saw was this – I saw belief. I saw the desire for belief. I saw the need for belief.

I saw little Abu.

81

Now you see why I wouldn't fit in, strictly speaking, with the roomful of gamblers.

Gentlemen, place your bets.

14

We had a little more way to go before the possibilities of what we were doing really kicked in. Apart from anything else we knew we had to be more careful now. I know bits of this story read like a rulebook – one of those pamphlets under the lid in four languages which always misses some vital point of procedure. So there is always at least one rule that's not finite, that is floating.

What it came down to was this.

Maddy's 'game' had had guidelines. But we were playing the game in ways they didn't cover; we'd taken it a step beyond anything Maddy had ever tried. It sounds good when I put it like that, doesn't it? Another step towards the dark. Very dramatic. Very Conrad.

So we needed guidelines of our own to cover where we were taking things. This all came from Rich, by the way. And I should explain that, usually, when Rich stopped listening and started talking, everyone else generally did the opposite, and shut up and listened. He talked way more sense than me or Rob could manage without clawing for each other's jugular.

The gist of Rich's ground rules was this: what the spirit had just promised us was exciting, but scary. We had to consider the magnitude – the potential for danger as well as opportunity – of what we'd just heard. I mean, we had been promised all the dirt we wanted on the future. But we were wary of asking just anything. We had to decide pretty quick what was safe to know and what was out of bounds. Define limits and stick to them. There would be no room for mistakes.

Agreed.

De acuerdo, as Rob would say.

Or, as Rob would also say, my priest was right.

Yes.

These were the ground rules: first, we don't ask about personal matters to do with us as a group, information about how we were connected. For example I vetoed anything about me and Rich, whether we would stay in love or drift apart, or get hitched and have children, whatever. Second: death. Nobody asks when or how anybody dies. Nobody leads a line of questioning anywhere which could pass too close to these subjects.

That pretty much covered everything we could think of, which when you look at it is some pretty big stuff. Love and death is big stuff. And we reckoned that if we stayed within these guidelines – our own guidelines – we would be pretty safe.

But something still felt bad, like there was still more to be wary of. So much which could go wrong by accident. We just didn't know.

So, do we go on? Do we pack it in before it gets too messy?

Not a chance. We all knew it. We'd always be too curious. Always be ashamed of the night we chickened out. We had to take this to some kind of conclusion, no matter what that was.

To a Conclusion.

So that was that. We drank to it, to playing the game by our own rules, to being careful, to staying in control. We drank from plastic cups like the one upturned before us on the board. We drank to ghosts.

Cut back to the seance:

'To ghosts!'

'*Fantasma.*'

*   *   *

84

And cut again:

Jump forward a few conversations. You've seen enough rehearsing. I've shown you enough of these rituals by now for you to play the game yourself.

So here's a summary, with our new ground rules in mind:

Now we know what the stakes are, how do we start?

With something simple. Something that doesn't matter too much to any of us.

Something to test the water?

That's right.

How about politics?

Politics, that's a good one. No one gives two hoots about politics any more.

Okay, here goes: Who's the next Prime Minister going to be?

A name.

The cup spelled a name.

We knew the name.

It bloody worked.

Not the guy we expected. But from the right party, a young guy. And spelt right. In our hyped-up state it was more than convincing enough. My notepad could have been the dead sea scrolls.

Hallelujah. We believed.

But *what* did we believe?

'Jesus!' Rob gasped. He was freaked, we all were. 'Think about it. We know who the next prime minister of Britain is going to be. We actually know. I mean, we absolutely *know*.' Words to that effect.

Again: *what* did we know? Did we know this was a great game? Did we know we were excited about the cup spelling big words that weren't in any of our minds to start with? Did we believe in what was coming out of that cup simply because no one was cheating, that it wasn't the result of lies?

Yes. And more. I think we were ripe and ready and prepared

to believe absolutely anything that wasn't something we already knew to be bogus. And this was certainly that. This was something new.

But did we *all* believe – that was vital for me to know. I couldn't go on with this if I thought one of us was hanging back. But no one seemed to be doing that. Group madness. I didn't need to ask, but I did ask. I asked the boys half a dozen times. Are you convinced? Because I am. Are you with me in this, with me completely? Like I said, I needn't have asked. Yes, yes, yes, they told me each time. It was like a prayer, an act of affirmation. An incantation of absolute faith. I loved it.

I couldn't say anything after that. The power of what I thought was happening was too much for me. For once I was happy to let Rob prattle on, bless him.

'I mean, that's a fact. From the *future*. And we *know* it!'

And more of the same type of thing, blah blah.

And then he said this.

'I tell you what, I wouldn't mind having a few quid on that come the next election.'

And there it was. That's what clinched it. That's what banished the last doubt.

I said, what do you mean? He said, stroll down to Billy Hill's tomorrow, stick a few quid on this joker, take a price, let the odds do what they will. Come the big day, we collect a packet.

A packet.

Rich said: Say that again.

Cast your mind back to that bargain we made. Trust, the roomful of drunks, remember? Now, a drunk will believe anything she wants to believe. And three drunks will believe everything – times three.

Rich said: say that again.

Rob said we'd make a packet.

And the last of our earthly reason seemed to go awol. This couldn't be happening, it had to be a joke. But the point is we were letting it happen. We had opened our arms wide to all of this. Everything was a blur. We were wired, tired, laughing, back-slapping. Fuck it, we were already rich. This was what we were saying. The rest was going to be easy. Just picking up the winnings. Thank you very much. *Gracios y buenos noches.* Warnings? Guidelines? Who he?

15

Will you help us to make money by giving us information about the future?

YES.

Information we can use to bet for profit?

YES.

Will you help us to win money gambling?

YES.

Clear as crystal, don't you think?

Nothing to fear. Simple as that. Every variation got the same reply. Yes. No problem. Ask away.

We were going loco trying to control our excitement. We wanted all kinds of answers *yesterday*. But the thing was getting tired, moving slower and slower between YES and the centre of the board. I asked it as much.

Are you getting too tired to continue?

A laboured crawl to YES.

We would have to release it soon. It made sense to release it now; our energy was thinning out, it was too risky trying to go any further tonight. Except we just couldn't wait. Who can wait?

So, we didn't wait. The $64,000 question suggested itself via the politics slant. This was a by-election week somewhere in the home counties, safe Toryville. The plan was simple: get the result from the spook and place a bet. Now, there was no money in this. The outcome was never in doubt: one of those midterm protest votes would overturn the government majority and give the LibDems the seat until the general election. Labour would come its usual sad south-east third. We'd get diddly odds – if we played it straight. But we weren't going to play it straight. With our sources we could play it any way we wanted. We wanted to try something different.

What we came up with was numbers. Something no one else would have the brains, balls, or stupidity to try at home. So, we requested of our obliging spirit the precise numbers of votes which would be cast for the three major parties. The odds couldn't help but be spectacular. Who could accurately predict such a thing? It was not possible – unless . . . The bookies would wet themselves laughing as they took our money under the plexiglass, then quake with nausea as they handed it back plus obscenely massive winnings. We'd be dirty mucky rich by this time next week. Just like that. Test tube Tories. Are you getting all this? Jesus.

If you're starting to think there are three people in this story spending way too much time between the four walls of a small flat, you could be absolutely right.

The cup was painfully slow coughing up the three numbers, but they came. Added up they made just under 50,000. A figure of 60,000 for the average UK constituency had stuck in my mind from somewhere – I must have read it. Anyway, our numbers sounded okay. We said many thanks, and put the spirit to bed.

We were going to be rich.

But how could we be sure?

For one thing the buzzing noise was back, big-time, there at the table. And I was awake. No, not quite true. I didn't feel awake, or even alive exactly. I've tried for six years to accurately recall my state of mind in those days. I haven't come closer than to picture it as walking on a kerb. Not much of a thrilling mental picture, I know, but the image has solidified with me now. I even feel comfortable remembering it.

It's a narrow kerb in a street with a high path on one side and a low road on the other. The street is deserted. I am walking on the kerb which in my mind represents a cusp, a border of some kind. I am walking and wobbling, swaying alternately towards both sides of the kerb, the high path and the low road.

The world of the living and the world of the dead.

I think that maybe without the buzzing I might have let it all go, dismissed it as mumbo jumbo and too much rich food and cheap wine. I would never have suggested it to the boys, although it had probably occurred to them too, but I know I took the buzzing as a sign.

And so I was sure. We were talking to the dead and they were promising to help us, offering us a way out. An escape from working in bars, from worthless degrees. From not having the start our parents' generation took for granted. Certainly from crashing in a fugitive drug dealer's flat. If this worked I could forget all that. I could forget that there was that world, and live in the one of the board, of my new certain future, of free money for me and all my friends. Why would we not believe? How could I ignore this feeling?

But nobody was a millionaire yet. We had an answer, three numbers. But that was all we had.

We adjourned to the kitchen table again. The night was almost gone but strangely no light was leaking under the skylights. We were drinking coffee and eating dry cereal, our last solids. That was it. There wasn't anything left.

I noticed something. It's hard to look street and chic with a mouthful of dry branflakes – it's hard to look anything but constipated – but Rich was thinking again. He'd put on a tape for background to help him think. It was someone doing old Woody Guthrie songs. Pretty new to me, but *How Can a Poor Man Stand Such Times and Live* sticks in my mind. How old was this stuff? My all-seeing, all-knowing lover pushed away his bowl and placed his elbows on the table, clasped his hands, and creased his brow.

'Thif mummy,' he said.

We waited.

'Thif mungy –' picking brown clumps from his back teeth with his spoon handle '– if not juff mungy.'

'You mean the money we're gonna win?'

He nodded.

'Enlighten us.'

He raised his hands: be patient. 'This isn't just about money, is what I mean. It's about knowing – and therefore maybe playing a part in altering – the future. D'you see? I know it sounds like Dr Who, but that's what's supposed to happen. You know the future, you have the power to alter it. Yeah?'

Aw, fuck. I could see what was coming. Where did it end?

He went on. 'Perhaps not just our future.' Rich's turn to gesticulate. 'We're taking away variables. If – when – this works, we're going to be rich almost without a thought. Think about that.'

We thought about that. It was an easy thought to think about.

Rich sighed. He wasn't getting through to us. 'Without effort. Without having to try. We're simply gonna be rich, and any time we want more *dinero* we just go back to the table and get more answers and win more.'

Rob: 'Man, what a drag.'

'But that money will change us, don't you see? Because

it's not like getting money any other way. As long as we keep going back, as long as we remember where that money came from –'

'From William Hill. Ha ha.'

'This is not from William Hill, Rob. As long as we remember where that money came from and who – or what – gave it to us, we will be part of where it came from.'

It was starting to sink in, at least with me. I looked up at Rob. Bless his sensitive heart, he wasn't quite there with it yet.

'We'll be indebted,' Rich was continuing, 'at least in some part of our consciousness to this other world. The world of the dead. Understand? This is dark stuff here. Do we know what we're doing? Can we cope?'

'I can cope,' I said, too quickly.

'But can you? Really? You've said yourself you didn't sleep last night, that you're half-living with the dead already.'

I felt my cheeks flush. 'You said you wouldn't tell Rob.'

'I told Rob because I was feeling the same. I wanted to check it out. And it turned out he was, too.'

'It's true, Trash. I got the same thing with the buzzing noise. And feeling high, like walking on a wall – you said a kerb, didn't you? But it's the same feeling we're talking about, and it ain't pleasant.'

Me: 'What do you reckon it is?'

Rich: 'I know what it is. It's messing with the dead. Think about the timing of it, the order it all happens. We talk to them, we go to bed, we try and sleep. We let these people – these dead people – into our dreams. They're probably running riot in there, hence the buzzing. Do you see?' He shrugged. 'That's my theory, anyway.'

'I don't know,' Rob said. 'It might just be us getting hyped-up and excited.'

Rich: 'I don't think so. You don't get a spooky buzz like that just from being excited. And think back. Did we all start

92

getting the buzz at the same time? Right after the seance with Maddy? Before we thought about betting?'

Me and Rob looked at each other and nodded.

Rich said: 'Okay.'

I said: 'It feels horrible. And the way you put it makes it worse. It gives me the willies.'

Rich put his hand on mine. 'Yes, love. But it's a good sign. It's horrible, but it bodes well for all this ghostly stuff being true.'

Rob: 'Although with the slight drawback of slowly but surely driving one up the proverbial wall.'

Rich patted the table three times, and said firmly: 'Exactly. It is not pleasant. Do we want to feel that for the rest of our lives?'

Aw, damn, damn, damn. 'I am coping. And maybe it wears off. It has to wear off if we stop betting, say. We don't have to bet for the rest of our lives. Just make a killing for two or three years, or five, then stop.'

'That sounds okay,' Rob offered.

Rich: 'Well, it's getting there. At least we're thinking. But there's still the money. What do we do with it? This money from an unnatural source – don't forget that. If we're having nightmares now, how are we going to feel once we start dipping into Beelzebub's current account?'

I allowed myself a chuckle at that. It was a nice picture. 'Do you want to stop?' I asked Rich.

'No, I don't want to stop. I want to think.'

'We're not getting into selling our souls or anything here.'

'I didn't say we were. And I think we can cope. As long as we know what we're coping with. What I'm getting at first is that we've got to be careful who this money touches. We've made our decision regarding ourselves. But we have to remember it's not natural. If we spend it on other people, families and friends, aren't we involving them? Changing their futures?'

'But that's true with any money,' I said.

'But we won't have *any* money.'

There was no arguing around it. We were going to have to postpone collecting our riches for yet another unbearable ten minutes while we invented more rules. Jesus, whatever you did, even when you found a miracle cure for the whole of life, a way out of all the shit you could imagine, a method to beat the spiralling world at its own game, there were still rules; and then there were probably more rules about rules. Rich was right as usual, clever bastard. When did he come to all these perfect conclusions? Whatever, the fact remained that he was right, that we needed ground rules for betting, and for spending.

Ah, the sound of guns being jumped. Chickens being counted.

The new rules covered two categories: moral and practical. The moral rules seemed simple enough (hear those alarm bells?). Initially we'd keep the money a secret, not allow it to touch anyone we knew. How we thought we were going to manage that I can't conceive. It didn't seem important. But our spending would have to be discreet. And it went without saying that the method was the biggest secret. If, after a while, it was pretty clear that no funny business of any sort was resulting from our activities, perhaps we could redefine the rules about spending. Perhaps we could even be open about betting. How do we do it? Oh, we're just lucky. Luck and research.

The practical rules weren't so simple.

There were types of betting about which we knew *nada*. I hadn't admitted it to the boys, but I'd never even stepped inside a betting shop. Our stuff with the dogs was always on course. So, maybe we didn't know about bookies, but we knew they didn't like to lose. And we knew that, against us, they were going to be losing with great regularity. So we'd have to vary our targets, possibly for each bet, maybe over the whole of London. Each bet would have to be small and inconspicuous, but we'd place sufficient of them to add up to considerable and regular winnings. As those winnings grew, so would our available stake money. We'd mastermind a network of apparently insignificant wagers which together would amount to a king's ransom. Or a fortune for life for three people.

We were trying to stay calm, and not succeeding. We talked wildly about weekly, monthly, yearly winnings. We wrote down massive figures. Then we strayed into crazy plans for what we'd spend the money on. But we managed to step back from that, because it seemed like tempting fate. We agreed. Let's win some money first, then we'll talk about how we're gonna spunk it. And then we came back to the question – when should we stop? There was no clear answer, but we all knew it would have to happen. The main reason for me was that, okay, I was coping with the buzzing now, but I wasn't sure how long I could keep it up if it lasted. If this stretched into years I'd become certifiable. There was a limit to how long I could stay on that kerb.

Some more talk, and we had a kind of plan, beginning with the by-election. This was our test wager. Were the spirits lying to us? Was our collective imagination addled by too many dashed hopes and late nights? We'd soon find out.

16

And then the sleep.

And then the dreams.

And the noise like a drug.

It had to mean something. It had to be worth something.

We were each to place a separate five-pound bet in a different local venue, taking whatever odds we could get – the odds themselves weren't important at this stage. But three bets were better than one. So, Rich would wander up to Tottenham Lane, Rob down to Finsbury Park, I'd stay in Crouchy. We'd rendezvous to watch *Late Night Election Special* on BBC2, prepared either to celebrate our impending untold wealth, or return in honourable defeat to the surface of the planet. It was a simple test: are we mad?

A fine plan but for one thing – we had nothing to bet with. We'd spunked the last of Robin's money on *Jurassic Park* and sweets. It was Monday, the election was three days away. My giro was due Thursday, for all that was worth. Rob didn't get paid until Friday; we had nothing to sell. So we'd just have to hope the cheque came. The next three days were going to be tense.

And we were out of Bran Flakes.

But at least Monday was cleaning day, and if the manager of the Barbarossa – I forget his name – was not around, or was holed up in his office sleeping off the weekend, the boy could just load on up. And bingo, Rob tipped up that evening with enough frozen tuck for a good sized UN relief convoy. Turkey breasts in tarragon sauce, king prawns, mushrooms in garlic butter, corn on the cob, crab claws – yum – pork ribs, breaded squid, even a bottle of Gordon's. The stuff of surfeit, a taste of things to come. But stuff we still had to steal, and which, besides the gin, we were way too wired to enjoy.

Three days.

Thursday we were at our stations around the kitchen table long before postie was due.

Had the buzzing noise, the sensation of being only half alive, stretched miserably over three empty days and nights? Oh yes. Every night the dreams, the noise, every night the drug. Rich had it, too. We all had it. But we didn't mention it any more. It was bad stuff to mention. Although to anyone else we must have looked like zombies. I was tired, on automatic, running on fumes.

But when the brown envelope fell through the slot on cue it was as if we'd already won, and someone was just politely letting us know. The cheque's arrival was like a fix. We were suddenly relaxed and re-enervated. There no longer seemed to be any hurry. We lingered over coffee and strolled the hundred yards to the Post Office arm in arm, smiling, strutting. I noticed things in shop windows. Rob scanned the back pages of a couple of newspapers . . . Arsenal nil . . . blimey . . . We queued without shuffling or speaking. We got the money.

This was it.

In less than an hour I was back at the flat, my forehead pressed up against the mottled glass pane in the door, my fingers shaking out of control trying to guide the spastic stupid key into the lock. Let me in, get me into the flat and out of the world was all that mattered to me. Let me in; let me hide.

No sign of the boys. Dumping my jacket on the floor I ran into the m.b., crawled over to Rich's side of the bed, collapsed and sobbed. I was shattered. I didn't know if I could face the boys. The buzzing back in my ears and now my eyes, I cried long and loud. And then I think I slept.

But of course my dreams wouldn't let me sleep. They were there, waiting. They were loud. LOUD.

The boys tipped up together an hour after me. I remember wondering how that could be, and feeling left out by it – conspired against, almost. I heard them in the room and felt the duvet pulled from my puffy face. As soon as Rich sat down and held me the waterworks resumed. Sob, sob. Pat, pat. There, there. I was sure I could smell the pub on him, but I ignored that.

'I (sob) couldn't do it (sniff), Rich.'

'I know.'

'I fucked it up.' More sobbing.

'No, you didn't.' He sounded surprised. We were at crossed purposes. But I was enjoying my cry.

'Come one,' I heard Rich say. 'We need some mud.' Then I felt him lift me from the bed. He carried me to the kitchen. It has its moments, this being weak and feeble.

I told my tale of woe while Rob sorted the coffee.

As I said, I've never been inside a betting shop in my life. Once in the door of William Hill's on Crouch End Broadway, I froze. I remember wondering what all those people thought I could possibly be doing in there on my own. All these men, and not even men I could look down my erstwhile sheltered nose at, not drunks and deadbeats and the like. But just ordinary guys watching telly and smoking and betting, which threw me. Just people, normal people. I was psyched up for something else, some low-life tableau like the *Star Wars* cantina.

Glancing nervously about me I clocked the slip dispensers on the walls. I hadn't noticed anything like them at Catford or Wembley dog meetings. At the track you just went straight to the TOTE.

There were two types of slips. The larger ones looked like pools coupons. The small blue papers I thought must be for horses. I wasn't here for football or horses. So what next? I had to do something besides admire the walls.

I watched someone pick up a stubby blue biro – well, what do you know, I'd discovered the secret of where stubby blue biros came from – and squint at his *Daily Mirror*. Everyone seemed to have one of these little pens. In fact, everyone seemed to have a *Daily Mirror*. (Mental note to myself.) I picked up a pen. And then I just stood leaning against the shelf where I'd found the pen. My spare hand drifted up to my neck and began twirling a lock of hair.

I suddenly recalled how that simple unconscious gesture and what it implied had infuriated my mum when I was a little girl, and I stopped doing it. I remember thinking: I don't belong here. Maybe I'm not this kind of gambler. And still I leaned. I'd probably turned bright red by now. I'd probably still be there today if the black girl behind the plexiglass hadn't come to the rescue and asked, yo, did I want something? Hallelujah, yes, I want something. But then things just got worse. Much worse.

I described the bet, the way we'd planned. She looked at me as if I was on some very bad, or very good, drugs. Then she made me repeat myself, then said the whole thing back to me again in a south London twang. West Croydon, I guessed, or Herne Hill. Worse and worse. She shouted to someone invisible behind her, and a door opened and there emerged a mug of tea with a man behind it. Well, half a man anyway. I had to go through the bet once more for his benefit. I could feel myself turning from red to green. Matey put down his tea and scratched the back of his neck. Oh, I get it, that other hand's for your balls, one for each scratch. I looked him over and shivered. What a dish. Pasty-white skin, chunky gold ID bracelet, chocolate-brown staypress. Nose like a knuckle. In a strange way he was a reassuring presence, more like the kind of specimen I'd expected to encounter.

Well, he told me straight: No way, love. Long slow shake of the head to drag out his mastery of my sorry situation. Mental note: *I. Hate. Men.* We can't take a bet like that, darlin'. Not a chance. I could tell he was desperate to laugh, but just about human enough to wait until I was out of there. Only he didn't think I was on drugs. He thought I was just a stupid tart. And I couldn't feel annoyed because, at that moment, the odds were on his side. I stood there dying, he stood waiting to laugh. To show there were no hard feelings he dipped his eyes to my chest and allowed them to register his approval. It was a surprisingly sophisticated gesture for a man of his stature and appearance, and it almost made me puke.

I turned and staggered towards the door. It seemed to take about five years.

The boys listened in silence to my story. Only they didn't look surprised or angry, didn't laugh. In fact, they looked like they could use a good weep themselves. Why don't men cry? How do they manage without it sometimes?

Rob solved one mystery (I'll never know about the crying): 'They wouldn't take the bet anywhere, Trash. I tried two places, Rich hit three.' Rich nodded in verification. 'Last place they were waiting for him. The branch he'd just come out of phoned ahead. They knew all about us.' He shook his head. 'They told me the bet was too bizarre. That was his word, bizarre.'

Rich looked up from his drink and sighed. All he said was: 'They have a point.' And he smiled. We all smiled.

How could we have been so naïve? So. Utterly. Fucking.

Stupid. The thought seemed to hit us simultaneously, and then we weren't smiling, but cackling hysterically. A serious post-nuclear collective giggle fit. We were rolling around, laughing with tears in our eyes. Desperate to see the funny side.

Oh, boy. You learn your lessons. So, this time all we could do was watch. The result was going to be the same whether we had money on it or not. We'd still know for sure come the wee small hours. This was still the first step.

Holy moly.

There was so much we didn't have a clue about. We expected to be able to make a fortune and keep it secret. We couldn't even get past a dwarf in brown crimplene. I don't recall exactly what we did for the rest of the day. Mainly we waited.

Waiting.

In the days and weeks which followed I was to learn a whole lot more about waiting. I waited and learned and waited so much that the days seemed more like months. Time took on a stretching quality like it must do in prison, or when a loved one lies in a coma, or maybe how it must be for addicts between fixes. Hours become longer, thinner, emptier, begging to be filled although there's nothing inside you to fill them with. And then the emptiness spreads into your self like a hunger, like a space in the throat and the gut. I know we all felt that hunger.

At 12.15 a.m., extended *Newsnight* – the one with all the pie charts and blue and red wall maps – kicked off, and we were ready, suggestively squashed onto a couch meant for two with a big bag of Butterkist. A thigh sandwich, me in the middle, boy on each side. It felt like cup final day. The buzzing had died down, the calm was edging back.

The count was fast, a record apparently. At 12.50 the returning officer read out the number of votes cast for each party. On Peter Snow's chart in a corner of the screen a computer-generated blue hammer was pulverising a forlorn red rose, its petals disintegrating into perfumeless red cyber dots. In the seconds of anticipation before he began speaking I felt the standard weakness of the knees, the familiar butterflies.

But these were sensations of the living, and they were a trick.

'What the hell happened? No, what the HELL happened?' Robin was shouting.

'What about our MONEY?'

Rich was slumped forward with his face in his hands. I was sitting quietly. It had been a long day.

Rob was still shouting. 'I was just going to get fatter and FAT-TER and BUY women. What am I supposed to do now?' Then something dawned on Robin, and he stopped shouting. His face grew some sharp angles and he said quietly, 'I'm a cleaner.'

17

But for the TV the room was silent.

Rob crawled over to the set and turned it off, and slumped back down in front of the sofa. His anger was visible and heavy, and I thought for a nervous moment he was going to cry. But his anger was also a tired anger. And the viciousness he felt now manifested itself in fatigue as opposed to rage. Either is always equally possible, but for now at least, the space left by the TV silence had been filled by just a nothingness which blanketed us all.

At the other side of the room Rich leaned back and let his eyes fall shut.

No one moved. Time passed – maybe hours. I don't know what time it was. It hardly mattered – the sleep we were missing was just that damn buzzing anyway. We drank gin, taking turns to refill each other's plastic cups. I occasionally glanced at Robin's and Richard's grey expressions. I wondered how I looked. My cheeks and lips and eyelids felt doubled in weight. What had we lost? Just another piece of innocence, and you can survive that if you leave it behind neatly enough. No one outside the three of us would ever know what we had done, how ridiculous we had made ourselves, so we could mourn what had happened without the fear of embarrassment. Just another money-making scheme that wasn't viable after all. Just another daft piece of hope.

After what really must have been a couple of hours, Rich spoke. He was propped against the far wall by the bed, his legs folded before him like a Buddha, hands upturned on his knees. We heard a deep sigh, and saw the white circles of his eyes open wide, and waited expectantly for the wise and weighty words which would break the bad spell.

Finally Rich's lips opened and he intoned, 'I'll put the kettle on.'

He disappeared off into the kitchen. I felt better. I could use a coffee. Rob still looked distant. 'What's up, babe?' I asked him.

'I ever tell you about the time I got sacked?' His voice had a dark edge.

'Which time?'

'There was only one. The others I left entirely of my own accord.'

'Allegedly.' We laughed for a second.

'No, the time I was seriously sacked.'

'The Luau Lounge? Rich has mentioned it, but he never went into detail.'

'Seriously tacky place. I jest you not, you could get drinks in half coconut shells.'

'Ouch.' I chuckled. 'Whatever possessed you to work there?'

Rob shrugged, and felt around on the floor for his cigarettes. 'Money. The tips were on a shared basis. The girls got tipped and I got a slice of that. And they didn't mind because I looked out for them.' He found a lighter and lit two and handed me one.

'How do you mean?' I shuffled closer to listen.

'I looked out for them when punters got difficult, too physical.'

'What, like a bouncer?'

'No, no. More subtle than that. You couldn't really throw anyone out. Because no matter what wankers they were the

104

management always wanted them back. They had a lot of money. The more money you had the more of a wanker you were allowed to be.

'No, by looking out for them I mean talking the punters down when they got over excited, bless 'em, getting them cabs, politely suggesting that their attentions were becoming a little too conspicuous. The girls were gorgeous. Some real model types. It was all diplomat stuff, that job. I never felt cut out for it. Which is possibly why I ended up getting sacked. Christ, what a shitty job. Why should anyone be expected to do something like that?'

I looked at the floor and thought about it. 'I think it should be the other way round. I think everyone should be made to do a shitty job like that for six months, then they'd know what it was like and they wouldn't give the people on the receiving end such a hard time.'

'That's not a bad idea, Trash.' He looked at me. 'Sometimes I think you may not just be an ugly face after all.'

'Get on with the story.' We both inhaled and the red tips glowed in the dark.

'I got sacked because the wanker I twatted was rich, and I was just a cocktail barman doing the right thing in the wrong place.'

'You hit someone? How is hitting someone doing the right thing?'

'He wouldn't leave one of the girls alone. Pauline.'

As if on cue a woman's scream reverberated somewhere in the streets outside, followed by laughter of indeterminate sex, then another scream. We turned our heads to where the noise might have come from. But as long as we were inside, the world was someone else's problem.

'So he wouldn't leave her alone, and he got very physical, and she ended up in tears. And I stepped in. And he made an issue of it with me. And I decked him. I tell you what, it felt really good. My hand hurt like buggery for weeks. But I couldn't feel bad about slapping that prick at all. But I did need that job.' He shook his head. 'Cunts.'

'God, and they sacked you? They should have called the police and had the bastard arrested.'

Rob laughed nastily. 'That's not the worst of it.'

'Why?'

He looked at me. 'They sacked her too.'

I was stunned. 'Pauline? Why?'

Rob replied in his most matter-of-fact tone. 'Because they failed to understand Pauline's problem with having this gentle-man's fingers in her knickers while she was trying to do her job and serve some drinks.'

I suddenly felt uncomfortable. The way he was looking at me in the dark, and Rich away in the kitchen. Perhaps he'd been sitting here brooding too long. 'Why are you telling me this now?' My voice was shaky.

'Money.' Rob leaned forward until his face was only inches from mine. I could see the red veins in his eyes, thin dark lines like rivers on a map. I heard the hiss of him stubbing out his cigarette in something damp, and I jumped. 'My point is money. What it does for you.' He dropped his voice to a whis-per. 'What you can get away with.'

He was still close up, staring at me. Then I heard Rich in the hall and Rob moved away and Rich was in the room, handing out the mugs.

Maybe it never happened, I told myself. Maybe I'm just tired and we never had this conversation. Maybe I made it up. It was a strange night, after all.

Rich came over and sat beside me and put an arm around my shoulder. But I felt oddly disloyal and distanced from him. I wanted to feel different. I needed a distraction.

So I crawled around to the other side of the sofa – around Rob, who didn't move – and picked up the pad. I'd written out all the figures, predictions and actual votes, side by side. I don't know why I wanted to look at the pad.

Tear it up, Trash.

But I couldn't. And as I stared at the page an idea began buzzing away. I recalled fragments of what Maddy had told us about the dangers of the game.

Stop, Trash, it's finished. Forget it. Go to bed. Sleep in the night and wake in the day.

Think, Trash. Sometimes they lied; okay. Sometimes messages got jumbled. Sometimes they were misspelled. Other times they were unreliable or just inaccurate.

I said it to myself again: inaccurate.

That word kept sounding better.

Inaccurate, inaccurate.

It doesn't mean anything. It's just a thought. Go to bed.

Were the figures *merely inaccurate*? But *essentially correct*? I jolted upright. My heart began spanking like mad. I grabbed Rob's thigh and shook it. 'Boys,' I gasped. They ignored me. Rob hung his head. 'BOYS!'

Rob looked up then. 'Let me die, Trash old friend. Save yourselves, I'll only slow you down.' Half of a half-hearted smile.

'Stay alive. Look at this. You too, Rich. Look at these numbers.'

'I've seen the numbers,' Rich said. But he opened his eyes.

'Yes, but look at them.'

'Leave it, babe. I've seen the numbers. What about them? They're wrong.'

I gave him a second to show I was the one being reasonable here, then said, 'But they're right. Look.' I held up the pad. 'Don't you see? What's wrong about them? Almost nothing. The result is right. It got that right, one to three, the parties in the right order. And the figures are not far wrong. In fact they're almost spot on. The furthest out is only two hundred and something votes off the actual figure. Can you see what I'm saying?' I knelt up and stuck the pad out at arm's length. 'Can you see what happened?' I gave them another second. 'It's just a problem of accuracy. Accuracy,' I repeated. 'Maddy said this might happen. She said the spirits make mistakes. She said they get lazy, they get tired, they get sloppy.'

Rich: 'Stop it now, Trash. Stop it all.'

'Our guy was *tired*.' I let that sink in. 'We even asked him if he was tired, remember? Are you too knackered to go on? Yes. YES. We didn't listen. So it's no big deal, you see? It's just our silly fucking fault.'

Now the boys were paying attention. 'What I'm saying is there is a way to do this. There has to be. We can get it right. There must be a right way, a safe way.' They were beginning to believe me. 'That's all we have to do. Find the way to eradicate these mistakes. It's just total accuracy, that's what we have to ask for, to get through to the spirit the need to be absolutely certain about what it's telling us. Not ask it questions when it's too tired to answer them accurately, that's one thing – that was our mistake, we fucked up. But we didn't lose any money. Look at me! I'm sure about this. I'm sure it can work!' I left a good pause then and checked my audience. I almost had them. 'I'm convinced,' I said finally, and put down the pad.

The boys looked at me, then briefly at each other. Rich shrugged.

Rob said quietly, 'Of course it could make sense. But then again –' He shook his head. 'Fuck it, why didn't I see it?' He picked up the pad, curled a corner of the top sheet. He shook his head again, but in a way that meant yes, and said, 'Look at these figures. We were close. We were *this* close.'

'I suppose we lost nothing,' Rich said slowly. 'We had no money on it – the spirits might even have been protecting us, not letting us lose money. Maybe I'm clutching at straws or I don't know exactly how to say what I mean, but it just seems right that we lost nothing with this.' He paused and sighed and then, turning my face towards him, his hand under my chin, said, 'I think Miss Trouble here could be right.'

Rob: 'What are we going to do about it, then? We can't wait for another by-election. I need some money. We need some answers. We need something else.'

No one wanted to suggest anything. There was silence for a good couple of minutes, punctuated only by the odd sniff and scratch, fags being lit. It was late, so late. Then, very quietly, mumbling really, Rob spoke again. 'It's the numbers.'

We ignored him, carried on thinking up foolproof, brilliant new plans.

'We could talk to the spirit again,' Rich was saying. 'D'you feel up to it now?'

'I don't know about now,' I said.

'It's only the numbers!' Rob said again, loud this time, slamming the flats of his big hands down onto the carpet. That got our attention. Okay, so it was the numbers.

'The numbers are all wrong, but only the numbers, I see it now.' He began to gesticulate, with his head as well as his hands. 'Of course you're right about accuracy, Trash. Of course you're right about the spirit being tired and getting things wrong. And it's the numbers. We can't give them huge fucking numbers to spell out. Of course they might get it wrong, of course they might fuck up! We're just asking a bit too much.' Rob drummed his index finger hard on the pad. He was speaking so fast he was almost babbling. 'If you think about it these are minor errors. So we didn't fuck up, not fundamentally. We're not wrong. See? It tried to help us. It got the result and figures as close for us as it could under the circumstances. But we asked too much! We stretched its capabilities. With what we know now we can do this again and get it right. Minor errors – but they count.' He may have been babbling, but his mind was keeping pace. 'Man, Trash is so fucking right. This is about *accuracy*. We have to be so careful what we ask. We were way over-ambitious. These huge numbers. Twenty-odd thousand, ten thousand blah fucking blah. This is a plastic fucking cup, for christ's sake. We can't trust it with five-figure numbers.' He stopped and took a deep breath. I suppose he needed one.

'So what now?' I asked.

Another big breath and boy wonder was off again. 'So now we keep it simple.' Now the ideas were coming faster than he could speak them. 'Like names. Names have got to be simpler than numbers – we already have the name of the next Prime Minister – that one's gonna make us a fortune. What about horses' names? Even if the cup spells them slightly wrong you can still work them out. How many horses in a race anyway? It's got to be easier.' Another idea nosed ahead and he ran with this one. 'And if we do use numbers let's keep it simple: two-one; three-two; one-nil – footy scores! The simplest combinations of numbers and names! Look, I could guess the name of any football club in the country from the first three letters of its name. So could Rich, it's a piece of piss. All the spook has to do is get a rough idea of the name and two lousy one-digit numbers. It has to work. It has got to be possible. Certainly –' pointing for emphasis, '– certainly more possible than fucking by-elections. Yes?'

Rob sighed, and the pace in the room slowed down to take it all in. No one spoke, but it was obvious we were all thinking in the affirmative. Lord, help us to believe. Rich laughed and stretched his legs way out in front of him. The knees of his faded Levi's were grey with cigarette ash and purple with spilt wine. The colours we lived with. All our clothes were stained the same, all our lives hunched on this carpet, waiting for the big joke to be over, waiting for the scheme that worked, sweating for a fix of new hope.

And here it was, the latest one. Hallelujah.

I jumped across the sofa onto Robin and, panting and laughing, wrestled him onto the red and grey carpet. He put up token resistance before letting me mount his big chest and pin his wrists to the floor. When I was completely in command I drawled, 'Boys, we're back in business.'

18

What happened that year?

199–?

Was it a leap year? Don't know. Olympics? World Cup?

Nope, sorry. Did Princess Di induce puking and 'fall' down some stairs? Was it that year?

Not a clue, your honour. I'd have to look it up. Not a Danny LaRue. Was anyone born? Who died and got their picture in the Sadly Missed double-page spread in January? Who got caught straying from the marital bed? Who was granted tabloid resurrection, reborn and forgiven? Who made the headlines in 199–? *Who won the war, in 1964?* Who's Who in 'Trash's Full-Colour Chronicle of 199–: Only £19.95. The complete record of a very special year'?

I do not know.

I cannot remember.

I cannot remember a single thing that went on in the world that whole year or, if I can, I can't connect any events to calendar time. No, about the only thing I can recall has to do with the bets. That and the weather.

Yes, the weather. Somehow that sticks in my mind, although at the time it didn't register any more than anything else. But it has gradually returned to me that the weather was good. Not just good: legendary. People talk of the summer that year as one that will always be recalled and commented on in their lifetimes. But although I am aware of it now, it almost completely passed me by.

Because we spent a spectacular Indian summer hiding indoors, isolated, scheming, ignoring the simple luck of being in the world on such days. It has a vicious ring to it, doesn't it – scheming. Thinking about £money£, and only money, conniving with the buzzing noise, that taunting promise to pay. And as if to rub it in, my memories of everything we did are played out against images of endless summers, six-month heatwaves that don't really happen.

This one, though, happened for a while. The light and the heat lingered long into the autumn, extra long days like unexpected gifts, when against all odds the sun poked in everywhere, even through blond Bob's bashful skylights. And there are odd moments now when, of all the impressions I have of that time, my silliest and strongest feelings and regrets are for the perfect Indian summer we wasted.

The *Sporting Life* might as well have been in Sanskrit. We burned a whole pack of Marlboro Lights dissecting it, with negligible results. The day's race times got closer and we got none the wiser. *No comprende.*

Nov Chase E 2m 4½f (£3,236) 7 runners.

The stuff below the horse's names made even less sense.

ch g No Risk (FR) by Revelation (USA) 1990–91 2m 1f good/soft (Hereford). £1,115.

And there was worse still. We looked for help to the opposite page where the text was bigger and the pictures of the jockeys' colours looked reassuringly like football kits. I don't know why we thought that helped.

It shouldn't have mattered; the paper was purely supposed to be a checklist. But it would have been preferable to understand the mechanics of what we were planning to subvert. At the very least it would have been a nice touch. Whatever, we would give the board the times of three races and ask for the three winning names. No innacuracies, no half-way right answers. This was really it: three names, three races. We would have our proof. And the first of many wins.

A seance in broad daylight? In for a penny. We even lit our usual candle. As for each session we also made a new board. Our ragged origami contribution to the lore of the black arts. I would even say a kind of calm was in the room this time. It may surprise you, but there were these moments. Moments when I was not fighting my light-headedness, but felt in harmony with the buzzing. When the things we wanted seemed not only possible, but obvious, inevitable. It was another tease, another hook. But I couldn't resist. In those moments the rhythm of the buzzing was hypnotic and circular, purring in sync with the film of events. In those moments I could balance on that kerb.

At the table the response from the cup was not slow and not fast, but steady. It felt right. We started with the essential questions, reestablishing the agreement with our ghost. It was tedious, but I had to hammer home the point.

Will you tell us about the future?

Will you help us to win money by gambling with the information you give us?

Will you tell us the truth?

Will you be absolutely accurate?

YES to everything.

'Will you tell us your name?'

YOU KNOW MY NAME.

We looked at each other. This was our spirit. I wasn't going to press it further. The answer could be a riddle or a clue but I didn't intend wasting the spirit's strength trying to decipher it. But I did mean to make a point.

'Thanks for the information you provided about the by-election. But the figures you gave us were not entirely accurate. Whatever you tell us must be accurate. Do you understand?' My repetition was very deliberate.

YES.

'Good. We'd like your help again. Will you help us now?'

YES.

'We'd like to know the winners in some of today's flat racing. Do you understand?'

YES.

'There's no room for mistakes – even small mistakes. Mistakes will hurt us. Do you understand?'

YES.

'Do you want to hurt us?'

NO.

'Then will you help us by being as accurate as possible?'

YES.

And a bit of a wild one at the end:

'Will you enjoy helping us?'

Wait for it . . .

YES.

That seemed pretty thorough to me. Nods from the boys. So, I asked questions and wrote down answers and compared them to the names of the runners.

So much for accuracy – there were no matches. This was not what we'd asked for. For a few moments we were uncertain.

But the cup had moved easily enough, and it hadn't seemed tired. If anything it seemed confident, if that's possible. Perhaps these were errors we could deal with, interpret? And at least we weren't working with huge, unwieldy numbers.

Yes, we were sure this was different. There were no exact matches, but it could all be made to fit. The spirit was willing, and we had the flesh to overcome the weaknesses. So, despite the spelling variations we felt pretty good.

Matching some of the words was a struggle, but for each race we managed to settle on a name which looked more like one than it did the others. We accepted that, for all our insistence on accuracy, this may be as close as we were going to get. And we felt sure it would be close enough. We had the runners in front of us, and names on the pad. I was wired up for anything.

And that afternoon we took our marked-up copy of the *Sporting Life* with our three names and fifteen quid and change to William Hill's on Crouch End Broadway. And lost it.

19

I could tell you the names of the horses.

Fuck it, it can't hurt. Our first was called Believe Me, and was beaten into a close second place at the line by Mr Bumby. They're not very similar, are they? We missed that one.

We weren't downhearted.

Our next race was a stroll to the line by Mr Dreamy.

However, our five was on a camel called Do Ray Mi. He finished a lazy third. If they really do shoot horses I hope someone gets round to popping a cap in that one. No, I don't mean that. Mr Dreamy and Do Ray Mi. They don't sound hair-splittingly like each other. Not similar enough for the chance we'd taken. This was serious, we had money on this, more than we could afford if we wanted to eat all week. What were we thinking? *What rubbish were we prepared to believe?*

Downhearted we now were.

In a numb trance of blind faith we went ahead with the last race and put five-fifty including tax on a 25-1 outsider called Land of Plenty. We stood to win one hundred and twenty-five quid plus our initial stake. I don't recall what we were thinking by the time it came in trailing by four lengths to a dark shadow called Band of Twenties.

Now, they are quite similar.

How had we missed it?

HOW HAD WE MISSED IT?

Shoot me, not the horse.

Why oh why were we determined to self-destruct?

All our bets were to win. Over three races we lost sixteen pounds and fifty pence.

We had a booth in the Elbow Room. The boys debated our next step at intervals while I turned my glass and watched the bubbles burst in the foam, and pretended to pay attention and thought of other places and other problems, problems with wonderful, helpful solutions that made everybody happy. We sipped pints of Guinness – the black stuff, like our mood. The Elbow Room was as small as its name suggested and it always seemed to me that at least half the patrons could hear your conversation just by choosing to, although that wasn't true.

Robin's post mortem:

'There's no reason to stop believing.' Silence. 'It's just taking time to get the hang of this.' Silence. 'There's obviously a formula.' Silence – you get the idea. 'There's obviously one single right way to do this. We're *this* close. Look at the names of the horses. How close can you get? We were this close to winning a bundle today, especially on Band of Twenties.'

Band of Twenties. The name made me wince. Land of Fucking Plenty.

Rob lit up, as if a cigarette would help his case 'Look, they keep giving us answers. It's not as if they say no, or give us some wildly outrageous predictions. They haven't done anything wrong, so far. If anything it's us that's been wrong again.' His non-smoking hand was tapping the edge of a beermat against the bridge of his nose. It looked painful. I hoped so. And on: 'There is a way to do this and we will find it and we will win our money back a million times over. No question.'

I had a question. What about my sixteen-fifty? I had other

questions as well. But I shut up. If I'd contradicted Rob then, if I'd opposed going on, I'm pretty sure Rich would have backed me up, and I might have stopped it all. What does that suggest to me? It's no use thinking about that now.

But what else was there, anyway? When all this was over, what would be left? Just a big fucking heap of reality. Perhaps even a void in my relationship with Rich, which I felt increasingly afraid for my ability to fill. After all these wild dreams would little lousy me be enough?

So, just let Rob talk, Trash. It's not doing any harm. Let him talk and let him take the blame, and keep thinking it's only sixteen-fifty, it's only sixteen-fifty, that's all anybody's lost or is going to lose. I promised myself that.

So Rob talked. And I nodded my head.

Finally bored by my own thoughts, I snapped back to the talk. With exaggerated interest Rich was saying: 'What do you suggest we're doing wrong?' His tone went straight over Rob's head.

'For a start it's the wrong game. I still vote for football. It's simpler. Less to go wrong.'

Rich banged his glass down. 'Football, netball, Johnny fucking Ball – wake up! There's more to this than that, for fuck's sake!'

This wasn't like Richard. And Rob reacted. 'Easy, tiger. Spat your fucking dummy out?'

Easy, *compadres*.

There was a dangerous lull. Rich would have to conclude this. After a time he spoke, slowly. 'I don't believe it's just the game that's wrong, *Robin*.' He was the one drumming a beermat now, but on the table, chipping at the loose varnish, threatening to expose more raw wood. 'Think about it. If we're going to be allowed to win we should be able to do it with any kind of betting we like – even by-elections. It works or it doesn't. It should be up to us. Answers are answers. They should be the right ones. But it's not happening. So, what's wrong has to be something else.'

Rob, reluctantly: 'Go on, then.'

Quieter: 'I don't know. I don't know, but there's something we're missing. Some vital part of the whole ritual is not being performed, and it's stopping the information getting through to us as it should.

'The spirits want to help but they're holding something back and it must be because of something we're not doing.'

'Go on,' I said half-heartedly. I looked around when I spoke – still paranoid – but no one was paying any attention to the three of us.

'I can't. I don't know what it is yet. But there's something more they want from us, I'm sure of it.'

'Let's *think*,' Rob said.

If only.

'Think,' he said, and started up with the beermat again. His nose looked red. 'We're polite, we're respectful, patient. We're up-front and we don't lie about how we use the information. What else could they want?'

'Perhaps they're testing us?' I suggested.

It was just a thought. Talking for the sake of being heard. I looked around again but we still weren't being spied on. Of course not. Calm down, woman. I watched someone drop coins in the jukebox and was surprised to hear Steve Earle's *Good Ole Boy*. They must have had 'The Best of' CD.

I was born in the land of plenty, now there ain't enough.

'Testing us.' Rich nodded. 'That's good. It might well be something like that – but more than that. More.' Rich was still working on something. He rotated his pint on the table top, looking for answers in the dark liquid. 'Yes, more. Testing us isn't worth much if we only lose fifteen quid.'

'Fifteen quid's fifteen quid – and it was *my* fifteen quid,' I reminded him.

'Yeah, but it's not much of a risk, is it?'

Oh, cheers, I thought.

'What did you say?'

Rich stopped playing with his meal-in-itself and looked up at Rob. Then he slowly repeated his last words, listening to himself say them. 'I said it's not much of a risk.'

Suddenly all the lines left Rob's face. My mind began working, trying to get into his. He had something. But, god, his face. Then I could see it. See how something had become so clear to him that, for just one moment, it had levelled all the lived and honed edges of his features to the absolute flatness of blown white sand. But then something replaced the clear white. There was still clarity, but now under a dark blanket, as if a wind had spread black dust over the white. As if what had become clear to him was something dark to the core.

I felt a chill.

'What is it?' I asked him quietly.

No answer.

Rich leaned across the table and said: 'You know, don't you. You know what's missing?' He leaned closer 'You have to tell us.'

Rob nodded slowly and exhaled. He looked into Rich's eyes as if deciding whether to tell him. And in that moment he carried the sole burden of the knowledge himself and, just for that one moment, the responsibility of sparing us something. Then Rob opened his lips and mouthed one word across the table. His face and Rich's were close together and, as Rob spoke, I noticed Rich lip-sync the same word.

'Risk.'

That was the last thing anybody said for a while.

What was left of my dole money, together with Rob's and Rich's which both arrived early Saturday, came to approximately two hundred. That same afternoon we watched it disappear. Nobody said anything then, either.

Give or take, we blew our last two hundred pounds on the day's nine premier league fixtures, at twenty a match plus tax, simple fixed odds. It seemed like an awful lot of money to us. It seemed like an awfully big risk. For every game we had the correct result; every team won or lost as the spirit had predicted – no draws. But for every game the scoreline was exactly a single goal adrift. A single goal and two hundred pounds. It was as close as we had come, closer than the horses' names, certainly.

All we could think to do was to go home and make another board.

After some hesitation – as well as a good deal of cursing – we asked if risk was indeed the sticking point, if they were waiting for us to show some big commitment before rewarding us. We came up with all kinds of questions. YES, they told us. Haven't we risked enough so far? we demanded. NO. What is it we have to do? RISK, they said. Risk what? RISK EVERYTHING, came the instant reply. Simple as that.

And spelled perfectly.

RISK EVERYTHING.

PART TWO

20

That night I dreamed the Madeleine dream again. She was sitting at the red bar, holding a plastic beaker, looking in my direction. Her lips were red. I almost touched her. But then the other dreams came.

But first another night all but gone, another morning without light. Another kitchen conference and more dry cereal.

Another moment of not thinking, of just going along with what is your life. What happens if you don't just keep going? Is anything different? Does history get interrupted by the people who stop and think about what they're doing and try to alter the course of many lives? Or is stopping and thinking, is changing the direction of your own tiny life – or changing the whole world – all just a part of keeping going? Is it expected of a portion of us, and allowances made? Does the difference you try and make ultimately matter?

Matter or no, I think I like the people who stop and think, and who change things with violence: violent act and violent thought. Who engender revolutions and cause things and places to burn. I envy their instinctive, casual sense of destruction, on one condition – the change must be universal and immediate. I don't mind the thought of them collapsing my world as long as they collapse it for everyone. I would welcome that as a blessed relief. They can come into my temple and push away at the pillars, and I will fall into a peaceful sleep with them as the world screams in the aisles and falling stones from the roof crush the crowds. Nodding off, I will mumble to them (I may as well mumble because shouting will do no more good, but I must appear to tell them) I will mumble, don't run, don't worry, it's only polystyrene, I've seen the film and I especially remember this part, and the stones are only polystyrene and they don't crush the crowds of actors. But the crowds don't believe me – if they can hear me – and they believe themselves crushed and they lie down, like good little TV bodies. 'Then,' is my final muttering before sleep, 'we will all be crushed together.' And I close my eyes and snore at the broken fake walls.

Can anybody hear me?

Monday was only two hungry days away, but we couldn't count on Rob having a clear run with the supplies two weeks running.

We stayed up that night ostensibly to discuss our next move, but we all knew what it would have to be. I hated facing it, but when the food and the giros ran out, I ran back to mummy. It was the practical thing to do. But I hated admitting that I wasn't self-sufficient, I wasn't a big grown-up girl surviving on her own. The shame, however misplaced, gnawed at me. Of course that wasn't the only thing pouring on our parade just then, but we were too shocked and drained to discuss the money. So we sat in the kitchen in virtual silence and ate bran.

But there it was. However much I resented going home it was always the easiest solution to empty cupboards and coffers. I'd raid the teacher and the diplomat and return with a food parcel and a loan of twenty or thirty quid. Except of course it wasn't really a loan – they were never going to ask for any of it back. I suppose I took the piss shamefully, just assuming they had bottomless wallets. I wasn't to know that within three years my mum would be forced to go part-time for a different LEA, a victim of downsizing in the cut-throat, high-intrigue arena of primary education, but I should have known better and behaved better. All I can say in my defence is that I didn't feel good about it.

But I did it. I even hit my little sister for subs. My worst trick was to go back home under the pretence of a visit and not even mention cash, just mope around, sighing, until one or other of my parents, or better still both, offered me a little something until I was flush. And I'd go through the motions of refusing once, twice, finally taking the cash in a sulk, as if they'd hassled me into it. But most of the time I at least took the honourable route – just came out and begged. I begged my parents and my little sister for money and then took it with disdain. That can't be normal. How horrible.

When Rich was stony he usually went back north to work for a while for his big sister who ran, yes, a restaurant. Pride, bless him. But it was his sister's place where she'd make a job for him and pay him unfairly well, and even slip him his train fare, and the other staff wouldn't mind because they'd all been there, and they knew Rich would make a point of doing more than his share to make up for the special treatment. But that always took him away from me for upwards of a week.

We knew Rob would volunteer to do extra shifts at the Barbarossa, but he was supporting us already. And Rob pitching in wouldn't be like Rich working for his sister. Workwise, the boy wonder was at the end of his tether. He could just about hack the Bar-for-tossers as long as he didn't have to work extra, because that meant waiting tables. What's the big deal?

The big deal was he couldn't do it any more. He could clean up after the punters when they'd gone, but he couldn't wait on them. Not again. He'd reached the point where he couldn't stand by the table and say the line any more. Ready to *order*, sir? Education's a wonderful thing. He'd got a first class degree so he wouldn't have to be a waiter, and now he'd elevated himself to cleaner. No, Rob had done enough.

This was Sunday morning. Two days later Rich went away from me. Train fare arrived from his sister and he left to work in the bistro for two weeks, or for as long as it took. As long as it took to do what, he didn't say, but I thought I understood. In his eyes, he'd just lost us all our money, although that wasn't true at all. He felt responsible. He needed a fix of self-respect. We got the tube to Euston. On the platform, kissing him good-bye, I felt all the usual softness erupt and collapse inside me. Then watching him go, something stiffened deeper down. And then there was just the ache of goodbye.

I gritted my teeth and phoned home. Hi, mum.

Mum. The word tasted somehow salty.

I needed to impose on them until Rich got back? I'd imposed enough on Rob, you see?

It's a mystery to me how I'd become so cold towards the teacher and the diplomat – I couldn't even bring myself to refer to them as mum and dad – because as a child I was always terrified to be away from them for even a moment. For years I hated going to school because I didn't know where or how they were when they were out of my sight. And when I did get used to school it was only because I reinvented myself, became someone else in the seven hours I had to be away from home each day. Became loud and over-energetic, tomboyish. And when I was home I didn't want to play in the street, certainly didn't want to be out of sight of the weathervane at the top of the garage door. Didn't want to go to birthday parties or the park – not without them. It's a wonder my parents ever got the time alone to conceive Nicola. I was a scared child.

Maybe I became cold towards them because I sensed – or perhaps merely feared – that they would not always be there in the same way. Maybe I caused that to come true by fearing it. And it has come true.

Anyway the teacher – mum – didn't say anything except, of course you can come home. You can always come home.

Of course. I was afraid of those words, of their certainty and of something I knew about them, which was they were not a certainty.

Mum was trying to sound casual but I knew she was ecstatic about my visit, even though she must have known it amounted to me going home on hire. She didn't care about me bleeding her of money or that I still behaved like a shitty adolescent towards them all. She meant what she said, with unlimited love. I could always go home.

It wasn't as easy for Rob. But without me as a drain he could manage comfortably in the flat. He was still a cleaner, after all.

I phone Rich twice the first week he was away, both times during the day. But I couldn't get him. I got Frank, the Scottish chef. He had a nice voice. The second time Frank said something about Rich having mentioned heading out to the library. What library? In Manchester, Frank said. Hold on, yeah, that's it. The Central Reference Library in Manchester. It puzzled me, but I didn't think much of it. So then I phoned a couple of evenings, when he was working.

He was different. It was like talking to someone who was dealing with a bereavement. He didn't mention anything about a library, and it slipped from my thoughts. I didn't want to ask him about working in the bistro. He mentioned that his sister was being very understanding. Understanding about what? What had he told her? It was the same when I talked with Rob – the bereavement thing – and I was surprised to realise that I was coping better than the boys.

Perhaps because home wasn't so bad. The teacher and the

diplomat kept out of my way and there were no lectures, few questions. The teacher – my mum – only once asked me why I was so hard up all of a sudden, and I smiled and shrugged and told her we'd just gone a bit wild recently. Bad planning, I said. She forced a smile, but it seemed she was looking at me pretty carefully through that smile. Thankfully that was my entire interrogation.

But the olds fed and watered me and allowed me a position of respect within the family and their – our – home, far exceeding what my behaviour deserved. They were making it easy for me to be somewhere I did not want to be. I'd have been proud of them if I hadn't been thinking so much about myself.

Nicola, the Little Sister, came through with flying colours. We'd always been close enough, I suppose. But never really in the confiding, very close sense. Perhaps a year too many or too few separated us. I'd missed her most important years while away at college, and we'd developed separately. But look at her now.

She was a revelation to me that visit. She'd grown up. It was such a pleasure to find she existed now beyond a room full of *Just 17* posters and teddy bears. And she was smart enough to notice that something was up, as well as magnanimous enough not to make a big deal of throwing me a lifeline. The first thing Nic did was to rescue me with a trip to the pub – on her, of course. She never asked why I was broke, but helped me to some form of escape almost every evening I was home. If she was meeting friends in the Black Horse, so was I; if there was a film on good enough to kill two hours, we saw it; if her boyfriend took her clubbing, he took both sisters. No questions asked. I kept thinking: Nic must be spending a small fortune.

I counted a small fortune in my head.

*   *   *

The thing happened during one of Nicola's treats.

I hadn't left the buzzing behind in the flat. The feeling of existing halfway between life and death was becoming normal. I know that sounds obsessive and somewhat neurotic, but I was still on that cusp, I hadn't let go. And I needed the buzzing, now. I was comfortable with the headiness it gave me, the way a person who is sick for a long time can grow attached to their pain. But sometimes that buzzing needed to be drowned. To be able to live with it the rest of the time, more and more I needed to find myself amongst noise and darkness and light that was artificial. More and more I needed the contrast of dark and light. And when Nicola took me clubbing it served just such a purpose. Shallow light, deep darkness, anonymous music at pounding volume were all a kind of perverse cure. Like for the man who, in order to remedy an unbearable migraine, hammers a nail into his head. The first pain is cured. But how?

The Future Shock was a pokey upstairs place where few people could actually dance at once. It wasn't your usual spangly suburban nite spot. Its reputation was somewhere between pretty grubby and downright seedy, which is why I thought I liked it. The dance floor had those awful light panels built into the actual floor, and the bar area was backlit in a tacky, ghostly red. The red backless barstools were bolted to the floor. The forced closeness of the tables also made it easy for strangers to lean across to each other on some flimsy pretext and begin courting, which is the posh description for the Future Shock's principal function. In its way it was a good, honest, no beating about the bush place. And me and Nic and her boyfriend – I think he was a Steve, he looked like a Steve – were zoning out nicely there. Two or three drinks in I was beginning to feel as relaxed as I had since leaving blond Bob's. I was just contemplating shaking my thang when big thangs began shaking all by themselves.

A guy at the next table who'd been leching at Nic since we

came in suddenly slapped down his bottle of Sol and made a grab for his own throat. My first thought was: trouble, he's lost it. Until his eyes began to bulge unnaturally and stream, and he looked across to our table as if for help.

When I turned to Nicola she was holding her throat, then rubbing her eyes. Then Steve's hands were all over his own face and he was up and running towards the fire escape – alone, the chivalrous bastard.

I grabbed Nic by the wrist and followed without knowing why. Our chairs toppled over silently under the pulsing thud of the dance track. Then it hit me, like a cold rag rammed deep into my lungs, freezing solid the air I was trying to breathe. I sprawled on the floor and felt someone's shoes on my back and head. I tried to cough up what was choking me but my throat had clamped shut. Then my eyes were stinging, the pain making me feel sick. I could see Nicola trying to shout a word she had no breath to complete. The last thing I saw before my vision was drowned in tears and I succumbed to the urge to rub at my eyes was something truly beautiful – blind panic. No, that wasn't the last thing. The last thing was someone sitting at the bar. A girl. With short hair, and freckles, and white teeth under her smile. She wasn't choking, but smiling, lit from behind through the bloodshot bottles.

I couldn't have seen her. If she'd been there she'd have been choking like everyone else. No, I couldn't have seen her.

Then I was back in the panic. It was as pure and as fragile as any choreography I've ever seen; it looked planned, but was all the more perfect for being entirely spontaneous. Bodies and thoughts lunging in several directions but with one purpose – escape.

Get me out, get me out only leave him, leave her, leave my loved one, screw them only get me out.

In the instant I stumbled to my knees clutching for my sister's scratching hands, in the all-fearing all-seeing instant

132

before the fire exit sprung open like a trap in reverse and a hundred revellers fell onto the steel balcony and steps to suck in air, something of the possibility of that moment of blind panic seeped through the pain behind my eyes, settled in my mind, and stayed.

Out there on the fire escape, crisis over, I somehow knew the explanation – I've watched the news. Then the words were everywhere, being shouted, cursed, questioned.

Tear gas, CS, whatever it's called. Then the words died down. Someone's idea of a joke. Funny. It made you choke and rub your eyes and rubbing your eyes was the worst thing you could do because that made them hurt even more. But its effects wore off quickly, and before too long we moved back inside. The music had never stopped and our drinks were where we'd left them. I reclaimed our chairs and righted them. Steve was enjoying comforting Nicola, no doubt wondering how he could weave himself a hero's fuck out of his version of the story. Well, good luck to him. Within a few minutes the Future Shock would be back to business as usual, but with an unusual new pretext for strangers to make their moves. A night for heroic conquests, all courtesy of blind panic.

I thought about who I'd seen sitting at the bar. There was no one there, now. There had been no one there, then. It must have been the dream, coming back to me in the moment of panic, a moment my brain interpreted as a moment between life and death, like the dream. I saw it, and I needed something. I needed a laugh. I needed some light in my life. I needed more nights like this – only without the drama – and I needed a drink. I had several.

I found myself thinking about that wonderful gas. A few sips of my drink later I was still thinking about it. I was fascinated – it was something about blinding pain. If pain had a sound, this one would have been like my buzzing. Yes, I could hear the pain; I could hear the gas.

And then I could see it.

A black canister the thickness of a broom handle, and the length of a shot glass, was rolling towards me between the tables. Rolling straight for me. It seemed to come from nowhere, it could have been anything, but no, I was convinced this was the instrument responsible for the night's chaos.

Without hesitation I bent down and caught the thing under the palm of my right hand, and slipped it between two buttons of my geeky cardigan as I straightened up. I hunched over with it sitting in there between my tits, until I was sure I hadn't been watched. Then I fished it out with the intention of transferring it to my jacket pocket. But its solid freezing weight was too impressive to let go of straight away, I had to finger it and feel its shape. It didn't feel how I'd seen the words tear gas in my mind. It was cool and compact with just a depressor at one end and what felt like a small hole opposite that. Just a small aerosol, nothing more. Just a little spray.

21

What had he been up to at the library?

Not that there was any reason he shouldn't be going to the library – people go to libraries. But why the Central Reference Library? What was he looking for that would take him there? It may sound like a trivial thing, but my instinct had a hold of this one and it wouldn't let go. My instinct told me this would not prove to be trivial.

So what was so special about that place he had to go all the way to Manchester from his sister's? Was he studying again, was that it? Maybe he'd made a big decision or two in his time back home.

But why hadn't he mentioned it? You'd think he would discuss those things with me. No, I was ruling all these things out, eliminating possibilities. If he was planning to do some postgrad stuff, like an MA – no, I couldn't believe that was possible; postgrad was just another dead end, a way of putting off the inevitable, at the very most a tunnel-vision route into lower echelon academia, if you were lucky. And Rich knew that. But if he had shifted that way then why the secrecy? Would he tell me in his own good time? Should I challenge him about it? Would that make me look as if I was invading his space? We are allowed space, after all.

No. I was certain he wasn't studying for an MA. So what was he hiding, and why?

But that wasn't the only thing that was making me edgy.

*　　*　　*

When Rich was back – it was only two weeks – and we were together and relatively solvent again, it quickly became obvious that the boys had been calling each other almost nightly. I tried not to let it show, but I was hurt.

Hurt? I was furious.

I mean, *damn*! They'd discussed things at length without me. And what's more they weren't mentioning the library business. So they were both keeping it from me. That felt horrible. How dare they? It was an insult, and a mystery I didn't need. I couldn't shake off the thought that they knew something about all this that I didn't.

So our reunion kicked off feeling more like an adversarial board meeting. We manoeuvred around each other like nervous shareholders, unsure about who was allied to whom. That was the way it seemed to me. I couldn't wait to get Richard alone.

And then I thought about Rob – that maybe he was the one I needed to get on his own, and put pressure on. Yes, I knew he was nowhere near as discreet as Rich, who could clam up with extraordinary restraint. But not Rob the gob. Yes, that was the way to go. Rob would tell me everything I wanted to know, and not even know he'd done it. I wasn't comfortable about having to be devious. But it didn't seem to me like I had a choice. It was going to be rough, though.

I got my chance in the pub. It should have felt good going to the Hungry Horse, which was our favourite pub, and not having to stretch out three halves of Fosters. But it didn't feel good at all. For once we could afford what we liked within reason, and I was too wound up to care. And when Rich got settled into a conversation at another table with some people he hadn't seen for a while, I pounced on Rob.

What was that music? It was a tape, so I couldn't check the jukebox. It sounded like a young John Lennon. I was sure it was John Lennon, but it wasn't any Beatles song I'd ever heard. *You wanna be like the folks on the hill* was the first bit I caught.

Rob was chasing a Jack Daniel's and tap water with a pint of Stella, alternating sips. I was just on the Stella which I'd hardly touched – I don't even try to keep up with them. But I downed a good half of my pint now.

Rob affected a startled look. 'Easy, tiger. Night's young.'

'Why the secrecy?'

'What?' He put down the whisky glass and pushed both drinks away from himself slightly.

'What is there that's so important that you can't tell me?'

'I'm not with you.' He was being very calm.

I didn't feel calm. I leaned into him across the small round table. 'I know about the library. Scottish Frank told me. I know he went more than once.'

Robin's face was a total blank. I had to assume it was a lie, although I knew he wasn't that good.

'Library?'

'How much else is there you two haven't told me?' I nodded in the direction of where Rich was catching up with his other friends. There was a group of them and they were laughing at something, which grated on my nerves.

Rob drained his whisky and said: 'Let's rewind a bit.'

'No, let's keep going. I'd like to know why you don't think I need to know what you two have been talking about.'

'What are you saying?'

'I know you and Rich were in touch all the fucking time when he was back home. Every five minutes, by the sound of it. How do you think that makes me feel?' I leaned in even further. 'I hardly got to speak to him at all. Why is that, Rob? What are you hiding from me?'

Rob left a pause. Things were not clear to him. 'Look,' he said, cautiously. 'If Rich chose to discuss some things with me

137

rather than you these past two weeks, I'm sorry. I just assumed he was talking to both of us.'

'Apparently not.'

'I'm sorry about that. But we've told you the gist of what was said – which at the end of the day was very little.'

'That isn't true and you know it.'

Fire came into his eyes, and the human music left his voice. I shivered. 'Listen,' he growled. 'I don't care who you are. Don't call me a liar, Trash. Not now, not ever.'

I downed the rest of my drink. He was serious.

What now?

'What did you mean about a library?' At least his voice was back to normal, just about.

'I don't know.'

'You've started so you can finish. What's this about a library?'

I looked him in the eyes. 'That's what I was hoping you could tell me.'

Which was when Rich rejoined us.

'Ready for another, kids?'

Rob and me exchanged an uncertain look, which said, let's wait and see. I didn't like it. But for now there was nothing more I could say without appearing desperately paranoid. I wasn't happy. Now I didn't know who had secrets from who. I felt a wall of distrust go up between Rich and the two of us, separately. Two walls of distrust. There would be more about this.

'Oi. You drinking?'

'Yeah. Same again.'

'Rob?'

Rob was a long time in answering: 'Keep 'em coming.'

The John Lennon song was on a loop in my head as I tried to see through to the back of Robin's eyes.

But you're still fucking peasants as far as I can see.
A working class hero is something to be!

22

I pushed all this to the back of my mind, where it would be waiting when I needed it. In the meantime there were things to say. Decisions had to be taken about how to go on – it was taken as read that we would go on – with the betting. Two weeks with our feet on planet Earth hadn't lessened our collective sense that we were into something special. Rich, especially, seemed like a man with a mission. Rob noticed it too. Rob watched Rich very closely. Anyway, the minute we began talking in earnest about it all again the hunger, the starving fever, was back. Money was what we talked about.

Money.

Something was going wrong. What were the possibilities?

We were talking to the ghosts all wrong; we were phrasing questions carelessly, possibly even asking the wrong questions; we were mishandling the information, not respecting the magnitude of what we were being allowed to witness and be a part of. Yes, these could all be factors and, yes, they had to be scrutinized, but there had to be a way of breaking the code. And, yes, it would come.

But we kept returning to that cipher: RISK EVERYTHING. We worked our minds around it incessantly, like working your tongue over a bad tooth. This was what we slept on and woke up with – that and the buzzing. The two things, the riddle and the noise, seeped everywhere and pulsed through everything.

*　　*　　*

And then a couple of days later someone robbed the betting shop.

'Our betting shop?'

'The very same. *Los mismo*. Check out this headline, it's totally laughable. *Muy* bizarre.'

'What?' Rob butted in from the bathroom. ' "**GRADUATE MAKES ENDS MEET**"?'

That was funny.

Rich summarised from the front page of the *Hornsey Voice*: ' "**ALL BETS ARE OFF!**" And then there's a story. It's like this. Guy walks into Billy Hill's with a pistol – real one – and wearing a balaclava. Demands the cash. Only, Securicor have not long since been in and there's not really much money around. So this guy gets a major sad-on and starts waving his gun around and shouting, the upshot being the Plod reckon they've got an Oscar-winning security vid of him featuring a CD quality-recording of his voice. Aha, they reckon the net's closing.'

'The plot thinnens,' I said. 'How much did he get?'

'Whoever it was, two hundred quid of it's ours,' Rob called out.

That was funny as well.

'Two hundred and fifteen,' I called back, but my words were lost in the flush.

Rob shuffled into the early morning gloom of the master bedroom, still doing up his fly buttons, and flopped on his back on the floor next to Rich. They looked too big to be lying on floors at 4 a.m. It occurred to me we didn't see much daylight any more.

'Jesus!' Rich said.

'What?'

Rich shook his head. 'It says here he got away with less than a grand.' He shook his head again. He was lying propped up on his elbows now. He looked at home again. He looked like my husband.

I was listening from the bed, scanning the *Hornsey Voice*'s fraudulent Careers supplement, more for perverse entertainment value than in the hope of turning anything up. By far the biggest ad, covering almost one third of one page, read: **TO RECRUIT IN *THE VOICE,* CALL** (ansaphone number) ***NOW!*** Like I said, fraudulent.

Rich went on. 'To get involved with guns for so little money, it's just not worth it. It's way, way too much of a r–'

Wow.

Praise be. I know the meaning of revelation. I know the weight of the word and the precise course of its hard definition dropping from the base of the brain to the backs of your feet. Richard never finished his sentence.

The code was broken.

What that man did for almost no money, that was the kind of genuine commitment we'd been challenged to demonstrate. It had to be something like that. To risk everything for the guarantee of nothing. For a faint hope. Of course. Among a dozen other sensations in that moment – fear, excitement, more fear – was simple white light understanding. Satori, the kick in the eye. I understood risk, commitment, pure dedication. *Pure*, that was the word I saw. *Pure*. And that thought was what mattered. I suddenly admired that prick who'd knocked over William Hill's with almost no hope of getting away with it and negligible reward even if he did. I envisaged us on the same side, saw him proving himself to his own set of ghosts.

It was a long time before any of us spoke. The decision was made. To refer to it openly would only hasten the necessity of acting on it. But eventually someone had to say something. Rich closed the paper and said quietly, 'Risk everything.'

We knew it was true. Up to then we'd been playing, dabbling with the ouija board like schoolkids, risking nothing and getting exactly that in return. No meaningful answers, just a moving plastic cup. Anyone can do that.

Of course we questioned ourselves. We put a case for common sense. But the sole truth was that we could not stop. We had to see this through, our one chance of success. Limitless money. Surely it was worth this one risk.

'It'll take a big bet. The kind we could never afford no matter how many giros we pooled. And anyway this isn't about pooling giros any more. We will have to risk something getting this money. We will have to do something along the lines of matey in the betting shop.' Rich talked slowly, looking us in the eye in turn. He was sitting up now. 'We will have to steal this money. That is the risk.' He said this even more slowly, and slowly we nodded in turn. The words meant very little just then. They were unspecific. We had time to plan and to imagine that there were safe ways to do such a thing. We were just talking, after all. We could say anything and it still didn't matter yet.

'There's all kinds of thieving,' Rob said.

'Yes, but guns are out,' Rich said without hesitation.

I heard myself say: 'How come? Risk everything, remember?' I heard myself say it but I don't know where the words came from.

'Guns are out,' said Rich, 'simply because there's no way on earth we could get hold of one. Where would we start? This is Crouch End, not the Bronx. And I imagine they'd be a bit beyond our budget. Even if we knew where to get one we'd have to rob the bookies first to be able to afford it. So, guns are out.'

'Well that kind of narrows it down a bit, doesn't it?' Rob said. 'We can't do what that guy did, for a start.'

'We can't do it exactly. But there must be a way of doing something similar.'

'Pretend guns?'

'And very real custodial sentences.'

'Burglary?' I asked. 'Houses?'

Rich thought, and shook his head. 'No guarantee what you'll get, if anything. And I wouldn't have the first clue about flogging hot camcorders. Let's face it, we don't exactly have serious underworld connections.'

Not yet, I mused.

'Off-licences,' Rob said. 'They always have shitloads of money.'

'And security cameras and a whole family of tasty Pakis on the door. Worse than bookies. Come on, we're not thinking. There has to be something else, some type of caper we haven't thought of yet.'

'Caper, good word, good film word,' Rob put in. He made a gun of his right thumb and forefinger and aimed it around the room. I found the gesture disturbing. Rob never used to be disturbing. A loud idiot, yes, but never disturbing.

Rich went on, 'Something risky. Something absolutely audacious that we can pull off for a ton of money in one go, without guns – oh yeah, and not get caught. That would be a welcome bonus.' By the time he stopped talking he was smiling weakly.

'Yeah, right,' Rob frowned. 'Staring us in the face, I should imagine.'

We chuckled, then tried to look as though we were thinking. I tried picturing the kinds of felonies we were after, but just kept seeing an image of myself abseiling through a bank skylight in a fetching Armani catsuit and mask. Not much help. I shut up. We were all quiet for a while.

Until Rob said something.

'What did the restaurant do?'

'Hmm?' Rich rolled over onto his back. 'What restaurant?'

'The last place we worked together on Greek Street. They had shitloads of cash every day. What did they do with it?'

Rich's face cleared of everything else as he tried to remember.

Then he inhaled slowly and said, 'The same thing every day.'

Rob nodded. 'Interesting.' The boys looked at each other, smiling. 'Very interesting.'

I jumped off the bed and joined them cross-legged on the floor, hardly able to keep still. So I thumped Rich on the back. 'What? What's interesting? Tell me!'

Rich turned to me, intent on enjoying relating the germ of a plan, until Rob butted in.

He sat up. 'It's like this, Trash,' he began at the double. 'It's just a restaurant. But there's no Securicor, no videos, no nothing. *Nada*. And the best part is the money leaves the premises and walks, *walks* through Soho to the Midland at Cambridge Circus. It must be a three or four minute journey with a dozen busy corners on the way.'

'Wait a minute.' I was confused. 'What do you mean it walks?'

'Just that.' Rich got in first this time. 'Two staff from the restaurant walk to the bank every day during the afternoon quiet spell. Just before the bank closes, in fact. Same time every day. All you'd have to do is be there just as all that money is walking through Soho and say: Hand it over, ta very much.'

'And they just give it to us, do they?'

'They're told to do just that, dearest. It's standard hold-up procedure: Don't fight. Don't struggle. The money's insured, not worth risking life and limb for.'

I looked at him. 'I'm not a mugger, Rich.'

'You weren't Trash the gambling medium three weeks ago,' Rob interjected.

I felt myself blush, and was thankful it was dark. But he was right. And three minutes ago I'd been ready to abseil into a bank. I just didn't know what I was thinking. But I knew I didn't like the direction the talk was taking. 'We'd be using knives or something, wouldn't we? Someone could get hurt. And what if they didn't just give us the money? What if they chased us, or made us fight them? What then? What if someone piled in on their side? Soho's a busy place. Think of what could go wrong.'

'You mean think of the risks?' Rob again. He was really going with this idea now. 'Risks, Trash?'

'You're right, it won't work.'

'Eh?'

Rich to the rescue, I thought.

'Trash is right, but for the wrong reasons.'

Nope. Oh, fuck.

'We can't rob Toppo's coz the minute we start hanging round checking the place out someone's bound to recognise us. Between the two of us we must have waited half the tables in that street. But you're wrong about the other stuff. I mean, would you argue with a knife? When you're robbed you freeze. You give over the money and you wish you were somewhere else and hope that you don't get carved. End of story. And as for some have-a-go hero, no way. People get robbed blind in broad daylight every day in London. Getting away would be the easiest part. Only, if it's a restaurant, it can't be Toppo's. It would have to be somewhere far away.'

Rob: 'Somewhere else which takes a lot of money.'

'That's another thing,' Rich said, scratching his arse. 'What's a lot of money? How much are we after here?'

'More than that dickhead in the bookies got, bless him.'

Rich thought for a mo, realigned his knickers with his crotch, and felt around the floor for a lager. There were a couple left somewhere. 'Then a restaurant's out. Restaurants don't take that much money. Certainly by mid-afternoon.'

Now Rob was messing with his privates. It must be subconsciously contagious, like sneezing or coughing are for normal people. 'But these places open till two a.m. There'd be the whole previous night's takings.'

Rich shook his head and licked his teeth in a way which

145

somehow made him seem cleverer than us. He spotted the lager, reached for it, and cracked the ringpull. 'I can't see it. Half of that won't go through the books. Not ever. I bet it goes straight home to Toppo's and into a nice little safe behind "Monarch of the Glen" where the tax man'll never find it.'

Another conspiratorial pause for thought, during which I smuggled the open can over to my side, and Rich pretended not to notice.

'Well, what about a shop, then?' Rob suggested. 'A busy shop with shitloads of money that doesn't use Securicor, but banks the Toppo way? Shops have got to be more kosher than restaurants.'

'That's good. That's excellent, in fact.' Nodding: 'I like a shop.'

I wasn't sure I liked any of this. But the boys weren't allowing too much time for doubts. Rich just moved straight along.

'Now the method. We still have to know what we're actually going to do. Details, gentlemen.'

'"You were only s'posed to blow the bloody doors off!"'

Silence.

'What?'

'Michael Caine in *The Italian Job*.' Blank looks. Rob reddened. 'Never mind.'

There was a decent-sized pause.

I said, 'I don't like knives, Rich.'

'Trash is right, Rich. I hear what you were saying before, but I don't know what I'd do if someone argued with a knife. Things could get nasty. I just want them to freeze, hand over the cash, then we fuck off into the sunset. Roll credits. *Finito*.'

And then bells rang out, trumpets sounded, and I knew what we would do.

'You want them to what?' I said.

'To freeze, why?' Rob looked at me. 'What's on your mind?'

'Oh fuck,' I whispered. 'I'll show you what's on my mind.'

And I hopped to my stockinged feet and skipped to the foot of the bed and picked up my duffel bag. From the bottom of it I fished out a small black canister I'd all but forgotten about.

23

The Madeleine dream had become the only part of sleep I looked forward to. It was the only time the noises stopped. I could see her more clearly now every time, see everything about her I thought I could remember and knew I wanted to see again. And I could see the background, the red bar, all the surroundings becoming more defined. And every time I had the dream I awoke knowing I had recognised a little more, and that sooner or later the place she was in in the dream would become clear to me, that it would be a place with which I was familiar, and which I could find.

And meanwhile I watched Richard. And Rob watched everyone and everything. When I saw the way he looked at me I had to remind myself of certain definite true things I had always believed in; I had to tell myself he couldn't see into my dream.

In the meantime I was having my doubts.

It's not every day you sit down to plan an armed robbery.

Armed robbery is not an every day thing in most people's lives. And when you decide to stop being someone who doesn't plan and carry out armed robberies and become someone who does, it tends to play on your mind. You can even lose sleep over it. Ha ha.

But it's serious. The choices you make matter. They matter because they change your perception of You. Maybe this was something like Rich meant when he talked about how the money would affect us. But it's hard to make people understand you. It's hardest of all to accept someone else's interpretation of change. Like it or not, you change the picture of You that looks out from the mirror of the universe with the choices you make. Depending on the nature and extremity of your choices you don't even actually have to do anything physical. Just make a mental choice and you *are* different. The only way back – or forward – is through other changes. So did I change into an armed robber, and everything which goes with that? Is that what I became? I still can't grasp it after six years, six years which, it pains me to record, have not done their job properly. There are times when my unwelcome window into the past is way too clear for comfort. In those moments it seems that time just hasn't made a reasonable effort to diminish or to heal, and I feel downright cheated. I don't know if I can keep bearing the responsibility. I don't want to be an armed robber forever. It feels unfair; I'm far distant from the person I once was in so many ways. The person young enough and desperate enough to do a thing like she did and hardly consider the consequences. I'm not the girl who made those decisions. I'm the woman who's long since climbed on her shoulders and tried to disown her. Some-times I've wished I could kill her, and have another past.

But it was me. I mustn't deny my culpability by separating what Trash did then from what Natasha thinks of it now. Prisons, and not just the stone and cement kind, are full of those kinds of thoughts, the thoughts of people who'll spend considerable tracts of their allotted time thinking: but it wasn't me, it was someone else. I shouldn't be here. It was a person I may have been, once, but am not now. Lord, have I not paid enough?

The worst punishment of all is memory. Remembering the people who got hurt. I see it through the window of years, hoping on the worst days, like today, that maybe today my eyes will cloud, the view dim.

But the window is crystal. And I have to tell the story. We earned that perfect view of our history. We crossed a line. How does that happen? How does it happen to someone like me? At the beginning of this story were three friends getting by. Here in the middle are three people planning something unthinkable. I've told you the facts of how the first situation became the second. And while the window is still clear I must look back through it for the facts to finish this story. A part of me wants to say more, wants to try and force the process of repentance. But that is inappropriate. I'm here because of what I did. It seems that only that fact is appropriate.

We moved to the kitchen where I filled the boys in on the Future Shock episode. I kept it short. Stuck to what was relevant.

At first they didn't see what I was getting at, didn't seem to understand what the canister was. And then when they did their eyes flashed, their faces took on the same How the bugger did YOU get hold of something as cool as THIS? expression. Rob whistled at my description of the perfect panic. I was becoming worried about Rob. They turned the thing over in their hands, passing it back and forth. The boys liked the gas.

They made me tell them over and over again about Future Shock, wanted to hear every detail of how the spray affected people. The part where the canister just came rolling towards me out of nowhere had them gaping in awe. I felt certain that, somehow, I'd be included in all our decisions from now on.

The first thing they wanted to do was try out the gas. I was in no hurry myself, although I had to agree it made sense. I wasn't looking forward to it. But they really were. I think they were enjoying the idea of demonstrating their manly indifference to extreme blinding pain. Boys have some funny ideas.

We did the test in the muddy alley which ran down the side of blond Bob's terraced block. The sun never reached in here, hence the mud even in summer. It was predictably unpleasant. The gas worked just dandy in the open even with the briefest of sprays. Rich pressed down on the canister for only an instant and a weedy mist genied out of the nozzle, but we were incapacitated in seconds. Rob was first out of the alley, wheezing and coughing, but we weren't far behind. There was reluctant agreement that we needed more practice; we had to get used to stomaching this stuff so as not to become victims of our own attack. So it was back to the alley for another squirt, and then another. After three gassings we were a mite ruffled. Make that traumatised. And we were in agreement: three tear gas attacks in one day was enough for even the toughest hoods to endure in the name of careful planning. We walked back to the house to the tune of the dawn chorus, hurrying red-eyed from the rising sun. No one passed us in the street on the way. If they had they'd have seen a pale girl and two equally pasty grown men crying.

Back in the kitchen Rich leaned back in his chair, lit up, threw the fags and matches down with self-conscious élan. Being a gangster suited him. 'We've got a weapon,' he said through the smoke. 'But we still don't have a lot else. Come on, people. Ideas. This needs a lot of planning.'

Smoke rings? That was new.

'In some ways,' Rob said. He was trying to look cool, too, but he didn't quite have it yet. He was too wooden. (Rob's the unfortunate kind who, whatever you dress him in, it looks like a former uniform. It was hell the few times he got new clothes. I had to wash them about a dozen times then thrash them about on the pavement before he stopped looking like Starch Man.

The things I fucking do.) Also he was experimenting with a mid–Atlantic accent. I'm not sure if the bloodshot, just-gassed look complemented or detracted from the image. Anyway, Rob went on: 'If these places send their money to the bank with a couple of goons every day surely you just follow the goons and squirt them.'

Goons? What, pray, are goons?

'Toppo never sent his money at exactly the same time every day – not to the minute. And the goons went in civvies. If you didn't know them you'd think it was just two punters coming out of the place. With a big shop it'd be even more difficult. We'd need to case the joint – probably for days. Get to know everyone who worked there so you'd recognise them the minute they left the place.'

Case the joint?

'There'd have to be practice runs,' Rob offered. 'We'd have to practise following the goons to the bank. Get to know the route they took – whether they varied it – and how easily we could get away and down what streets.' The ideas were coming fast – too fast. You could see it in their faces. All I wasn't sure of yet was which was Bogart and which was Pacino.

'Whoa, slow down.' Rich let his chair fall back onto four legs, then raised his hands and laid them flat on the table. Fag dripping from the loose corner of his lips. Pacino, no question. 'All that stuff is cool. But we haven't even got a target.' He patted his hands on the table in time to his next speech: 'I can't get this clear in my mind until I know exactly where we're going to hit. I need a focus. Otherwise we're just fantasising.'

Pacino needed a focus. Goons. They should have been hard to take seriously, except that I knew they were deadly serious.

Rob, blowing smoke around: 'I keep remembering what you said about central London. Fewer heroes.' Yep, Bogart.

'Definitely. Trash?'

152

I thought about it.

But I didn't want to think about it.

But I did want to be included. What they were saying terrified the shit out of me. What film did they think they were in? Was this their way of making anything they did okay? I had some nasty pictures in my head.

But I didn't want to be left out of anything. So I marshalled my thoughts and chimed in. 'Yeah. We could lose ourselves pretty easily. Two minutes and two streets away and nobody would know the difference. We could just walk home in broad daylight.'

Did I say that? Did those words come out of my mouth?

'Wow,' said Bogart. 'Jee-sus. Wow.' He had a point. This was all pretty hard to grasp.

'Target,' Pacino repeated. Trying to focus us. 'Come on, we need this settled. At least the type of target.'

'Well,' Rob said. 'Basically one that doesn't use outside help for its banking. I don't know how we can know that, though.' He shook his head. 'It's a basic problem but it could be terminal if we don't find a way round it. I mean, we can't just march in somewhere and ask.'

Rich grunted: 'True. Shit. Come on, where do we know? Where have we worked? Where do we know where friends have worked? What do we know that will cut down on the research factor?' He looked around the room for inspiration. 'Think, think think think.'

It made sense, using what we knew, sticking to the familiar.

Rob: 'But then there's the Toppo's factor. People we know.' He leaned forward and took the floor, so to speak. 'We can't pick somewhere a mate of ours might still work or where we might have been seen and remembered, even years ago.' That was true. We listened as he went on. 'Besides anything else I don't fancy jumping someone we know.'

Jumping?

153

'No worries.' Rich waved his cigarette nonchalantly. 'We'll plan around that.'

He meant around people – Rich felt okay about planning around *people*. I didn't like that. And I didn't like that word – jumping. Something had jarred in me when Rob said that and it took me a minute to recover. I was angry at Rob for using that word, I hated the sound of it, because I knew it was accurate.

Rob got up and stepped over to the sink. He ran the cold and splashed his eyes, patting them dry on his Barbarossa sweatshirt. The gas. 'Ouch. Jesus. Okay, fair enough.' He rubbed his eyes again but it wasn't enough. 'Jesus, this stuff's really going to put people down, isn't it? I mean, us, the goons, bystanders – anyone and everyone. I doubt this will pause to discriminate. It's gonna be tear gas carnage, Tiananmen Square.'

'Yeah. Only Leicester Square,' Rich said. Al and Bogey cackled at that one, heh heh, and I felt sick.

'Wait,' I said. They stopped yukking and turned to me. I tried to think about what I was feeling but there was something in the looks they were giving me which wasn't helping me concentrate. I said, 'Just wait, can we? Can we not talk about jumping people? Can we try not to sound like thugs? Listen to yourselves.' I was surprised at the anger in my voice. 'I mean, is this right?'

Two blank faces. 'Is it what?'

'Is it right? *Right?* You know?' And then the words ran on, spraying out like gas.

'It's like with the board. Like we said all along. We have to think about the moral side of this. We need ground rules. We're talking about spraying gas in people's faces and leaving them screaming in the street. It could be anyone. There could be children about or old people. This could go wrong. We don't know what side-effects this stuff might have. Just look at the state we're in.' The boys just stared through me; I wasn't

154

reaching them anywhere. I tried again. 'I just don't know what to think about all this. It's all happening too fast. I just don't want to hurt people.'

Rob chimed straight in. 'The gas was your idea, Trash.'

I looked to Rich for support. He just said, 'You're either in or you're out, Trash.' Then he took a fag from Rob's packet and lit it from his last.

He'd never spoken to me like that before.

He said more. 'Are you up for this? Because we've got to be sure of you.' And that was all of it. He didn't try and convince me, or refer to morals or try to reassure me. Apparently it was okay with him if I dropped out of the programme about now.

And he was absolutely right.

What we were into was going to be the same however genteel the vocabulary. You either did it properly – ruthlessly, with precision – or not at all. And if we did it successfully, if everything went according to plan, then yes, people would get hurt. Hurting people was part of the plan. I was in or I was out. Commit or just forget it. But I wasn't sure I could do that. I was thinking about what Rich thought about me. Did he think he knew me? Did he think I was a worse person than I'd been three weeks ago? And what did I think of myself?

But there wasn't time.

The boys waited, facing each other, sucking and blowing white smoke. I looked at the pack on the table and made a decision. I slid out a cigarette, lit up, and said quietly: 'I'm in.'

Rich: 'No more doubts.'

Trash: 'No more doubts. Talk about it how you like. Just let's do it properly.'

And that was that.

In for a penny.

*   *   *

So how would you do it? How would you sift through all the businesses in a town the size of London, pick one out and say: this is the place we're going to knock over? What processes of elimination would you use?

Hang on to that phrase.

What I'm getting at here is that although on the surface this is a pretty haphazard modus operandi, that's exactly what it is not. I wanted to show you this process, how we picked our target. And I've done that. And you see how little there is to it in the end? Isn't every process we encounter just one of elimination? And it doesn't begin or end there, either. Wind it back, reel in the logical *re*gression, and you see that even the processes themselves are chosen for us, through other processes over which we have equally dubious control. When we make choices we aren't doing much in the way of choosing. I'm not saying we're not responsible for our choices, as far as that means anything. Just that whatever you try and break away from, those processes are all in the script, waiting to find you. I think.

On the other hand, philosophy aside, we used my little sister.

24

It was that morning I got the letter from my dad.

Why would my dad write me a letter? He'd never written me a letter. Apart from anything else I'd just been home for two weeks. If he had something to say to me, he could have said it then, surely? What I could decipher of his scrawl on the good Foreign Office paper didn't make much sense. Incidentally, I know I call him the diplomat, but that was just something I started saying as a tease and which subsequently stuck. He was really more of a grey civil servant type, and not a big shot except to me and mum and Nic. Anyway, the stuff in the letter was very emotional which, frankly, embarrassed me. He kept going on about how I could come home for good any time. And the word 'unapproachable' in relation to myself came up a couple of times. Was that fair? Then there was something about him not blaming Rich. Not blaming him for what? The bit that jolted me, though, was when he started on about drugs. I stared at the word on the page, not wanting to be reading this stuff or thinking about it at all. Where was he getting these ideas from? I wasn't to worry, he kept repeating. I was just to come home, and they'd always love me and help me get over whatever it was.

I see now that the message in the letter was clear – my family needed reassurance, a little meaningful contact. But I couldn't spare the time or the consideration. And besides, I had other things to think about. I had to be focused. I made a mental note to drop the daft old sod a brief line at his office, to reassure him I wasn't a junkie, then promptly forgot about it.

The year I left college and she finished school Nicola worked for the summer in a bookshop, a big four-storey tomb of a place with an old and hallowed name in the trade. There are bookshops the whole length of the street it's on, new and second-hand, some warehouse-sized, others little more than stalls. During my student years I trawled the area regularly, burrowing for bargains.

Whatever its history and reputation, the establishment in question had long since deteriorated into a sprawling low-tech junk shoppe. Labyrinthine chaos. Old stock never seemed to be cleared out, flattened cardboard cartons covered holes in the floor, and dust was as sacred as cows in Delhi: disturb at your own risk. I suppose someone must have liked it that way. According to legend, the owner, an old guy rumoured to be about a hundred who ruled the place with a rod of iron from a vast office cum cobweb on the top floor like something from Dickens, wouldn't hear of changing a thing. Probably still hasn't. This is mostly hearsay and probably bullshit – whatever. But Nicola had worked there and had mentioned seeing money taken to the bank by staff from the shop, and no men in blue crash helmets in evidence. What lodged that shop in my mind was remembering how she always said that if they ever asked her to go with the money she'd refuse *because it didn't seem safe*. At the time I worried that if it came to a confrontation over the issue Nic would probably lose her job. But I admired her courage in sticking to her guns, which she certainly would have.

And that's how I thought of it. Recalling how Nic said she wouldn't feel safe. And then, for a moment, I thought about Nicola walking money to the bank and not being safe. Someone

I knew. And I thought about me doing it and I didn't like that thought either. And then I told the boys about the place anyway, and it seemed like a horrible betrayal.

That's what I meant by using my sister. I said: I've thought of somewhere, and I explained about Nic's bookshop, and they slammed their palms on the kitchen table and told me I was a genius, although I felt like a snake, and Rob ranted. He said, 'Safe? You fucking bet it won't be safe. That's our place! Yer fucking right it's NOT FUCKING SAFE!'

And I don't remember whether I felt sick or happy.

You see? Not much of a process, is it? It's all elimination, all decided before we tumble on it. No mystery. There are choices waiting to be chosen. People we know waiting to be implicated.

Is that how we treat the people we know?

Fuck. And for once everything was going according to plan.

Action time. This is the part in the film where you see them planning and rehearsing the job. Rendezvous, synchronise watches, pay attention double-oh seven. Thrilling stuff. Flesh and guns everywhere.

They wouldn't show the preparation in our film. Remember casing the joint? We patrolled a bookshop for ten days. Ten joyous, riveting days. *Reservoir Dogs* it wasn't. Casing this particular joint effectively meant spending the best part of ten dog day afternoons, mornings and long hungry lunchtimes hanging around this mausoleum in the Charing Cross Road pretending to be transfixed by AA restaurant guides or the new A. S. Byatt scrabble-fest. I shudder to recall. For ten days we browsed. Dirty work. But necessary.

It was like this.

We had to get to know everyone who did the bank run by

sight. The only way we could think to do that was to watch for any two or more of the dozens of staff leaving the shop together with a likely looking bag. The first few days we missed them every time. We didn't even know all their faces by then, and we shouldn't have expected miracles straight away. And our patience paid off. With every supposedly wasted hour we became more familiar with everything about the relevant staff. That was the challenge about this part of the job, trying to keep your brain working at absolute optimum while it was prone to slip into cabbage mode for minutes at a time, missing something small but vital. That's what we were watching for, little things. People whose actions betrayed their familiarity with the place; people who didn't wear coats, didn't look at the shelves, didn't want to be there – staff. Stay awake, that frizzy-haired lass on the stairs might turn out to be an undervalued employee. But not to us; we value you, Ms ——. We know your worth. (Listen for her name, log her face, she might be the one.)

You catalogued their faces in your memory (I still have them all). You overheard their names being used and you memorised them. And back at kitchen HQ you plotted against them: 'At two p.m. slim James left with little Erica carrying an American Retro bag, but they just went for lunch in Soho Square. I think James is shagging little Erica. However, I cannot confirm if Martin (Erica's official bf) is aware.' Poor Martin.

It was a weird way to spend your day, trying to spy on these people, memorising their routine while ideally remaining invisible yourself. But among all the tourists and students and suits it was easier than you'd think. The place was an absolute warren of cubby holes and corridors. A shoplifter's paradise. I even thought about it a few times out of sheer boredom. I could have nicked a whole library. James could have carried on an affair with little Erica and no one would have been the wiser. Perhaps he did.

160

It was Rob who made the breakthrough, following two people from an unmarked door near ASTROLOGY – bingo, the safe room – through MYTHOLOGY and, hey presto, out the front door, just like that, broad daylight. He tried signalling us but we were in different parts of the ground floor, blending in, boiling our brains. But Rob had them. Straight out the door they went, no pausing, no window shopping or tying laces. Just straight down Charing Cross Road past their diverse competitors to the Midland at Cambridge Circus. The same bank Toppo used.

'Sweet.'

That was Rob's word of the day when he rounded us up outside the shop. 'Sweet,' he kept saying. Dulce. 'Couldn't be simpler. No one gave anyone a second look. I just walked twenty yards behind them all the way and watched them turn into the bank. It's just a routine. They just switch off.' Rob laughed and pulled at his cigarette. 'Sweet.' He laughed again, then leaned forward intensely. 'They stood for a whole minute waiting for the lights to change at Cambridge Circus.' He pointed his cigarette at me for emphasis. 'A whole minute. I stood right behind them, breathing right down Erica's sweet little neck.' He dragged hard again, savouring the smoke, shaking his head and looking smug. 'Erica's cute. Quite a fox.'

I shuddered.

'Cambridge Circus,' Rich repeated slowly, deliberately.

Every day after that at least one of us caught them on their way out and tailed them to the bank. It began to look easy. They couldn't vary their route without taking a risky detour through Soho's sidestreets. So, straight down Charing Cross Road to Cambridge Circus. One of the hairiest crossroads in the city, a regular pedestrian abbatoir. Throng, confusion, daylight robbery. When people think of that road junction they think of *Les Misérables* and Pizza Hut and the constant screamings of the fire engines skidding out of the Shaftesbury Avenue station. Total noise, ordered chaos, pure poetry.

161

I think of something else.

They left for the bank at pretty much the same time every day, always shortly after twelve. Once we knew that, we didn't have to station someone by the door the whole day. Besides the boredom factor, the less time spent hanging around there the less chance there was of arousing suspicion.

The next twist was Saturday. The day after Rob's first success was a Saturday. Problem? No banks. Now, we assumed Toppo just took his cash home at the weekend. But a place this size would have to do something more with it.

Saturday was a nervous day. Twelve o'clock came and went, then one. We stuck at it. Rob stationed himself near the door with an atlas and wouldn't move. He had his jaws locked around this particular little teaser. I saw him get his wallet out a few times and look through it speculatively whenever he spotted a store detective nearby.

Incidentally, they were the first people we sussed out. Most were about as effective as drugged extras from *The Bill*. Everything about them was a dead giveaway, and we had them and their routines down pat before we knew many of the staff by sight. I actually saw them collar a few people, and had no sympathy whatsoever. If you couldn't evade these jokers you deserved to be caught and beaten senseless with a Beatrix Potter boxed set. If you ever see someone acting really, really suspicious in a large shop or a department store, you've spotted yourself a plain clothes store detective. Either that or it's some idiot casing the joint.

At four o'clock we conferred by the side fire escape. Maybe they weren't going today. Maybe they kept it in the safe overnight. But it just didn't seem right. All that cash till Monday? No way. We went back to our posts, and we waited.

Shortly before five, two chumps approached the door with the magic bag. Bingo. Out the door. Straight down Charing Cross Road – this time it was me following them – and straight to – straight to where? To the Midland's nightsafe slot. Out with a key, a couple of clunks, and down the shoot slides £?ooo. Lovely. Even easier than normal. No need to worry about them entering the building. Even more people around.

Turning to begin the short walk back I felt well chuffed with myself. I had something to report which might help us a lot.

But what was this coming towards me – straight down Charing Cross Road, blah blah blah, following the route? Two more chumps – my trained eyes found their faces instantly, even among the crowds outside the Palace theatre – and a second magic bag. *Que pasa*? And twenty yards behind, Rich shadowing them. I was foxed. I didn't know whether to acknowledge him or swish straight past and back to the shop. But he stopped me.

Twice. They went to the nightsafe twice. But why? What was in the two bags? It didn't matter now. It just meant that Saturdays were too complicated. Two bags. How much money in each bag? Was it money or a week's worth of cheques, no use to anyone? That decided it. Tuesday. Why? Well, barring Saturdays, now ruled out, Monday did the best trade that we could see. And Tuesday at noon was when Monday's money walked to the bank.

Sweet.

Sweet? I was shaking in my cotton socks. But we had taken a decision. Now things would happen.

Sweet.

You get a good view of Cambridge Circus from the window seat in the Marquis of Granby. An equally passable panorama is presented from the Spice of Life, and perhaps the best from the Cambridge Arms. Molly Moggs is a dead loss. But there's no one view which is perfect, no complete perspective.

By the time we ran out of pubs we knew the junction with

our eyes shut, or with our vision blurred by booze. We knew each burger stall, each shop and office, which were open for business and when and for how long, which were boarded up or available to let. We knew the short Asian guy who put fresh supplies of prostitutes' business cards in the phone booths, and the poorly-disguised MP who must have been using them to wallpaper his hall. We could tell you which letters were missing from the *Les Mis* sign that week. We could recognise the different *Big Issue* vendors by smell. We sat in the pubs and discussed every option. Every street to escape down, every corner to approach from, every alley to duck into. Every bus to run out in front of. Jesus Jesus Jesus Jesus. Every every every.

It's a thorough business, armed assault. You have to cover all eventualities, prepare for every possibility. I. Was. Scared.

But I had no doubts any more, I was aware of what we were going to do and I wanted to do it. I knew what would happen. I was scared, but who wouldn't be?

25

We were to be in place at eleven-thirty, no earlier, even if keeping it tight meant cutting it fine. We'd never seen the money set off before eleven-fifty, but we couldn't take a chance that today of all days it would go ahead of its usual schedule. At the same time we didn't want to hang around in the open for too long in our nervous state, drawing attention to ourselves – this time two of us would be outside. So the timing would be tricky.

The plan panned out like this.

Rob would be waiting further north up Charing Cross Road, the wrong side of the shop for Cambridge Circus and the bank. He was to watch for me coming out of the shop, and to follow me following the money. As our little convoy approached the crossing outside the Palace theatre he would overtake me and I would drop back.

Then Rich would move in.

Rich would have been waiting near the theatre, keeping his eyes peeled for the mules (another of Al and Bogey's new words, bless 'em) and for Rob approximately ten yards behind them, and finally me bringing up the rear. As the two goons stopped to check the traffic Rich would make his move. Rich would be carrying the gas. Rob would be there to block any escape to the rear, and to add weight to Rich's quiet but firm demand for the money. If necessary Rich would use the gas immediately. Whatever happened, once we had the bag, he would use it anyway. In the resulting confusion no one notices a young woman take the bag from one of the two (or was it three, or four?) hoodlums. Having hung back from the action she is unaffected by the mysterious stinging in everyone else's eyes and throats. The two men instigate a scuffle with the incapacitated mules, and beat a noisy and conspicuous retreat in different directions, but empty-handed. With the bystanders concentrating on the two men making their escape, the young woman, discreetly, unnoticed, walks away with the bag. Just walks away.

Sweet.

That's what was supposed to happen.

This is what did.

Tuesday morning was really beautiful. Which was really rubbing it in. I didn't want to think about the world being beautiful. I didn't want to hear the birds in Holly Park, or see the old woman who always appeared to feed the stray cats with stale cakes and chicken skin. I didn't want to smile at Linda the Scottish postwoman, or want to wave at Iris the cleaner through the window of the Tap & Spile. I didn't want to smell the chillis and mangoes outside the West Indian grocers on Stroud Green Road, or notice the wonderful colours of the parrot fish in the French fishmonger's window, or fall in step with the reggae music from the radio in the fish van opposite the World's End. Tuesday was a really beautiful morning in the world, but I belonged somewhere else.

Beautiful day or not, it felt cold inside the bookshop. Either that or I was shaking. I mean I was shaking, there's no doubt about that.

Whatever, I was committed. I was listening to the wrong angel, the little red one on the left shoulder, I think it is. The one that looks like fun. (The angel, not the shoulder, ha ha.) Yes, it was nerves. Of course it was nerves. I feel them now just talking about it.

So it wasn't cold, but I was. I was shivering like a bugger. I began rubbing my arms to keep warm. Which is when the store detective clocked me. I knew her by sight straight away. A big butch brunette in a shell-suit and impractical heels. No problem, Trash. Just keep calm. You've seen her before.

But something wasn't right. Today of all days, after a week of looking straight through me, she decided to put the serious eye on me. I wasn't supposed to notice of course. But it's like I said.

What was I going to do?

I had no choice. Down the stairs I went – the stairs from the safe room. Bastard. Six steps. I counted them for the tenth time that day. I went and stood by BRITISH TRAVEL GUIDES. I remember I was carrying a copy of *Paradise Lost*. Now, following me would mean the store dick showing her hand, as far as she was concerned. And if she did follow me she'd probably give me a minute's start, a chance, if she thought I'd sussed her, to ditch whatever she thought I was carrying out of the shop. She couldn't have seen me hide anything on my person, because I hadn't.

Fuck her, let her sweat. Surely she couldn't stop me if she hadn't seen me hide anything. But in the meantime I couldn't see the door of the safe room any more and I wasn't sure I would hear it open and close when the goons came out. I might miss them.

I couldn't do that. At this stage it was all on me. If I fucked up now the boys would know who to blame. This was my stage of the operation. What if I fucked up and they thought I'd done it deliberately, that I'd let them go, not wanted to follow them? What would they do to me if they thought I'd bottled out?

And for the first time I knew I was actually afraid of my two best friends – of my boyfriend. They weren't acting and talking like humans. They had their doubts about me, I knew that. I had to do this or I didn't know what would happen.

So I had no choice. I'd just have to stay put and keep my eyes open and hope.

But it wasn't going to happen. Oddjob was back, and she had my number. I could smell the adrenalin oozing out of her ugly big pores. Stupid, stupid bitch. She was following me. Perhaps she'd convinced herself I'd lifted something and she was just waiting for me to make my break for the door. And when – if – I spotted the goons with the bag and went after them, I would look guilty as hell and she'd be sure she was right. And she would pounce. Fuck, she was huge. She'd pulverise me. It didn't matter that she was wrong. It would be too late. Game over. Fuck. There was no way out of this. The moment I left the shop I'd be collared, the centre of attention, and any future plan involving me in this place would be scuppered.

But it wouldn't be my fault.

It hit me. Thank you Jesus! That was my way out of this. I would be off the hook for everything. God, let me clutch at some straws. Maybe we weren't meant to do this? Maybe we'd risked enough, proved enough, and now we could bail out? I'd be stopped and searched, Oddjob would find nothing. It would all be over. Relief flooded over me in a wave of sweat.

Which was when I saw Rob.

Correction. Which was when I saw Rob walk past me stuffing a boxed set of Dante under his grey GAP jogging top in full view of Oddjob. My heart sank. What was he playing at? What was he even doing in the shop?

Okay, he was reasoning now that Oddjob couldn't follow both of us. Then something else hit me – he'd followed me inside. Rob wasn't supposed to be in the shop, but he'd followed me in there. And I knew why. He didn't trust me to do my job.

No time to think of that now. Too many things going on. Just stick to what you came here for. Okay, Oddjob couldn't follow us both, but she could still get one of us. So what was Rob doing?

I tried to get some eye contact, but Rob just looked straight through me as he marched, hunched over, towards the back of the shop. He couldn't have looked more conspicuous if he'd been wearing horse blinkers and a flasher mac. Oddjob was clearly livid. So livid that she broke all the rules and looked me straight in the eye. I shuddered as she clicked heavily past me, in the direction Rob had taken. He'd done it, he'd got her off my back. Then I did what I knew Rob meant for me to do, which was to take up my post again outside the safe room.

About ten seconds later I heard what I imagined was a heavy book hitting the floor, followed immediately by a sound that resembled air being expelled from a large bag. Then more falling sounds, and finally a second heavy impact like the first.

I didn't pay much attention to the noises; I was watching the door. A few scattered customers turned around briefly. One or two looked disapprovingly at Dave, a nearby part-time member of staff I'd twice followed on the bank run. Dave pretended to be engrossed by the shelf in front of him, a gesture which said that if a display or table had collapsed, then someone on more than three twenty-five an hour could be the mug to fix it. Dave didn't want to know.

Then Rob was back. He'd evidently shaken off Oddjob. But how? I was impressed. He was coming towards me now. I could ask him.

But he didn't stop. All he did was to very deliberately deposit the Dante boxed set at my feet before walking away and back, I assumed, to his post outside. He had done all this and not even looked at me once.

169

Where was Oddjob? Why had he left me the Dante? Perhaps he'd put a message between the volumes. ABORT or CARRY ON AS PLANNED maybe. I looked down at the heavy hardback set and almost screamed.

One edge of it was dented so deeply you'd swear someone had used a sledgehammer on it.

I remembered the noises I'd just heard.

Every manifestation of fear and shock, every final destination of my nervous system jolted alive and threatened to trigger a general release: I was going to be sick; I was going to cry; I was going to pee; I was going to shit; oh god, no, I was going to have an *orgasm*. Thank god, the glut of sensations lasted only a second, and I didn't expel anything more toxic than a few litres of sweat. What had Rob done? No, I knew that. Then where had he done it to her? They would find her and raise the alarm. I had to get out.

Then I thought about it.

No one was going to find her. Rob had been very thorough, I was convinced of that now. This place was like a warren, that was what we'd said. That was what had made it so easy to stake the place out. Oddjob might not be found for hours. That was the gamble he had taken. I was sickened and terrified by Rob in that moment, by the single-minded purity of his vision and focus. I didn't want to get on the wrong end of that focus. I wanted to be far away from him.

But I admired him as well. He had put things right. We were safe because of him. I went back to watching the safe room door and tried to empty my mind of everything else.

At twelve-ten I finally saw the safe room door open and close. I saw our old friends James and little Erica saunter out lethargically, Erica holding the bag. I clicked into gear.

The adrenalin was back big time. I was fired up, but I was

cool. Oh, man, this was it. What was happening to me now? Suddenly I forgot the dented Dante. This was sex. I felt so alive, so hard. Fuck, I felt like a *man*. I wanted Rich to see me like this, see me carrying out the plan. I wanted him to watch me and want me as he took in the casual professionalism with which I tailed our unsuspecting victims out through the big double doors. I had no doubts. I felt no mercy. I wanted contact. I wanted money. I needed release. Rob was right, Erica was cute. Delicate. No mercy.

I remembered in the nick of time to ditch *Paradise Lost*.

Straight down Charing Cross Road to Cambridge Circus straight down Charing X Rd to Camb Circ straight down CXR to CC don't look back Rob's behind you are you there Rob god please be there you cunt you bastards in front don't deviate don't deviate DON'T DEVIATE thank fuck I thought they were gonna cross the road then you scum from hell what's on the other side of the road what the FUCK am I doing Rob where are you die screaming in hell my part of the operation your part of the operation you'd better be there boyo I didn't see him outside the shop he'd better fucking be there he better not have missed me altogether a slow death you limp cock and still be waiting there the prick oh fuck oh fuck I promise anything you want what the hell am I doing don't lose sight of them Trash there they are Molly Moggs not far now look behind you can afford to look behind you want to know Rob's there to know when to fall back you've got to look behind you won't lose them now Palace theatre phone the box office what am I thinking my knees don't work properly I want to wee but I don't want to where is he look back look back NOW.

He was there.

Hallelujah.

My knees almost gave way when I turned to see him just as

he overtook me and moved in. He winked at me, but in a cold way – pure business. My legs were turning to salad cream and he was winking. He was so cool. So ready.

And suddenly I knew I wasn't.

26

I couldn't do it.

I couldn't move from the spot to carry out my part of the plan. Paralysing doubt had leapfrogged all the discipline and resolve of the preceding days, and that was that. About the only thing I felt capable of right now was crying. And that wouldn't help.

The boys started to move. I was now seeing the action in that pitch black slow motion of inevitable disaster. From a good thirty yards away - uselessly far – I watched as Rich strolled through the milling Lloyd Webber afficionados, stationing himself to the right of the goons as they waited for the lights to change. I saw his hand dip into the pocket of his faded Levi's jacket.

I willed him to stop. To walk away.

But the film played.

Rich pulled the CS canister from his pocket.

And raised it in an arc from waist to shoulder, like a gun.

And dropped it.

And I watched it roll harmlessly into the Shaftesbury Avenue gutter.

Rich froze in one hard, spastic non-movement. People were in his way on one side; on the other, traffic was squeezing past at speed, and way too close. I could sense his panic.

I stiffened, clenching every muscle. Now I actually found myself willing him to pick up the canister, to restart the plan. Something sharp like good speed shot through me and I was thinking again.

But Rich just stood there. Even from thirty yards away I could make out the unmistakable facial contortions.

He was going to cry. What the *fuck*?

Maybe seeing Rich on the verge of tears was what thawed my legs and got me running towards the crossing. I can't pretend it makes any sense, but sense was hardly a part of this now.

Meantime Rob was still standing a couple of people back from the goons. The crossing was as crowded as I've ever seen it, and I realised that he couldn't know what had happened – he was still waiting for Rich to make a move. So, for the moment I was on my own.

But I was almost at the crossing now, pushing and slapping people out of my way. A dozen accents and languages squealed protests as I barged and punched my way through. I'd never have believed myself capable of shit like this. Me, little Natasha. I poked eyes and slapped faces and people twice my size recoiled in surprise. I made it to the kerb where the people didn't seem to move aside so much as become elastic in their attempts to keep out of the traffic. Keep out of the road, their brains told them. And keep out of the mad woman's road. Perform contortions. Become thinner. Mutate.

I got to the canister and snatched it up.

Both of the boys saw me now, and for one moment we could alternate eye contact. Everything was relayed in that moment.

Rob and I moved. I shoved away from the kerb and stood facing the goons – still too far off. I'd lost sight of Rich, but I saw Rob rivet through the people still crowding at the lights, forcing his face from behind into Erica's ear. Erica had the money. I saw Rob's mouth work threats I couldn't hear. But she didn't drop the bag.

Someone stepped briefly in and out of my line of vision and I had to strain to see. Rob was all but biting Erica's neck now, his eyes wide and blazing, his anger connecting with mine.

She still didn't drop the bag.

And then I knew it wouldn't work.

Damn it. He'd frightened her too much, and she'd gone too far into the fear. She was far beyond threats, now, away somewhere in her head, a distant meadow or a quiet church and nothing Rob threatened her with would make any difference when she simply wasn't capable of doing anything as conscious as telling her hand to let go of the bag. She probably couldn't even hear him.

James was staring sidelong at Erica, his own fear refusing to locate himself here next to her, his panicking and slowing mind wondering what was happening, wishing it wasn't. When Rich slipped through the crowd and faced him James's knees buckled and I thought he would fall. There was no fight in James. Fuck, if he'd had the bag we'd be gone by now.

Then, behind me, the lights changed.

Traffic slowed to a stop and people moved out into the road. But the boys weren't letting our two little friends go anywhere.

Now the sheer weight of pedestrian traffic was forcing me into the road – away from the money – and it was all I could do to stop myself going backward. Shit. We had them there and I couldn't get to them. I couldn't see how the stalemate over the bag was going to change without the gas. And I couldn't get close enough to use the gas.

But I had to try. I had to try now or forget it all. The money. Our future. My place to live. This was the one chance. Risk everything. RISK EVERYTHING.

I jerked my arm up straight and tried walking forward against the people jostling me backward.

It was useless.

And then the source of the pressure reversed and I was

175

being carried forward – of course, the people crossing from the opposite side of the road had reached me and were propelling me right into Erica and the money.

This was it. The one chance. Our victims hadn't budged an inch. The boys had somehow managed to separate them a few feet from each other, effectively isolating them. They were stuck: little Erica was too scared to run, James couldn't bring himself to abandon Erica.

James and Erica were at least five feet apart when I pressed my finger down. I had to get both of them. I skipped sideways along the grain of the moving body of pedestrians, dealing out the gas in a long slow curve, watching as, one after another, they fell. Erica. James. Then a lot of people.

I hadn't expected so much screaming, or I'd at least expected it to sound different, like the screaming in a disaster movie, maybe – muted and rehearsed, expendable. But it wasn't like that. It turns out real screams are different. Real fear, not movie fear, is different. I think I know now what mothers mean when they compare the sounds of some birds and animals at night to the sound of crying babies, and they shiver, and wish those sounds on someone else.

Erica screamed and her fists flew to her face like magnets – the right one still clutching the fucking bag. Rich was pulling at it – somehow he and Rob had contrived to swap places and victims – but Erica didn't even know he was there. She had a dead man's grip on the bag and he could have pulled at it forever and got no more back than broken nails. Erica was lucky it was Rich and not Rob on her now. But we needed that bag.

This was all wrong. Stuck. I moved in close – close enough for the gas to rake at my throat and fizz in my eyes – and jammed the canister point blank into Erica's screaming mouth.

I felt her sharp little teeth scrape my knuckles as I pressed down hard on the gas.

Erica's new scream ripped into my ears and stopped time. People stopped their own screaming to wonder at this noise. They saw her face change into something alien. What had I done?

Erica released the bag.

There was a moment of suspended animation, then Erica's screaming became more self-conscious and natural sounding, easier to hear. James got up to try and go to her and was blocked by Rob's boot in his back. The whole street heard and felt that blow, and the next, and the next to his head as he hit the pavement. But nobody tried to help. James met each impact halfway with preemptive sobs and grunts. What Rob was doing was excessive, but that didn't surprise me at all. Rob carried on kicking James, and I looked away.

Rich had the bag now. We could finish it, and we could go.

Then, for no reason that had anything to do with anything, Rich turned and took a run up, and kicked Erica in the stomach so hard the force of it lifted her off the ground. It was totally out of the blue, and I was as shocked as anyone. I could hear the effort he put into that kick and the grunt when he connected. Her eyes in that moment were huge. The girl landed on her left temple, hitting the pavement like someone dropping a plastic bowl, and you could feel the panic vibe thickening all around. Then Erica was quiet. The pile of still limbs looked like a big pink doll. The blood didn't look like blood. I was breathing hard, and grimacing.

Why did Rich do that? Where had I seen that kind of impulsive force before? Where did I think. Where have we all seen it.

And then I understood. It wouldn't have mattered. She could have let go of the damn bag straight away and something like this would still have happened. This was what violence meant, and it had nothing to do with any plan. This was the thing the boys had known, and what they hadn't wanted to talk about. And they were right. They were right to keep this from me, because I would have wanted out in a minute. In for a penny, Trash.

From then on we were able to revert to something like the paper neatness of plan A. Fists and shouts from the boys, perfect confusion, people helping people and moaning for help, other people entreating someone, anyone to call the police, but unwilling to get that involved themselves, of course. If they could just extricate themselves.

It was just what we'd predicted. Anybody could have been anybody; we could have been victims. And also this: people walking away. I swear it, you know it. People just walking away, don't want to know. Don't want to acknowledge that anything out of the ordinary is going on anywhere near me.

Rob and Rich were gone in different directions, shouting and laughing – yes, laughing. The area around the crossing began returning to its normal state of chaos. I dropped the canister in my pocket and turned away from the people still crouching or lying on the ground, and from the dwindling crowd of onlookers, and shucked the bag a little higher on my shoulders. No one paid me any attention. Then for some reason I glanced back at Erica.

She hadn't moved, but the pool of blood under the left side of her face was still spreading, and shining in the sunlight. Her jaw had slipped sideways into the pool and her protruding tongue was dipping in the blood. Her eyes were open, and fixed on mine. I told myself she was unconscious, and that if I moved away the eyes wouldn't follow. Then a bubble of blood ballooned out of her left nostril and burst in a splash over her cheek, and I staggered and cried out. I felt a hand support me from behind and knew I had to pull myself together. I closed my eyes and shook my head hard from side to side, and took

several deep breaths, then turned and walked away with everyone else.

The whole operation from the moment Rich had dropped
the spray, to me collecting the bag from him and walking away
down Shaftesbury Avenue towards Piccadilly Circus had taken
no longer than forty-five seconds.

27

It was the quickest fuck of my life, but quite possibly the best. Rich butted and bit me. I dug my nails deep into flesh – his and mine, it didn't matter – our hips bucked and hammered and clashed out of sync. He moaned with the pain and loved every bit of it.

Maybe it's hard to imagine any understanding between the two of us after the preceding days' silences. But it was there in those moments, a rare connection. Two people on a line to each other's immediate need, for what it was worth. It was there briefly, and then it was gone. But I clung to hope. Where does sex like that come from?

It comes from guilt, and from the fear of change, and the failure to recognise yourself.

We knew it. And we feared the onset of this change. That beautiful last fast fuck was our try at capturing a life in a moment, at pinning down our old souls. Because we weren't the same people we'd been an hour ago. We'd assumed new characters. We'd be living by new codes and facing new consequences now. Not least among these would be guilt and remorse, and memories we would never have chosen or deserved in our old lives. But for now if we could hold all this off, even for a few minutes, we would do it however we could. So first we fucked, and it was good.

That's the highbrow reason why it was good: the psycho-profile reason. The other reason of course, the honest, nasty reason, is that control and violence like we had just experienced make you horny as hell.

Rich had beaten me back to the flat by about three minutes. Rob was still on his way, so we had the place to ourselves for the romantic interlude I've just described. Anyway, Rich was right about the getaway – nothing happened. We had made our way home like anyone else. Like ordinary violent criminals getting the tube after a hard morning's aggro. It was that easy. Strolling back from the tube, stepping to the buzzing, the bag with the money slung over my shoulder, not really thinking about it or about anything at all, I saw it all fade in my mind just as we'd predicted; I saw the crime scene evaporate and the repeating rhythms of the ordinary day return with sinister speed and nonchalance. London is a crime scene; we can't tape it all off. It goes on. Nothing bigger than a few small lives is ever visibly touched. With and without us it goes on. We fade.

Some things change quicker than others.

There was something I needed to know.

'How many times did you hit Oddjob with the book?'

We were counting the money, wads of tobacco- and leather-scented notes, in our old places around the table. But the good fuck was over. It was three new people counting money.

'What?'

'I said, how many times did you hit Oddjob? You know who I mean.'

'Remind me.'

'You don't need reminding. The butch store detective.'

Rich stopped counting his bundle and looked up. 'What's she talking about, Rob?'

Rob chuckled and slipped a rubber band around five hundred in tens. 'Oddjob. Very good. Like it.'

'Rob, what's she talking about?'

'*She* has a name, thanks Rich,' I said with an edge.

Rich had stopped counting and was giving all his attention to Rob. He waited for an answer.

Rob answered me instead. 'Once,' he said, cool as you like, then made a show of starting on a fresh pile of tens. He wouldn't face me.

Rich was shaking visibly. He looked scared. But I knew that wouldn't stop him thinking straight. 'When was this?' he asked. His voice was hoarse but controlled.

'Back in the shop. Trash got sussed.' Rob nodded towards me. 'A store detective took a shine to her and I bailed her out.'

'I heard two blows. And I didn't get sussed.'

'I hit her once and she went down. And you were well sussed, Trash. She had your fucking number.'

'That wasn't my fault. It was just bad luck. How could she have had my fucking number? I hadn't done anything.'

Rich: 'Where did you hit her?'

'Head.'

Rich sighed and said slowly, 'I mean where in the shop?'

'Don't worry. Somewhere – how can I put it? – secluded.'

Rich left a long pause, then said calmly, 'Did anyone see you?'

'No one.'

'Think. Anyone at all.'

'No. Even Oddjob – the detective – didn't see it coming.' He looked at me for the first time. A meaningful look. 'Maybe you saw me, Trash?'

'I didn't see you, but I heard you,' I said. 'And I heard you hit her twice.'

'I hit her once, she fucking went down. What is your *problem*?'

182

'I heard you hit her twice. Once which put her down and once after that. I heard it, Rob. You can't deny it. I was there!'

We were eye to eye, now.

'I hit her once, you heard twice – so there's a fucking echo in there, what's your point?'

'I heard twice, and there's no fucking *echo*. Once, she goes down. Then twice. Twice. Why, Rob? Why twice?'

Rob slammed fists and screwed up banknotes down on the table so hard it jumped. 'ONCE! What's your POINT?'

I continued looking at him, straight at him, for a long time. 'Nothing,' I murmured. 'Nothing's my point.'

Rob was sweating and breathing hard. I'd heard quite enough.

Rich was still looking at Rob, and showing no signs of resuming the count. Rob had lost his cool, and Rich had not looked happy with him. Stretching out every syllable for effect, he intoned, 'I want to know exactly what happened. I want to know what you were doing in the shop. I want to know exactly who saw you.' Then with less cool he growled: 'I want to *know* if you've royally fucked us up the arse!'

Rob sighed and leaned back. He waited until he'd regained some of his composure, then shrugged.

'All right,' he said. 'All right. I was in the shop because I thought missy here was going to bottle out.'

I gasped. 'You bastard!'

'She'd been acting funny all morning. You know it's true. I was there as backup. I know it wasn't her fault she got noticed, but it's a good job I was there, isn't it? Well, isn't it?'

All Rich said was, 'You changed the plan.'

That was it. Enough.

Everybody looked at everybody. Rich could guess the rest. And he knew it wouldn't do any good to say anything else to Rob. Rob had gone out on his own. We just looked at each other, and down at the table. Nobody trusted anyone. No one looked like they liked anyone. After what seemed like a long time Rich made a sound that sounded like 'count.'

We nervously turned our attention back to the money. There was nothing else to do. I counted. Numbers filled my head.

28

The cash was in two bundles and wasn't split with any logic that we could see. We burned the cheques, about £400 worth, on the spot. I wiped up the ashes with a damp cloth, and wafted at the grey smoke with a tea towel.

The small bundle in the paper bag contained just over £700 in tens and twenties. Rubbish, who am I just-overing? It was £730. I'll never forget. Give me five minutes and I'll break it down into denominations for you.

The second lot was the big payout. £5270 – and the useless cheques. Fives, tens, twenties, and a few smug-looking fifties. Making a grand total (pun intended) of exactly £6000. Six grand. Say it. Say it loud and in a variety of accents. Try Bob Hoskins, Sean Connery, Al Pacino, Humphrey Bogart. Michael Caine. They all sound good. Six grand. And not one dinero to spend. We knew what it was for. We hadn't lost sight of that. That was one thing that hadn't changed.

Why? We had all this money in front of us, why not just enjoy it? Because that buzzing just wouldn't leave us alone. You couldn't just knock your palm against your ear and hear the water trickling out.

No. We stole the money for a purpose, because of a vision we had. We didn't do this for a pissy six grand. We did this for everything, to risk everything and win it back, and back, and back again. In that sense this was not our money yet. To do what we did for a lousy six grand, to put ourselves and others through what we did, force ourselves to become what we had become, was to be no better than that loser pointing a gun in the bookies.

Not only that: it had gone wrong. It hadn't happened the way it was supposed to, not as far as I was concerned anyway. So this was not our money. It had not earned its worth, not cleansed itself through multiplying. And, lord, it had a lot of cleansing to do after that day. And I was ready before Mary and Joseph to knife the two gangsters at the table if they decided they felt any different.

Counting the money and arranging it in bundles again took us up to nearly two o'clock in the afternoon. Less than two hours after the robbery.

Then a strange thing happened. We were collectively overcome by a need to sleep. And it was real sleep, with no buzzing and no bad dreams. We went to bed and all slept straight through until the six o'clock news, which we watched in breathless silence. Although I don't know what we were expecting to see. I suppose it was just fear. Against all logic, the prospect of a nationwide manhunt nagged at the back of our minds. Hardly. We were small beer. We didn't even make *London Tonight*. Of course we didn't. And I suppose I should have been happy no one was badly hurt, that there were no Neanderthal, post-IRA fotofits of me and the boys staring out from every channel, no cops queuing up to break down the door. Of course there weren't. We were in the clear. There was nothing to trace us except maybe some fuzzy shop security videos of a crowd at a crossing. Six lousy grand, nobody dead, nothing to follow up. Six grand, as the Americans would say, is chump change. We had got away with it.

Having sat silently through those two programmes, plus Channel Four news, the boys began casually discussing the big bet. Apparently big pals again. It took all my nerve and wits to stay focused, then, to keep my shame out of my head, or at least out of my mouth.

'Horses.'

'I've got bad memories of horses, Robin.'

'Horses.'

'What happened last time?'

'No different to what happened with football. It has to be horses.'

'Why does it? Horses fucked us up?'

'It just feels right.'

All very civilised, yes?

No.

Problem. A personnel problem, not a horses problem. I'd earned my right that day to participate, to sit at the head of the table if I chose. To talk and offer an opinion if and when I wanted to, and to shut up if that was what I wanted. And that was the problem – what I'd done to earn that right. If I'd been paying the right kind of attention, taking everything in, I'd have noticed a bit sooner that the boys weren't looking at me right. Their eyes when they fell on me betrayed something. If I think back hard enough, get specific with my memories and impressions, I can see them flashing me weird glances all afternoon. But as always with your memory you sometimes give its victims the benefit of the doubt, and so I can't be sure how much of this I'm inventing. But if I'd seen it more clearly then, if I'd really been sure of the evidence, I'd have known what it was I saw and why, and I'd never have forgiven them.

They were eyeing me with revulsion.

They were *scared* of me.

It wasn't fair. They'd been in on everything, both been prepared – even eager – to do what in the end I'd had to. They'd been happy enough when my decisiveness with the gas saved the plan. And I hadn't kicked any girls in the guts and I wasn't lying about how many times I'd beaten a store detective over the head with Dante's *Inferno*. And I wasn't looking at them any different. I knew what we'd done. I had to forgive Richard that kick, because I was no better. In my own revised memory of events I've even claimed responsibility for it. I didn't kick her but I was there. I was there and the gas was there and I was with the gas.

But I didn't kick her. And they still looked at me in that way, just the same.

Maybe they figured it was all right for them. After all, they were boys. They were men and men do those sorts of things. I should have known better. Been better. Women should be better. It is what the world expects.

But they were talking over everything, and I couldn't be sure. I didn't realise a lot of this until later. So I listened to a few more rounds of verbal sparring about horses and dogs.

'Believe me, our name will not fuck up,' Rob was saying. 'We're only asking for one this time. We'll get it right.'

Rich was about to come back with another objection when I stepped in.

'It doesn't matter,' I said. There was instant authority in my voice, which was something new, and something I could tell the boys didn't like.

Rob said quietly, 'What?'

'It doesn't matter,' I repeated. Leaning forward in that way Rich liked to do, both hands out in front, I said, 'What did we do this for?' Tapping the wood, again like Rich, I answered my own questions: 'We did this to risk everything, because when we risk everything we are going to get the right answer whatever we bet on. Isn't that the point of this?'

They looked down at my hands as if confirmation was to be heard in my fingers. I drummed and then pointed with my eyes to the money where it sat between us. 'This is what we did this for. We've kept our part of the bargain. We took risks. Now we get rewards. That's how it works. Simple.'

They didn't argue.

It felt good having them listen to me. So good I could ignore it – there it was again, the way they watched me when I pointed at the piles of cash and reminded them of what 'this' had entailed.

At shortly before seven we called up the spirit, and by ten past we had what we wanted. I'm not going to go through the ritual again.

We went for a horse blind. Which is to say we had no racing form in front of us, so no names to compare with the spirit's tip. Nothing to confuse us there and then. We checked out the RISK EVERYTHING business and were assured we'd done well; we wouldn't lose. The spirit was pleased.

The plan: sleep late, buy a paper, check the runners, bet six grand. To win. No messing. RISK EVERYTHING. The name of the horse which was going to make our money breed? I Forget. I don't mean I forget the name. I Forget was the name of the animal. And there it would be in tomorrow's *Mirror*, no problem. Epsom, 3 p.m. I Forget. 7-2. For the first time things looked like they were going to happen.

But that was tomorrow. There were still things wrong with today. Apart from when I'd pressed Rob about Oddjob the boys hadn't mentioned the robbery. Six grand had appeared in our kitchen from nowhere. I didn't want to be the one to bring up the subject. The way I saw it I couldn't win. Either I'd appear weak for needing to talk, or I'd just remind them of the merciless bitch they now obviously believed me to be. Plus, none of us wanted to be in each other's company any more. Not the three of us together. Fuck it. We went to bed.

Only this time I couldn't sleep. When I closed my eyes I

saw Erica's head hitting the pavement, and then a close up of her tongue hanging out and that accusing stare. I tried staring at the ceiling, hoping I'd drop off without trying, but it wasn't going to happen. Then, more than anything, I wanted to make love. Not that thinking about that poor girl's battered unconscious form was a terrific turn on. I just needed some contact. I wanted to remember who I was in love with, and to kiss and hold and to push away the bad pictures. It was obvious Rich wasn't going to talk, so maybe he'd want something else.

No chance. I got the stiff back and the pretend snore. Rich was either thinking or trying hard not to think, and my sexual presence was unwelcome either way. So okay, if we can't fuck, let's talk. I don't care how we do it, but let's confront these two people in our house, in our bed – in my head. Not a chance.

So I was back to square one and feeling cold and hurt. So, if I couldn't talk I wanted to fuck. I suddenly couldn't stop thinking about fucking. I was angry and edgy: my traumatised energy was pacing the boundaries of the situation, looking for a way through the fence and into Rich's good thoughts. I'd have taken anything at that moment and been grateful – a soft word, a small kiss really meant, an unreciprocated blow-job. But nothing. I was angry and horny and lonely, all in approaching uncontrollable proportions. It even crossed my mind to just get out of bed, walk stark naked into Rob's room and fuck him stupid. It crossed my mind as a crazy idea and then lodged in it as a serious possibility. I was pretty sure Rob would have liked it. Rob would do anything now. Rob had changed a lot and we probably deserved each other. And I knew also that Rich wasn't about to stop me, nor would he have had anything to say about it in the morning. He would just keep on pretending to sleep. He'd just let me walk out of the room, and then be oblivious as to when or whether I came back. If he cared, I would never know.

And that stopped me from doing it, knowing Rich wouldn't care enough to stop me. Why would Rich be happy for me to go and fuck Rob? Did he think I'd changed so much that it wouldn't surprise him for me to get up in the middle of the night and go and fuck his best friend? Was it a test? A confirmation of his suspicions?

And so, no, I didn't go. But I should have. Rich was betraying me in those moments. Because he was the one who was somewhere else. I was here, and I wanted to make love or to talk or just be held, and if he wasn't going to be the one to do those things for me any more, then anyone, his best friend included, would do. I couldn't shake the idea that Rich believed I had changed for the worse. But if that was what he thought then he had passed judgement on me without a word to me about it. And that was wrong.

I wish I'd done it. I really wish I'd skipped out of that bed, the bed my dad had brought from home, and down the stairs to Rob's room. I wish I'd had the guts to stomp down there and whip Rob's horrible Derby County duvet away and climb on top of him in his stupid LIVE LONG AND PROSPER jimjams and tell him to shut up and fuck me or kiss me or just hold me while I cried, only somebody notice me. On this day of all days don't ignore me, because I have done things and seen things that will not settle in my head.

I should have. In that one moment of lonely lust I should have taken responsibility for all the changes and forced them down all our throats with everything else. Yes, I should have confronted the last-ditch lie me and Rich had wrestled with earlier on the filthy carpet. I should have because it would have been right. It would have been the honest thing to do because in my perversely righteous way of looking at things, it was the thing I really, honestly wanted to do. Just one honest, straightforward thing to end that day. The next few minutes before I slept passed in front of me as a cracked tableau, like a scene in a dream. Nothing happens the way it's supposed to. I wasn't supposed to touch the gas. Erica was supposed to let go of the bag. Rich wasn't supposed to kick anyone. But that's what did happen.

I managed about an hour's fitful sleep and then got up and dressed in my clean Levi's, old CAT boots, Kalashnikov-Babe T, and my washed-out geeky pink cardigan. I looked pretty good. The clock radio on the far side of the bed flashed midnight. Still early in some places. I knelt down and looked at Rich. His breathing was shallow and his face contorted.

I kissed him on the lips and he muttered something in his sleep. Then I turned and walked out of our bedroom and down the hall. But not into Rob's room.

29

I knew where I was going.

The Lock Inn was a glorified after-hours pub on Tottenham Lane. To get around the licensing laws it called itself a nightclub, and there was a small dance floor in the first room you came to. But nobody went there to dance. In another room you could eat, provided your arteries were up to it. The third and largest room was for drinkers. For nocturnal locals like me and the boys the Lock Inn was an oasis. It didn't open until ten, and then it filled up quickly, and the atmosphere was usually relaxed and civilised. The overflow of plebs from the pubs was minimal. And even these people, whatever their initial intentions, almost always behaved okay once they descended the steep stairs to the Lock Inn. All of which doesn't mean I was in the habit of going there alone, far from it. But tonight was different. Tonight I was looking for someone.

It was about twelve-fifteen when I hopped off the last metal rung and stepped up to the entrance. The black bouncer smiled in recognition, and waved me past the bleach blonde reading *Cosmo* in the pay booth, and I smiled back at him. I went to the drinking room via the cigarette machine and headed for the bar. The room was smart enough, done out in red and black, but mostly red, with only red lighting in the whole room. The stools at the bar and against the walls were padded red vinyl. I stepped up to the only free stool at the bar and sat down. I ordered a pint of something cold and a Jack Daniel's with the same again of water – I was drinking out of my depth but I sensed I'd need it. I took out a pack of Marlboro lights, and offered one to Madeleine.

Madeleine flashed me a wide, mischievous smile. I recognised the same perfume from the party, but she looked tired, and older than I remembered. Dreams flatter people, I suppose. She shook her head at the barman, who gave me back my money, and winked at me. You could hear the music from the other room, but it wasn't so loud you couldn't have a comfortable talk. I could smell food frying.

I said, 'Thanks.'

Maddy waved it away. 'Hello, love,' she replied, still with that smile. Those teeth. 'Long time no see. Who told you I worked here?'

I took a pull of the Marlboro and a long one of each of my drinks, all but killing the whisky. 'You wouldn't believe me,' I said.

'Try me.'

What the hell. 'Would you believe I saw you in a dream?'

Madeleine's smile softened to a nice, peachy shade. 'I'll believe it if you want me to.'

'No.' I killed the cigarette, which was burned only half way down. 'Don't bother believing that. Dreams are nothing. I don't know why it took me so long to remember it. Truth is I used to come here a lot when I was a student and I lived around the corner. And recently since we moved back to Crouchy.'

'Of course, your new flat. Your party.'

'Which you crashed.'

'No.' She smoked.

'No?'

'No. I came with Dean – the other bouncer. Rich invited him.' I remembered now. 'But he left early. And it was a good

194

party. And I didn't want to leave, besides which I had nowhere else to go. And then I met your friend.'

'Rob.'

'Rob. He's a nice guy. Funny. Good in bed. But a bit intense.' She looked me in the eye and mashed her cigarette slowly, playing with it until all the sparks were dead, then said: 'Are you good in bed?'

I felt my cheeks burn, but only briefly. 'My boyfriend was there.' It wasn't what I'd meant to say.

'He's not here now.' Maddy was flirting, but she looked concerned as well. Maybe the flirting was just to put me at ease. I suppose I might have looked pretty stressed out.

This wasn't why I was here. I sat up straight. 'Anyway, I must have remembered seeing you here once, and it took a while for it to sink in. Look, I've got some questions. That's why I found you. I mean, why I came to see you.'

'Ask away.'

There was something flippant about the way she was looking at me. I sensed it wasn't going to be easy getting her to take my questions seriously. 'Can you remember the game we played? With the ouija board?'

Maddy laughed. 'Oh, yeah.'

'What's funny?'

She looked surprised. 'Nothing, really. It's just a good game. People love it the first time.'

'Why the first time? Don't they love it the others?'

'It gets boring after that. Either that or it gets weird. People don't quite know how to take it further. To be honest, I don't think you can. So I always do it with people who've never done it before. It just breaks the ice. And it's a great way to flirt, of course.'

I sat in silence for a moment, then asked: 'Is that all you know about it?'

Maddy shrugged. 'What else is there to know? It's just a bit of mumbo jumbo. Anyone can do it. The answers never really mean anything.'

'But what if they did?'

She shrugged again, looked puzzled. 'They don't.'

'So you've never seen it taken further?'

'It never goes further. Look, Trash, are you all right? What are you getting at?'

I sighed and attempted a smile. 'Nothing. I'm not getting at anything.'

'Are you sure you're okay?'

'Yeah. I was just curious. I just remembered the game and decided to ask you about it. And I had a row with my boyfriend and wandered out –'

'To find me in your dream?' She smiled and I blushed again, then drained my whisky, and looked around for the barman. This wasn't going according to plan. 'Look,' she said. 'I'm on my break. I finish about two-thirty.' She looked down at her lap. 'You don't have to go home.'

'I should go.' But I didn't know if I wanted to go back to Rich. Why should I?

'Please,' Maddy said. She put a hand on mine. 'Wait for me.'

I didn't know what to say. What had I expected to find? 'I can't stay here till two-thirty.'

'I'll give you my keys. You can go to my flat.' She smiled and dropped her voice. 'I'll come by later and wake you up.'

That woke me up, all right. Before I knew it the words were out of my mouth. 'Madeleine, are you gay?'

I think she sensed I was getting away from her then, or that I'd never really been a prospect. She sighed, like she'd made this speech before. 'Let's say I have an open mind. I'm not really sure. There are people I like, and most of them are men. But sometimes I meet someone like you, and I see something in them. Didn't you realise it that night at the party? Didn't you know I was flirting outrageously?'

For the first time I noticed Maddy had an accent. It was definitely middle class, maybe higher up the scale. That level of breeding always makes me suspicious.

Suddenly she wasn't mysterious any more. Suddenly she just reminded me of a few other people I knew. I snapped out of something, or back into something. There were all sorts of real life questions, and this wasn't a dream. Maddy wasn't unique. She wasn't some black magic diva I'd dreamed up.

And suddenly I knew that – like it or not at that exact moment – the place for me to be was at home with Rich. We were in the middle of something. We had things to finish.

'Look, Maddy.' I took her hand and squeezed her slim fingers. 'I think you're lovely. I'm flattered –'

'Stop. Please. Don't say it. Call me vain, but I don't believe we couldn't find something interesting to do for a few hours. And I don't believe you wouldn't like it. But it's really obvious you've got a lot on your mind.'

I smiled and meant it. She'd been sweet, and I certainly didn't feel any worse than I had when I walked in. 'I'd better go.'

'You know where to find me.'

I nodded. And we got up from our stools and Maddy kissed me, on the mouth, for a good long time. She was right about one thing: I didn't dislike it. A few heads turned. And then I left.

I was about two hundred yards from the Lock Inn, just too far for the bouncer to hear me scream, when a muscular arm slid from behind around my throat.

30

I tried struggling and got a slap to the solar plexus for my pains. When I could stand again I didn't have the breath to scream, and certainly not to run. Next thing I was against a wall – we must have been in an alley, but I had my eyes closed – and I was still gulping for air.

When I opened my eyes I thought I'd been rescued. I saw Rob holding me. Had I blacked out and missed some time? What had happened before he got here? And then the truth hit me, and a shriek escaped from somewhere deep in my chest. When I could catch my breath properly I spluttered, 'What are you doing?'

'Twice.'

'What?' I looked around me. We were in an alley. I'd never noticed it before. There were no doors off it that I could see. No chance of someone coming along. Opposite the alley was a building site you'd avoid in the dark if you had any sense. We were going to stay very, very alone.

'Twice. Oddjob. I hit her twice. Once to put her down, and again when she was on the floor. Twice. Satisfied?' Rob was speaking in a calm, singsong voice, and still holding me by the throat and by the hair.

'I knew that.'

'Then why ask? Why put me through that today?'

'I wanted to hear the truth. I wanted to hear you say it.' I coughed and winced at the pain in my abdomen.

'Well now you've heard it. And I want the truth from you.'

198

I said feebly, 'What truth? Let me go.' It was hard to talk – I was focusing all my strength on not collapsing.

'You treacherous bitch!'

'Rob, please let me go.' I was crying.

He leaned in close enough to kiss me. Then he whispered, 'You've got one chance to tell me. And don't try lying because I'll know. I know where you were tonight. I know who you were talking to – on your own, nice and cosy. Why was that. Trash? Why on your own? But I want to hear it from you. And I want to hear it from you –'

'Rob, it's me. You're hurting me. Please, I –'

Rob's knee jabbed into my left thigh and I collapsed with an agonising dead leg. My head swam and I sobbed and gagged. He dragged me coughing to my one good foot. 'That was your one chance, Natasha. I gave you that chance because we're friends. Now you're no one. Give me the truth, no one. Just remember, I can go on all night.'

I knew I had to start talking, but the pain was still pulsing all the way up to my stomach. All I managed was a gasping 'I'll tell you. Please. I'll tell you.' But before I could talk I started to cry again.

Then instead of hitting me, Rob let go of my throat and my hair and lowered me gently to the ground, and then we were sitting side by side in the alley. And then he did something that truly surprised me – he produced a handkerchief. I mean a *clean* handkerchief. Never in all the years I'd known him had Rob carried so much as a length of scabby Andrex about his person. No, folks, we were definitely not our old selves any more.

I looked at him and something in his face had changed. He looked like a child. Innocence is not a look I'd ever associated with Robin.

I dried my eyes and talked. In a few minutes Rob knew everything. I was still unsure about what he would do next, but I didn't feel in any more physical danger. I sensed he had more to tell me himself.

After I'd filled him in, Rob said, 'So it was nothing special to her all along?'

'Not to her. No big mystery.' I sniffed and blew into the hanky.

'And your dreams?'

'Just memories. I just remembered her.'

'So she can't help us with how far we've taken it?'

'We're on our own.'

'And all that weird stuff was just to get one or both of us in the sack?'

'Yeah. And you know what, Rob? I know she's cute as a button and all that. But she's really nothing special. Just a bit lonely and confused.'

'I knew that.'

'Smartarse.' My voice was still watery. 'She did say you were good in bed, though.'

Rob giggled. 'I could have told you that.'

'You have, plenty of times.' Tired laughter.

'Trash?'

'Yeah?'

'Were you tempted?'

'What do you mean?'

'With Maddy? Would you have done anything.'

I shook my head and raised my voice. 'You sad bastard. That turns you on, doesn't it? You're such a fucking cliché.' I knuckled him hard in the ribs – well, I thought it was hard – and he laughed like a schoolkid. He was okay now. He wouldn't hurt me any more. Why did that seem acceptable?

'I had to ask.'

'Wanker.'

He stopped laughing. 'But would you, though?'

I didn't even have to think about my answer. 'I love Rich.'

'We all love each other. It's just been a strange day.'

'Yes. *Oooh* yes.'

'Trash?'

'Mm hm?'

'I'm sorry for hitting you.'

'You sorely will be.'

'Sound sorely tempting.'

'It's sorely fucking true. What's the matter with you, for fuck's sake?' But I didn't wait for an answer. 'Come on, help me up.'

'On your feet. Hup!'

We were about to start walking, but Rob took my arm and held me back. I turned my head and he was looking in my eyes again.

'I love Rich,' I whispered, but he wasn't listening. His eyes were off somewhere else now.

'The second time,' he said.

'Let's go home, Rob,' I said.

'The second time I hit Oddjob, you were right. There was no need. That's what you were getting at, isn't it?'

I took his hand and tried to lead him out of the alley. 'It's okay, Rob. It's finished.'

'But it was totally unnecessary. I had to tell you.' There were tears in his eyes, but he wasn't sobbing. He was drained. He was in pain. 'I did it –' he closed his eyes as if he were ashamed to go on. 'I hit her again because I enjoyed it. Because it was exciting to me that I could do it and get away with it.' It took him a long time to get the last part out. He needed deep breaths. 'Because it was sexual. She wasn't even attractive. But hitting her and watching her fall turned me on so fucking much. And then she was on the floor and I just felt so fantastic. Trash, that's sick, isn't it?' And then the tears rolled down his face.

I don't remember who touched who first after that, it was

201

all unspoken. It felt right and, at the same time, all wrong. A symptom of everything. I remember his hands in my clothes, and the night air on my cool skin, and holding him for a long time before guiding him inside me where we stood. He lifted my behind so I could clasp him in my legs. I remember that strength. I remember knowing I loved Richard, but knowing it felt good to finally relieve the burning and change the pictures in my head. I remember the feeling of simple uncertainty, and the simple confusion and ordinary comfort that feeling brought. I remember Rob's careful touch, his gentle instinct which didn't surprise me any more. I remember conceding something, and taking something: letting things happen, and making things happen.

Rich was up when we got back to the flat. He didn't ask where we'd been, as I knew he wouldn't. He smiled a smile which told me nothing, then went to the kitchen for another two plastic cups – those damn plastic cups. It was going to be a long night. A good night, hopefully. Dylan was on the tape deck, *Knocked Out Loaded*.

The song was *Brownsville Girl*.

We're going all the way, till the wheels fall off and burn.

Rich picked up the bottle and gave me a long look, and this one I could read. It said: Whatever you have done, you have done on a day when the rules were not the same, and I forgive you for this one day. I returned his look with one which said: This day is finished, and I'm back.

Then my lover poured the whisky and we started to wash the day away.

31

A little later I heard the door handle of the master bedroom turn and Robin cough a couple of times before he closed the door quietly, and just as quietly stepped across the room and sat down. Despite what I thought had just passed between Rich and me, I felt the potential for trouble, or at least awkwardness, that the moment carried. Something had to happen.

As it turned out, what happened next was possibly the strangest thing to occur all night. Even stranger than being propositioned by a queer clairvoyant, or than being unfaithful in an alley with my increasingly unhinged flatmate and, now, partner in crime.

What happened next was precisely nothing.

Rob lit three cigarettes and crushed the empty pack and passed them around, then made three fresh drinks. He put on the tape of Leonard Cohen's *Various Positions*, and we listened in intense silence to the first two songs. Or at least I listened. Beautiful, beautiful songs of pain and forgiveness.

That's what happened. We smoked a cigarette, drank some whisky, and played some music. And we listened to the other tape playing under the music: the interconnecting loop of our thoughts. There was no confrontation, no accusations. We were all at fault for something both on the surface of our lives and way, way down deep in the dark places where we had never expected to have to see. Throwing blame around on a night like that, after a day like that, would have been, well, downright indecent.

Besides which, Rich must have noticed the worrying changes in Rob. And he must have been as wary of needling him as I was.

After a decent amount of silence and of Leonard Cohen, we talked.

It didn't take long to fill Rich in about Madeleine, and about Rob hearing me leave the flat and following me. Of course, Rob had to confess to having harboured a good deal of suspicion and paranoia over the past few days. Paranoia. A word. Just takes a second to say it. But what took most of the remains of the night was reestablishing some kind of mutual trust. The silence had been relatively easy, but now we were talking again we had to re-cross a bridge, back into the land of small talk and awful jokes and shared silliness, everything we were used to taking for granted. The whisky helped.

So, kiss and make up all round. Almost.

There was one issue still unresolved, and I knew Rob was still biding his time on that one too. It was the small matter of one of us making secret visits to a library. It probably meant nothing, but it was the secretiveness that bothered me. As for Rob, in his present state of mind, I didn't like to think what scenarios he was building up around Rich's clandestine reading trips. Still, this was a night for secrets, if secrets would help along the delicate process of re-bonding. And Rob and me kept quiet.

Eventually, tired and numb, we dragged ourselves to bed. That was another awkward moment, getting back into bed with Rich. But we were too numb and wasted to think any more.

The good news was I'd stopped dreaming about Madeleine.

The bad news? Erica had taken her place. Boy, was that fun. In the nightmare she was an ugly life size rag-doll, blood and pus oozing from her gashed cloth head, attempting to climb floppily into bed beside me, then dropping in a heap on the floor before dragging herself up for another go. Then she had Madeleine's voice telling me I was going to enjoy making love to her. And then a long wet tongue slithered out and licked her lips, followed by a bubble of mucusy blood. Nice. I jolted awake when the doll's leg swung over the side of the bed and bounced on my belly and one of its damp eyes plopped out on to my breast. Jesus. The second time it woke me I decided I'd just had enough shit for one day. I lay shivering and sobbing for a good minute, then cursed both Erica and Madeleine to bloody hell, after which I felt empty, and better. And then I slept okay for the last couple of hours dreaming, for some reason, of friendly nuns. Who knows.

A new day, a new twist. The transformation in the boys the next morning was amazing. Far from being the pariah of the previous day, I was now their hero. I'd have been livid if I wasn't so relieved. Still, yesterday afternoon was forgotten. Today everything was: Trash saved the day; Trash is hard as nails. I didn't know what to make of this new mood, but I was just happy things were back to normal. Of course, what was normal? But perceptions change. We were acting happy again, whatever the situation, and I was willing to go with that. In fact, I was on a high. Anything was better than having to think about my nightmares of bloody rag dolls, and of what I'd done to deserve them.

So, it was another big day. We had the money, we needed the attitude to go with it. Things were going to get better. We had to be professionals again. First off, it was clear there had to be a hefty degree of ceremony and sense of occasion involved. We found it over breakfast at a Jamaican restaurant near the Barbarossa, hoping some of the influence would rub off from the voodoo decor. Or is voodoo from Haiti? Okay, so it was the best we could do, but the food was excellent, and we felt suitably black-artish. An early morning beer to toast the living and the dead.

Fed and watered we swanned into Ladbrokes two hours before the race, just to soak up the atmos and dig the vibe. We were ready to win. There she was in black and white, our baby – I Forget. 7–2. Beautiful. 7–2, a haul of £19,250 on a £5,500 bet (£550 tax), plus stake making a grand total of £24,750. Oh, baby, come to mama.

This was our lucky day – in quite another way altogether. It was our lucky day because, despite ten miserable days spent planning and staking out the perfect crime with a view, ideally, to not getting caught, we immediately went and broke rule number 2.

Rule 1: Don't get caught.

Rule 2: Stay not caught; i.e. don't do anything to attract attention to yourselves and hence give the game away. Seen *Goodfellas*? Remember that bit after the Lufthansa heist where the crooks meet in a bar to celebrate? One turns up in a new pink Caddy, another in a ten grand mink. They get their bottoms seriously kicked by the cool-headed Mr de Niro for jeopardising the whole deal in their hour of triumph. Good film. Well, the moment Rich sauntered over to the counter to place that bet, I began feeling antsy. At first I couldn't put my finger on why. And then I knew. First, the girl behind the screen signalled to the manager to come over and sign something. Then the manager glanced at Rich and picked up the phone.

He picked up the phone.

My stomach flipped and I felt that cold sweat that comes just before sickness. Common sense told me that he was merely calling someone higher up to clear the large cash bet. No problem. But it threw me, and I could have kicked myself lame for betraying my nervousness. But I wasn't the only one. I caught

Rob's eye in time to see him turn grey and break into a sweat. For a moment I thought I might have to go over and hold him up, but that would have attracted even more attention – I'd already clocked the manager giving Rob the once over. Rob looked different, these days. No, stay put.

Of the three of us only Rich remained really cool – presumably because, being on the spot, he had no choice. His back was to me, but I didn't even see him flinch or tighten up. Jesus. It occurred to me somewhere in that daze of panic that somehow, sometimes, everyone gets their moment to shine. Hero time, Charlie Brown. Me and Rob had both John Wayned it at different times yesterday, today the show was all Rich's. I don't know that Rob and I wouldn't have just turned and run out of the place if it hadn't been for Rich's cool in that one moment.

That's all it took. Someone picking up the phone, someone else keeping their cool. The difference between success and failure, between blowing everything, and just another ordinary day in the lives of three armed robbers. It was hard at that moment to think about things in terms as simple as, say, a process of elimination. But that's what was going down. Sheep and goats, de Niro and the other blokes. We'd had a warning. And this time we'd got away with it. This time.

I'm not a big horse racing girl. I'm probably deluding myself, but it just seems that little bit more of a mug's game than other types of gambling. At least with poker you get something for your money, win or lose, while horses is strictly spectator betting, like the dogs but less relaxed and informal. And in this instance, knowing the outcome, we were even more detached from what was going on. The whole vibe was nice enough, but after twenty minutes of basking in it we were confident bordering on bored.

Why not? That's what low-dosage adrenalin feels like before the big fix kicks in – boredom. We had every right to feel blasé. Our horse existed with a real name, for once, not like the red herrings of our first effort. We'd gone for this one blind and there was nothing else remotely similar-sounding in the whole meeting. As far as we were concerned this was the last guarantee, the final piece of the puzzle. We had fulfilled our part of the bargain. The wretched buzzing could stop, the winning could begin.

It was a flat race – I don't know the distance or terminology in miles or furlongs. We settled onto high stools like the ones in the Lock Inn, and exchanged knowing smiles. We watched the horses and riders jolt out of the traps (do they call them traps, or is that just for dogs?) and hurtle towards the first bend and I admit that, despite what we knew, there was a thrill in that first drum roll of hooves.

I Forget, a big grey thing with a white nosebands took an immediate lead, the jockey shining in black and purple silks. Yes, it was some kind of thrill, seeing your horse, knowing it really was your horse, pre-ordained, knowing how you'd come by the tip. And for a minute I felt something like the high and the sense of certainty of our very first seances. For almost exactly a minute, in fact.

I Forget led for about forty-five seconds before being overtaken on the inside by a black horse whose name I forget. That isn't supposed to be funny. The strange thing was, I relaxed even more, leaning back on my high stool, anticipating the elation of a strong late finish. That would just make it perfect. I felt like an Arab tycoon. But when our horse slipped a gear and threatened to drop back into a hopeless third I sat up dead straight. How about a very strong, very late finish? I Forget was fighting for the race. He was two lengths behind the horse in front and fighting a losing one with the bastard nag in third.

Fuck.

He wasn't going to win.

Should I panic now? Was that appropriate?

For the second time in a quarter of an hour I felt the sickening sweat, and this time it stayed. I felt myself leave the stool and hover towards the door. People saw the look on my face and made way for me. Before running from the bookies I heard it, and turned in time to see it on a dozen screens. I saw I Forget charge to the line with a ferocious second wind, pulling safely away from the brown in third, which was being vainly lashed by its bobbing jockey. I saw him, my horse, my hopes, strain in the effort to stretch its whole body into something else, something both liquid and solid, something which would be enough. And I felt liquid and solid merge and separate inside me as I Forget crossed a dozen finish lines still half a length behind the winner.

I shouldered open the door, staggered straight ahead, and vomited into the gutter. Tears dripped onto the mess, and then something that looked like blood. I was shaking and gasping. Then I could feel the boys, not holding me, not comforting me, but simply lifting and dragging, one arm each, along the street in the direction of blond Bob's. People must have been watching, but I didn't care. Every twenty yards or so I tried to stop again as I needed to be sick. But the boys weren't going to stop, and I was forced to spray it out on the move, over my chin, chest and shoes, again and again until there was nothing else. Shoppers gave us a wide berth. Gradually the tears dried and I fell into step with the boys as they silently frogmarched me to the house and through the front door. Rob's wrists were jerking spastically and I thought I heard him muttering to himself, although I couldn't make out any words. I was breathing heavily and half sobbing. I was exhausted from the vomiting. It was finished.

But it wasn't. After helping to sling me onto my bed Rob marched out to the kitchen, slamming doors behind him. I heard a radio flicked on – I hadn't known there was one in the kitchen – and turned up too loud, followed by swearing and general banging about. It sounded like he was punching the walls. Then through that din I heard the buttons of Rich's Levi's pop, and the swish of his sweatshirt and T-shirt over his head. And then his hands were working at me, yanking off my messed-up trainers and then my jeans, throwing them across the room. My knickers he ripped painfully away, making me wince as the elastic snapped. I heard all this and, as my damp eyes dried, I saw it. But I did nothing. I waited for what was going to happen, for Rich to lash out and hurt something, and take out all his hurt on me. I heard his breathing accelerate into something uncontrolled. I think I heard him try to speak.

And all I could think was: poor Richard. Poor man. For the first time his hard penis looked dangerous to me, a thing I didn't like and didn't want to touch. His face looked red and ugly and weak, as if all the confidence and certainty and humanity had been slapped out of it by someone bigger and meaner than he was. He looked bullied and beaten, and dangerous.

But I loved him.

Poor Richard, poor man. I lay there on our bed and the tears returned, slower this time. I held out my arms to Richard as I quietly wept, haggard and bruised and stinking of sick, and he came to me, and sobbed in my arms, all his violence gone. I stroked his hair and held him and we both cried for what seemed like a long time. And then it was finished.

While Richard slept I took a shower and changed into my long loose skirt and an ancient jumper. Being fashionable wasn't a priority just then. I assumed Rob was in his room, and I listened at his door for a few minutes, but I didn't hear anything. I picked up my keys and cigarettes and a lighter and left the flat. I walked over Crouch Hill to where you can get down onto the parkland walk. It was a nice day. The parkland walk is only a disused railway line with the rails removed, flanked on both sides by trees, but any patch of green in the city is prized by someone. I decided I needed time alone with the quiet and the air, and so I followed the walk all the way down to Finsbury Park, and strolled over to the boating pond. I let the breeze fill my ears and the sounds off the boating lake, the flapping of the Canada geese and the squealing moorhens and the splashing of oars, nudge out my anxiety. When I was relatively sure I was feeling stable enough to let reality back into my head, I took another look at our latest fuck-up. At what had gone wrong, and why.

There didn't seem to be much to it. Madeleine was right. It was all just a bit of fun, just garbled signals. We read into it what we wanted to. Yes, we had contacted something, but it was something meaningless and without power. Except, it seemed, the power to mislead and hurt us. As if there weren't enough pitfalls in just surviving in the world of the living, we had to wander into the afterlife with big targets on our backs, big signs saying I AM GULLIBLE, TAKE THE PISS AT WILL.

I did a circuit of the pond and then the running track, and watched the black guys training for American football, marvelled at the pointlessness of it all, and backtracked to the café by the pond. I sat smoking at one of the empty picnic tables, and hoped no one came to take my order. I didn't have any money.

A memory came into my head. A flashback of me and Rich just a few days after moving into blond Bob's. I closed my eyes.

It's the wee small hours. We're moonbathing. Which is to say the curtains in the master bedroom are pulled open and the full moonlight which is lighter than the room's normal nighttime dark blue is bathing our blue-white bodies. The duvet is away on the floor. We have been straining our eyes at the far off star to see mountains and craters and the shape of a face in the shadows, and talking about where and whose the face might be, and if it's away on the dark side. But now we are just lying in the dark light.

It's surprising how much extra noise the curtains keep out. We can really hear the difference now they're open, when there's a joy rider or a night bus or someone screaming blue murder from the flats above the Seven-Eleven.

We are just lying here. We haven't made love tonight but we might. There's a feeling of good possibility about everything in this rare pale light. A feeling of familiarity, which is what will make it good if it happens. Yes, not the surprise, not the unusual, but the familiar, the knowledge of touching the same places with the same places every time. Of things remaining the same. I stir to sweep a hand over myself from thigh to neck, to remind myself I'm really here, my fingers and my wrist riding the warm curves on the way. I am the same. I shift position slightly. I am the same. Here I am, it's all I want to know. I am the same. I want the room to stay this colour of dark and my lover to sleep beside me in anticipation of the familiar for as long as there is blue moonlight and naked white bodies. Because all naked bodies are a kind of white under a full moon, and that too is familiar and certain and nothing has ever been so inevitable and so fundamentally familiar and certain, as nights like this. I run my hand over myself again, back the other way. I am the same.

And then there is another noise, maybe not even a noise, maybe it comes from inside my head. But something snaps on like a bad painful light, jarring me. And I remember really

212

where I am, and why I am here. How long will I be able to stay here? Will blond Bob come back in three months or three weeks and say he wants his flat back? Will I have to move again, or go back home? And now the spell of the night is ruined for me and I will have to find my way back into it another way. I'll need to talk my way back into the night. But the things that are in my head now I don't want to say, because they are not things to say on a night like this. But something comes out.

I say: 'What's your dream job?'

Rich answers surprisingly quickly. Perhaps he has been thinking as well. Perhaps I misjudged the whole mood. He says: 'Sorry, love?'

'What's your dream job?'

'What a daft question.' He has left a short pause before answering, presumably so it can sink in what a daft question I've just asked.

'No it's not. I want to know what your ambitions are. I want to know what you want from life. Come on, play the game, it's one of the classic discussions: what do you want to be more than anything in the world?'

Another pause. 'Thin.'

'No, seriously.'

'Thin.'

'No you don't. You're not bothered about your weight, and you know I'm not. Thin is for girls – I should be worried about thin. Come on, you're not trying, answer properly.'

Now he really does think. 'I don't think I have a dream job. Not any more. Not the way I used to.'

'How do you mean?'

'I mean the way the teacher would ask you at primary school, and you'd have to write a little essay about it. What I Want To Be When I Grow Up, by Rich.'

'You mean If you grow up.' I pinch his thigh. 'So what did you want to be?'

'Kevin Keegan.'

I giggle. 'What?'

'Kevin Keegan, and all the usual things. I don't think I was that different to anyone else. You had the usual smartarses who wanted to be Prime Minister or Superman. But mainly the boys all wanted to be a variation on Kevin Keegan, or an astronaut or a train driver or a fireman. We thought they were the everyday jobs that had to be done. We thought there were thousands of astronauts and Kevin Keegans, that we could all have a go at being each one till we got bored. That's how it seemed.'

I giggle. 'I never had to write that essay at school.'

'They'd probably wised up by the time you started school.'

'How do you mean?'

'No sense building your hopes up. "What's your dream job? Getting four stars on me Mickey D badge, miss."'

'God, how depressing.'

'So, go on. What's your dream job?'

I think seriously and simply for a minute. Then I close my eyes and say: 'One that exists.'

'Amen.'

'You? Still want to be an astronaut?'

'You're the only star for me, baby.'

'Yuck.' But I grin.

'I don't know what there is any more.' Rich enters the talk properly now. He is allowing me this. 'But if there is something I can do, something I'm good enough at to be paid for my time and my skill, I want to do that. But I don't know what there is, and I don't know how you get to do it. Applications and job descriptions are scary jibberish. I don't know what people want. And if you get to an interview you still don't know what they want. They don't ask you straight questions. It's all that psycho bollocks shit.'

'Psychometric.'

214

'Whatever. I think I probably did have a clear idea once. Serves me right I suppose. All in all I'd still settle for Kevin Keegan.'

The noise over the Seven-Eleven starts up again. I wonder what they're discussing.

I wonder what their dream jobs are, the people who live above the Seven-Eleven.

And then I'm back by the pond in Finsbury Park, and I'm wondering why I happened to think of that particular memory. And it suddenly seems a long time since Rich and me had a nice talk about something.

32

'We have to accept it, don't we?' I said. 'It's over.'

I'm going to have to report a different type of conversation. I don't like doing it; it tastes bad. But I need you to hear our voices; I need you to hear how well we were trained in self-deception. How we thought we could still sound like our old selves.

These were things said in the aftermath of an idea in tatters. It was a strangely calm aftermath. A long dark night of the soul among the newly soulless. Although this is by no means all that should have been said: nothing about Erica and James or about the shameful wrong we perpetrated against people who had done nothing to us. It always happens like that, the way you choose your targets. If we'd really understood and felt the social pain of our situation as I've claimed, if that was something we cared about, then we should have been striking out at the people – if there were such people – who had done something to us, rather than turning in on our own class. Divide And Rule. It's hardly a new conspiracy. When will we wake up to it? When will we target the cause of our situation? But I don't know anything about that. I wasn't a revolutionary, I was just broke and clueless. I didn't have the resources to fight anyone bigger than myself. Which is why this will keep happening the way it has always happened. I'd fight back now, now I know things. No, that's a lie. I wouldn't fight back.

See? Still thinking about myself. No, we weren't big enough to think about anyone else yet – we didn't deserve to. We were still perpetrators, and as such hadn't earned the right to feel as victims. We couldn't claim to understand their pain, or even to really listen to our own guilt. This wasn't all that needed to be said, not by a long way, but it should have been a start. And we should have been listening to our own words.

So here are two conversations, and neither is any better than the other. The first went something like this.

Rob: It was never gonna work, was it?

Rich: Never.

Rob: It couldn't. God. How fucking stupid. I mean Premiership stupid. All that stuff Maddy showed us. We were never meant to take that seriously. And you talked to her just last night and it still didn't sink in. It was just supposed to be fun. A couple of minutes' fun. Look at what the fuck we have done.

Rich: A waste of fucking time.

Me: Is that all this was?

Rich: Come on, take it easy.

Me: I'm waking up now. It's dawning on me.

Rob: I don't mean the time. I don't care too much about the time – what else were we gonna do? Get a job? But I feel so cheated. I really believed in something.

(Deep shame.)

Rich: How do you feel?

Me: I feel lots of things. And I feel poor.

Rich: Again.

Me: I really thought that was it. I thought that was everything.

Rob: We risked everything.

Rich: Too fucking right. Jesus. We risked *everything*.

Rob: We could have gone to jail.

Rich: Fuck.

Me: I think we risked a bit more than that.

(No response.)

Rich: So, we have to accept it, don't we? It's over.

Me: All over.

Rob: Roy Orbison.

Me: Gene Pitney.

Rob: Whatever.

(Pause.)

Rich: Definitely Roy Orbison.

Rob: Think about it. If it worked there'd be people doing it. Someone would know. Someone somewhere would have opened their gob and the word would be out. Someone would fucking know – bookies might even know.

Me: But we did talk to spirits, didn't we? All that stuff was true? It wasn't for nothing. I can't believe it was for nothing.

Rich: Start believing it. But I don't know what's true.

Me: But you were there.

Rich: We talked to something. Energy, spirits, call it what you want. I'm tired.

Rob: Your aura's knackered.

Rich: Ha ha.

Me: But we did contact something?

Rich: We may have talked to ghosts. I suppose.

Rob: I feel such a twat.

Rich: You think you're a twat? I even spent good time and money researching how to be a twat.

(Quiet.)

Rob: What do you mean?

Rich: Promise you won't laugh?

Me: No promises.

Rob: No promises.

Rich: But this is embarrassing.

Me: So's spunking six grand. Spit it out.

Rich: All right. When I went back to Rose's this time, working in the bistro, I did a bit of reading up.

Me: Go on.

Rich: You'll laugh at this (no laughter), but I even went all the way to –

218

Me: – to the Central Reference Library in Manchester.

Rich: How?

Rob: You mentioned it to the chef, Rich. You told Frank. If you were trying to be secretive about this you didn't do a very good job. The point is, why didn't you tell us at the time? I spoke to you every day when you were up there. You never mentioned a fucking dicky bird about this.

Rich: Because nothing came out of it. I didn't come up with anything solid.

Me: Which is totally beside the fucking point! Do you realise me and Rob have been watching our backs for weeks because of this?

Rich: Why didn't you say anything?

Me: No, why didn't *you* say anything? It wasn't our place to say anything. We shouldn't have had to ask.

Rich: Oh, come on.

Me: No way, I'm not letting you get away with this. It doesn't show much trust, does it?

Rich: There was nothing to tell.

Rob: So why the big secret? You wanna know what I thought? I thought you were doing something like that. Finding stuff out. And you know why I thought you were finding stuff out? So you could stab us in the back. Yeah, you can fucking laugh. I didn't want to think it, but I couldn't help it. I thought you were planning a way to do this on your lonesome and keep all the money. I mean it. What would you think? And think about this. Can you imagine what might have happened if I'd kept thinking that?

Rich: What are you saying?

Rob: I'm not saying anything. Just think about it.

Rich: You psychotic bastard. Who's talking about trust now?

Rob: Well I had good fucking reason, didn't I? You deceived us, Rich. It didn't feel very nice. You're lucky it wasn't you I was following around.

Rich (with meaning): Yeah, I reckon I am.

Me: Look, let's forget it. There's no real harm done.

Rob: Not for want of trying. (Pause.) Jesus, look at us. We can't even concoct a decent conspiracy between us. Fucking library. What a bunch of losers.

Rich: Can we drop it?

Rob: With pleasure.

(Pause.)

Me: Just out of interest, what did you find out?

Rich: You really wanna know?

Me: After all this time worrying about it? I really wanna know.

Rich: Nothing.

Me: What?

Rich: Really. A big fat *nada*.

Me: How long did you spend in that library?

Rich: I went four times. Four afternoons.

Me: And you found out nothing? Are you sure you went to the right place? Sure you weren't in the launderette across the road?

Rich: Jesus, you're not gonna let me forget this, are you?

Rob: Correct.

Rich: Nothing of any use, anyway. It was mostly toss, written by quacks. Some deeply sad stuff.

Me: Such as?

Rich: This is really embarrassing. You'll see why I didn't own up. I looked at a lot of stuff on the occult. I mean it, books of spells, biographies of people who reckoned they could talk to the devil. No matter how much we made that cup move on our paper ouija board, nothing could make you believe what was in these books. It was such a dead end. No pun. Waste of time. Certainly not worth all this trouble it's caused. Sometimes I'd get to a good section, and just as I thought the author was about to explain something he'd go off onto talking about a cure for warts, or alchemy, or astrology. That's what made me think that these people didn't really have any secrets to divulge or didn't want you to think they did. I look up what I thought were key words on the CD-ROM and then checked the indexes in the supposedly relevant books, and just got crap. The most impressive thing I found out was the meaning of the word ouija.

Rob: Which is?

Rich: Yes. Just yes. The French *oui*, and the German *ja*. Put them together, ouija.

Me: Yes? That's all?

Rich: That's all, folks.

Me: God, how depressing.

Rich: And seance means sitting.

Rob: Sitting? That's absolutely fascinating, Richard.

Rich: My point exactly. So now you see why I didn't bother telling you all this.

Me: Yeah, but considering our state of mind, don't you think it would have been sensible?

Rich: I assumed you wouldn't be phoning up to quiz Rose's chef.

Rob: You assumed a lot. Never a good idea.

Rich: Don't threaten me. Don't fucking do that!

Rob: Then don't lie to me!

Rich: I didn't lie!

Rob: You know what I mean. So don't lie to me and I won't threaten you. Agreed?

Rich: Okay, let it go, for fuck's sake.

(Pause.)

Me: Well, that's one jolly mystery solved, eh, chaps?

Rob: I wish I could laugh about it.

Rich: Oh my lord.

Me: We're never gonna live this down. Please, please tell me this is our secret until we die.

Rich: Amen.

Rob: I feel such a twat.

Rich: You look a twat. There, see? You nearly laughed.

(Long pause.)

Rob: *Calzoncillos.*

Me: What?

Rob: *Calzoncillos.* Spanish for underpants. I looked it up.

Rich: Did you need to go to the library?

And me and Rich alone, later.

Me: We have to re-think everything, don't we? We have to start thinking like creatures who live on the surface of the planet again.

Rich: The real world.

Me: Oh, I'm not sure what that is any more.

Rich: No choice.

Me: I mean, we've done so much. We've gambled. We've conspired, robbed, mugged. Rich, what have we done? We've done so many things that were never going to be a part of our real world. How can we slip back into the old one? How many different people are we now?

Rich: We have no choice.

(Gentle hug.)

Me: So why did we do those things then?

Rich: I keep saying it: we had no choice. It's just becoming clear to me now. We never really have a choice. It's all done for us.

Me: I think I see what you mean. Rob's right. I wish I could laugh about it. I wish I could feel anything but the way I do.

Rich: Be careful what you wish for.

Me: How could it get worse?

Rich: I'll have to go to Rose's.

Me: Oh, no. Not now.

Rich: Once again, no choice. (Pause.) You know why I never think about going home for good, Trash? It's not because I hate it there, because I don't. It's not because it's an uncool place – although that's true. But that's no big deal. The reason I don't go back is the same reason I left. Because there was nothing there. I thought there'd be more to aim at here.

Me: And isn't there?

Rich: I think there is. I have to believe that. I just haven't got it right, yet.

Me: Maybe this place is all a big myth.

Rich: I'll tell you what a myth is – I learned this at college, for what it's worth. A myth is when the hero leaves his home on a quest and returns with a gift that enriches his people. That's what a myth is. Now think about it. Of all the people me and Rob know who've gone back up north, how many of them have taken anything back? Yeah, I get it now. The myth is itself a myth. Very clever. Shit.

Me: Don't talk about going back.

Rich: I wish I had some money.

Me: I wish we had some, too. Rich, do you still love me?

Rich: No. You're too poor.

Me: No, really?

Rich: No, you're really too poor.

Me: Come on.

Rich: See? The real world. Yes I love you, ya peessa trash.

Me: And which world do you love me in?

Rich: Mm?

Me: Nothing.

Rich: Mm.

Me: Rich, we don't have any money, do we?

Rich: Nothing.

Me: I suppose I could go home. If I had to. What do you think?

Rich: Mm.

Me: Rich, pay attention. We have to decide. We don't have any money. I could go home. But I'd rather not. I'd rather we thought about this and came up with something. We could look for jobs again, anything. I'd rather do anything just so we don't have to be apart. I could wait tables, it might not be so bad. I want to keep us together. These have been some pretty weird times and I want us to come through them still together, not with a distance between us. Do you know what I mean? Are you with me?

Rich: Yeah.

Me: Rich, can you forgive what I've done? I mean, you were so strange with me for a while after the robbery, after what we did to Erica and Ja –

Rich: Jesus, those fucking names!

Me: But you were. And you were funny with me today, when it didn't work – when nothing worked. It's not like it used to be, Rich. Do you forgive me? Can you forget the bad things we've done in the last few weeks? Can we be us again?

Rich: Ain't nuthin' to forgive, darlin'. It be all history.

Me: I love you, Rich. (Kiss.) Rich, we don't have any money. What will you do?

Rich: Phone my sister.

I stole from mine – my sister. Not a loan. I didn't hit the teacher and the diplomat for a handout, didn't pester Nicola for a sub. She had a hundred and ten quid in her white dresser drawer, the one her dad knocked up from a kit when she was so high, and I took it and headed back to the flat.

The buzzing told me to steal it.

I'd been home for three days, miserable days. Family guilt, lame explanations, concerned looks, a few tears from the teacher. Really tedious stuff. Some very weird looks from the diplomat, who didn't seem to be himself. I vaguely registered

224

that him and mum didn't seem to be talking, even seemed to be avoiding each other. But I had other things to think about. I kept everything brief and businesslike: found the money, waited until everyone was out, and fucked off.

The phone was ringing as I opened the door to blond Bob's. It rang again for a long time while I was in the shower. The ringing sounded lonely, like someone in tears. I couldn't listen to it any more so I went out to try and find the boy Robin. I expected he'd be waiting tables at the diner. Sunday lunchtime was good tips. But Rob wasn't there.

Oh. When will he be working again? When can I catch him? (Nice smile.)

You can't. Robin resigned. I'm looking for a cleaner and a waitress. Interested?

What? Erm, might be. Gotta go.

What the fuck was going on? What had that bastard gone and done? How would I eat? I couldn't go back home now. My giro wasn't due for another week. And the hundred and ten quid wasn't for food. I began to be just a wee bit scared and to think I'd gone too far. I'd burned all my bridges. But the buzzing kept me going. I had to find Rob. And anyway, would it work with just two of you? I didn't know. I had to get Rich back from his sister's. I had a hundred and ten quid. I had a lot to do.

What was I doing?

Against everything I still believed. The buzzing believed, my fear and my dreams believed; still the same dreams, the souls and the voices screaming for life. That was all they wanted. And it made me believe something.

I'd done it all now. Cut all the ties. The parents, okay. But my sister, the closest there is. Would she keep it from the folks? I had no right to expect her to, I know that. But that didn't matter right now. I had the money. I had my part of the bargain. I'd done the worst thing: I'd taken it home to my family. Now

I couldn't run home any more, even if they'd have me. And I had to live with the knowledge that I was the worst kind of thief. Now, in my eyes, I really had risked everything.

I didn't know the half of it.

33

Rob woke me late afternoon. He was standing over my bed, his daysack at his feet. He was wearing the blue M&S fleece he called his travelling jacket, although he never travelled anywhere. He didn't look surprised to find me. I sat up and rubbed my eyes and he took off the fleece and threw it over a chair and sat at the foot of the bed. He looked at me in a way that made him look calm and attractive and reliable. A way that made me recall some of that night in the alley.

He took Marlboro lights and matches from the zip pocket of his daysack and lit up one each. He slipped Steve Earle in the deck. We listened to some of *The Devil's Right Hand*. After a good smoke he cleared his throat to speak. I was still settling in to the cigarette, still a bit sleepy. Rob looked straight at me and said, 'How much did you get?'

'Hundred and ten.'

'Parents?'

'Sister.'

'That's too bad.' He was pretending to look around for an ashtray.

'What about you?'

'Oh, parents. Seventy-five. There's more but I have to pay back Sally at the diner. The train fare.'

I laughed weakly. 'You borrowed money so you could nick a few quid off your folks?' I laughed again. 'Oh, Rob. You're not much of a gangster, are you?'

Rob went red. 'It was necessary. All right, look. I was

going to rip off the diner but there was just no chance. They've got a tight system. Then when I thought about it this just seemed better. The right kind of risk, you know what I mean?'

I thought. 'Yeah.'

He sucked and blew smoke. 'And then I jacked in the job because having the job is no risk at all.'

'Do your parents know?'

'They will by now.'

'Oh.'

'They never did like banks. And they really do keep it in a biscuit tin.' He laughed and I joined in. We were thieves again. Laughing went with the territory. It filled a space meant for something else. 'My mum. It'll break her heart. We were a close family until I moved away. She'd have a hard time thinking of me as a thief. But knowing I'd steal from her? I don't know what it'll do to her.' He mashed out his cigarette on a crushed beer can. 'This had better be fucking worth it. Because my mum is gonna take some fucking buying back.'

I looked into Rob's eyes and felt a flash of something. I could see it now. I could see why this was what we were meant to do. We'd proved our willingness to do bad things to get money to bet with, and it hadn't been enough. This wasn't about anything that easy any more. It was about sacrificing our ties with the people we loved for the sake of one more bet. Risking everything meant risking what was most important to us. Starting with our families. Okay, like most people we had consciences, and limits, and it meant something to us to do the awful things we'd done. Even Rob, for all his bravado and his twisted anger, was hurting through all this. Maybe his bravado was a symptom that he was hurting more than any of us. We were ordinary people. We were not career criminals and we were not cold; just because we had done bad things did not mean we did not feel the wrong of those things or the shame that went with them. But the spirit

228

wanted more from us, and maybe this was the start of it.

Rob rubbed his eyes and he looked old and drained. I stroked his fingers. He said, 'I wish it was enough just to rip off the diner. But I know it wasn't.'

I lifted his hand to my mouth, and kissed a fingernail. 'I know, Rob. I know.'

Rich robbed his sister's place straight after we phoned him with the plan. Actually there wasn't a plan. We just said we had money to bet with and if he wanted to be in he'd better get his sorry padded arse back here and be in – preferably with some cash – and if he didn't want to be in then we'd carry on without him. I think he understood everything that was implied by that. An hour later he was winging his way Eustonward with the best part of three hundred quid stuffed down the front of his *calzoncillos*.

When he dropped his black waiter's trousers and began gingerly producing bundles of damp tenners from around his privates I enquired as to why he had judged this the suitable method of transport for a large amount of cash – or any amount for that matter. His somewhat defensive reply was that that was where he'd stowed the money when he'd grabbed it, and he'd just never had the time or the nerve to transfer it somewhere more comfortable. Robin, facing a classic laugh or cry dilemma, went off to put the kettle on, while I rubbed moisturiser into Rich's traumatised willy. He winced and narrowed his eyes when I ventured to suggest there'd be no cock-up this time.

It wouldn't work.

It couldn't work. We knew that. Combined losses of £6,264.50 were testament to its being a hare-brained cockeyed mumbo-jumbo plan with as much chance of success as there was of a complete stranger walking up to me in the street and handing me the deeds to a luxury flat in Regent's Park (my favourite recurring daydream. Actually, it travelled the scale between that and a studio in Clapham depending on how far I was from giro day).

Four hundred and sixty-five quid said it would work.

The board said it would work. But what did that mean any more? No, if we believed in anything now it was in what came directly from within us. Instinct. Need. Frustration. These are better than nothing. And these were what we had. Risk everything. Lose everything. What's left? Whatever you can find.

The only thing left to do was unplug the phone. You couldn't think with that thing pleading in your ear, never stopping, never shutting the FUCK UP.

34

The odds said 15−1.

But maybe there weren't really odds on this kind of bet. Maybe you just lost, and losing was both an ending and a starting point for something else. Meaning: you lost and then you could start to atone, tally your debts and pay off the right ones in the right amounts to the right people.

This felt something like that. What it certainly didn't feel like was the start of a string of wins. It was a gradual dawning, but a welcome feeling. Perhaps I was starting to feel okay about being alone in the world. Was this going to be the moment I grew up and stood on my own two feet? If so, I'd come a funny route. But it was true. I wouldn't have dared mention it to the boys, but I was just about ready to face losing. There was something relaxed in the sensation, a quietness in my head. There were things I needed to face after this was over. I hoped the boys felt the same. I let myself think about that, that maybe you could lose with your faith intact, settle up and start again. Maybe call time on the biggest adventure in your lives and stay close to your partners and remember the times when you felt so alive you thought nothing real could ever touch you in a bad way again; perhaps even keep something of that feeling somewhere special inside you. Yeah, why not. Maybe feeling this way meant you'd always find something in life to believe in, while abandoning it half-finished meant believing in nothing ever again. But there were things I was forgetting.

No one said much over the fry-up. The meal was solemn.

You could tell the waitress sensed there was a kind of condemned persons' hearty breakfast thing going on. Never mind
dogs, all manner of waitresses have a sixth sense. Her doomed
demeanour was making me giggle, and I was attracting stares,
which made me giggle more. She kept appearing with more
coffee and toast, perhaps hoping to keep us there and postpone
some dreadful date with fate. When we eventually filed out she
didn't look comfortable about picking up our money. It was
funny but sad. If we'd left a tip I think she might have broken
down.

And I couldn't get that poor woman out of my head – I had
plenty of time for morbid thoughts on the way to the bookies,
as no one was talking. I wondered how her day would go, if
she'd be able to forget us, or whether she'd simply pick up the
vibe from the next customers to sit down – maybe someone
happy, perhaps a young couple in love. Boy, I'd really picked
up the doom vibes rebounding off her, though, and the next
thing I knew I'd resolved to look at things around me differently
from now on. It was one of those split second life-changing
decisions that never stick and just end up depressing you by
showing you how shallow you are. So maybe everything I'd
been thinking about all morning was crap. But for now I decided
that the sky was bluer, the light clearer, the air sharper than I
had ever remembered. This, I thought, was how a condemned
person must perceive their world: their final chance. Of course,
I had no right to think like that. I had no idea then how a
condemned person feels or what they think.

But it wasn't all in my over-dramatic imagination.

That morning I was sensing the process of change, to the
extent that I knew a life was about to end – not literally: no
one was buying the farm. Maybe metamorphose is a better
word. Yes, that's more like it: metamorphose, like caterpillars
and butterflies. Only this was the human version. In the human
version of metamorphosis it's the butterfly who wraps in her

wings and crawls into her shell and, after reassessing her options, crawls out again as a caterpillar.

It was that kind of day. The kind of day when the most you can expect is a dose of the truth and a fair crack at measuring up to it: at accepting caterpillardom with grace and honesty.

We didn't expect Hook Line & Sinker to win by two lengths.

We didn't expect to win six grand.

I watched it happen.

I saw the bastard beast fly home on a dozen TV monitors, a good two lengths clear. I saw it with part of me waiting – god, almost praying – for some crippled donkey to overtake and humiliate the representative of all my worldly hopes, so I could go back home and start my life over.

No, I should have stuck to what I now knew had been my unconscious plan all along, whatever happened, and strolled out of the bookies and on to Who Knows Where, leaving the £6,400 to the boys or whoever wanted it. I should have walked away to live with my guilt and come clean with everyone.

Instead I felt all the wrong things happening at once.

It wasn't even the euphoric vibes coming off the boys which set me off. When Hook Line & Sinker came home I was in there myself. The little red guy on the left shoulder was a nose ahead once again.

And I sprang off my chair.

And I screamed.

And I watched the boys scream.

And tears of joy blurred my vision.

And the last sound I made out coherently for a good fifteen minutes was Rob yelling over and over: it works! it works! IT FUCKING WORKS!

35

Believe it or not they didn't have six grand in cash on the premises. Either that or they didn't want to give us their entire float – it was still early in the day. They offered to send Securicor for the rest when they turned up for the bank run, but we said no way, we'd rather walk to the Tottenham Lane branch for the rest. On the way out of the place the manager said something – probably completely innocuous – which nonetheless set me off laughing like a maniac, and that set the boys off in turn. We were way too hyper. We were buzzing – yes, that kind of buzzing. The morning's quietness was lost, pushed out.

The noise would have to go.

It would have to be drowned.

There are maybe six pubs in the way from Ladbrokes Tottenham Lane back to Crouch End. In Crouchy itself there aren't actually too many – maybe half a dozen. But throw in swanky wine bars and you've got an awesome crawl zone. And forget food: Eating is Cheating, so ran one of our college mottos. So, even with all the adrenalin we were pumping out it was only a matter of time before the three of us were just slightly totalled.

We did the occasion magnificent justice. Only it was the *Goodfellas* thing again – doing it all wrong. Fair enough, have a drink to celebrate, have lots of drinks. But keep your heads down. Don't do the following: stagger from one watering hole to the next shouting, hugging, snogging, and simulating group sex; fall up to the bar of each establishment wielding a very tatty and vulnerable-looking duffel bag from whose innards you coax conspicuous fans of banknotes. In other words, don't draw the worst kind of attention to yourselves.

And something else. Where was the restraint? What had happened to the ground rules we spent so long moralising over? What about the respect for where this money came from? Never mind moral codes, what about plain common sense? Gone. Awol.

It was probably midnight when we were pro-actively assisted out of the Hungry Horse. I don't imagine we'd deserved any better treatment. Not for the first time that night we found we'd left the duffel bag behind at the bar. It soon caught us up, courtesy of the long-suffering landlady. In London lonely bags make people nervous about bombs.

Our bag had attracted all kinds of attention.

I'd noticed them by now, and amid the alcoholic haze the thought began to form that their presence spelled trouble. Three figures waiting outside the double doors of the pub, about twenty feet to our left. They'd waited until we were reunited with our bag and now they moved in. The boys had noticed too. They noticed three tall and looming shapes which materialised into one Nigger, one Paki, and one example of vicious pedigree White Trash. Dangerous people, unreasonable. Not, in this context, a black, a white and an Asian, but just what I said.

The next few moments happened faster than I could sober up. The next thing I knew the Black Guy had Rich by his throat against the wall of the pub and Rob was wrestling with the Paki, dangerously close to the edge of the road. The boys were being attacked and my consciousness had somehow skipped the moments leading up to it. Then there was another time lapse and the White Trash was trying to prise the bag from out of my hands, and I was fighting for the bag and shouting, and I heard my own voice filled with panic and pleading and fear. And everything became familiar to me.

36

I went for White Trash's balls with a scything hoof, but he knew that trick. Catching my leg one-handed, he flipped me hard onto my back. His other hand grabbed at the duffel bag. But I wasn't letting go.

Somewhere above me a voice gasped: 'Let him have it, Trash!' I couldn't place it at first. It was Rich, only the Black Guy had him so tight by the throat he could hardly breathe, let alone shout. There was a croaking sound as the Black Guy's grip tightened. Rob threw off the Paki's bearhug and made a charge for Rich's attacker. The Paki hit the ground hard.

Robin punched the Black Guy in the kidneys and Rich and the hurt man went down together. Was it my terrified imagination or was Rob enjoying himself? White Trash, meanwhile, nonchalantly began stamping on me where I lay clinging to the bag. He wasn't even going for the money any more – there was no hurry, he'd get it eventually – he was teaching the bitch a lesson. The lesson hurt.

Rob turned and came up behind White Trash, but not fast enough. The Paki was on him again and this time caught him hard on the back of the head with something that sounded like it should kill you. For a second I feared the worst.

But somehow Rob got up. What was inside this man? That strength of his worried me now – the force necessary to keep him down would probably kill him. He was up and swinging at the Paki but the blow on the head had slowed him down. The Paki simply stepped aside and let Rob slump to his knees.

I knew it was over then. Rob held his head in a delayed reaction, and stayed down. The Paki held up an arm as a signal to White Trash to lay off me, then stepped forward and flipped me onto my battered back with one deft toe poke.

I'd had enough. I felt like dropped fruit. I let go of the bag. The Paki calmly picked it up. White Trash turned around and delivered a running kung-fu kick at Rob's back which sent him sprawling. Then he turned and stuck a boot in Rich's guts. Rich and the Black Guy had been sitting side by side against the wall of the pub, nursing their separate wounds, looking like a couple of buddies exhausted after a jog. But, on being kicked, Rich vomited violently and it sprayed over everyone's legs and shoes.

White Trash and the Paki went mental, and the unnecessary phase was on us. Just like Cambridge Circus. The Black Guy crawled out of their way and they dished it out to Rich with their feet. It was sickening to see.

The gang's anger suddenly seemed unified and massive and efficient, and all of it directed at Rich. The vibe was as impressive as it was horrible. I had a brief flashback to the Future Shock and experienced a moment of clear thought. Not that it would help.

Then slow motion set in, and I watched the film, unable to move. Rob was clutching his head, probably unaware of anything going on outside it.

'Run!'

Rich's command to me seemed to trigger something in everyone. The Paki started off at a sprint towards the centre of Crouch End. Then Rob, with what I can only describe as a deep growl, was up and on his tail, staying as steady as he could. The Paki looked back, saw him, and accelerated, and then they were both gone into the black.

When the Black Guy turned to watch them go I made my move. I got up off the ground and scampered off in the direction of Muswell Hill. I could hear the white man laughing and the black man panting and gaining on me, and then I could hear him cursing his pain and he wasn't running any more. I owed Rob for that.

But I didn't stop. I went on and on and I changed direction. I was thinking and running at the same time. I had to keep ahead of what was behind me.

I ran until the pain of my bruised chest and back and ribs made it hard to get the breath necessary to propel me forward. Then I collapsed to the ground and sat panting and sobbing with my eyes closed.

When I opened them again there were lights around me. I could hear fast moving traffic, but couldn't work out where the noise was coming from. Had I run to the motorway? Surely not. The M1 was miles away. Staggering to my feet I looked around in the dark. I was standing by a high wall topped with a fence. At the very top was barbed wire. The traffic noise was from far below. I looked down and knew where I was.

The highest road bridge in Britain, Rich once told me. There's an urban myth about the place that goes something like this. A battered body is discovered in an open top lorry in a Glasgow haulage depot. The dead man is a bricklayer from Kentish Town in north London. What is he doing in the back of a truck in Govan? Fell onto the back of a lorry, maybe? Some bright spark eventually works out that's precisely what happened.

Anyway, this was Highgate, the road below was the A1, and I was standing on what Londoners call Suicide Bridge.

Assuming you don't jump, a short walk over the bridge takes you onto Highgate Hill. Highgate Hill, where Dick Whittington once thought: ah, what the fuck. The pubs around there have appropriate names: Whittington Stone, Whittington and Cat. Contrary to the spirit of their legend they are the kind of places that would drive depressed bricklayers from Kentish Town to take a short walk and a long leap. The biggest going concern at the bottom end of Highgate Hill is the Whittington Hospital's casualty department. I laughed at the idea, then stopped when I heard myself.

I was laughing while Rich might be dying. But it was okay because the streets were paved with gold.

I laughed louder.

I wandered. My head was spinning from booze, and probably some concussion, too. I tried to think clearly. It didn't occur to me to call the police. Of course not, we were on opposite sides. And I couldn't go home. Not while my boys were out there suffering alone. I couldn't think of anything to do, so I kept wandering, thinking strange thoughts. My efforts at lucidity drowned in a stirred and very shaken mental cocktail.

They say remorse hits you. And it's true. Sitting weeping and mumbling, curled under a tree on Highgate Hill in the middle of the night, the blows of remorse for what I had done one afternoon to a girl who sold books, rained down on my face, on my guilty body, on my marked heart. I saw the truth of what I had really done and what I had not done.

I had not been part of an adventure. I had not pulled off a daring robbery. I had not gambled and lost, won, and lost again. I had not emerged with honour from the pages of a story.

I had possibly caused something to die in someone. I had definitely fucked over at least one life. And I had not paid.

'Excuse me?'

What was that?

'Oi. Excuse me?'

I looked up, and through my tears saw two men grinning down at me. One was white, the other was black. So they'd followed me. What did they want? They had the money, didn't they? Shit.

I began to shake. I was so scared I stopped crying. I shuddered and felt heat where I was sitting and knew I was wetting my pants. White Trash smelled it or saw it and scrunched up his nose and cackled nastily. I began to cry again. I had run out of fight.

The Black Guy raised something thick in his right fist and then I felt an impact on my left shoulder that made me scream as I didn't know it was possible to scream. I saw a boot coming towards my chest and felt my back bend to fit the shape of the tree behind me. I thought something had cracked, and I screamed until something froze in my voice. That was when I started to drift. Each time they hit me after that I saw it coming but I felt nothing, or maybe just something like an ice cube being rubbed on my skin, but no pain, and I couldn't hear any sounds except my own breathing and a happy sound like someone laughing far away. It went on like that, me curled into a ball in my mind, until I heard the White Guy saying he was going to fuck me. Opening my eyes I saw his trousers around his thighs and the dark blur of his crotch, and then the Black Guy was holding my hair and pulling my head back, and then I really started to scream, and to lash out with my hands and feet. Someone put a hand over my mouth but I bit down hard and then there were two of us screaming, and I know the soles of my feet were hitting someone some of the time, and they must have panicked, because when I stopped the noise and stopped feeling what I was kicking, I was on my own.

I tried to stand, but I could only feel one of my legs, and I fell back down. I could feel sobbing coming from my chest, but I had no more voice left, and so I sat and wheezed. And all I remember after that is sitting under my tree and being very, very tired deep down in a place where tiredness does not normally reach, and wanting to sleep, and falling off into a place beyond fear where heavy doors close in the mind.

37

I came to, numb and freezing, lying by the front porch of blond Bob's building. The concrete had made patterns on my arms like burns. The moment I moved, my head began pounding. Almost as a reflex action I began to cry, dry, spent tears. For a few moments I just sat like that and tried to get a measure of my pain. And some pain. Every sound, every movement, every muffled sniff and restrained sob brought on dull spasms: I winced at traffic vibrations, and the light breeze playing around my neck and hair felt like a freezing blast.

Gathering my thoughts was a slow process. After about fifteen minutes of gathering very few of them I risked opening one eye. Five more minutes and I chanced the other. Fighting the urge to vomit, I told myself to move.

A quick check told me my keys and purse were still in my pockets. But loose change was scattered around my feet and wedged under my bum. I started to smile, but that hurt too much. Obviously I'd been taken for homeless. Judging by the number of coins I must have been lying there on the flags a while. Or the world had become generous overnight. My clothes were a mess and I smelled like a toilet. I glimpsed a memory of myself limping down Crouch End Hill, past the King's Head. I suppose I got as far as blond Bob's building and then collapsed.

I found myself gathering up the coins. I suppose it seemed like the coherent thing to do. More blurred lumps of time came back to me. A lot depended on how I dealt with this: I knew I could cross a line one way or the other. I had to be strong.

The flat was empty. I double-locked the door from the inside and checked the windows and scanned the streets below. I took a long hot bath, which hurt like hell all over. Then I forced myself to confront the full-length mirror in Rob's – Bob's – room, which hurt a lot more.

From the toes all the way up I looked like someone I couldn't imagine. My physical proportions actually looked altered where I'd been kicked. I seemed dented, like a toy doll used for a hammer. I tried seeing myself as someone else, someone naked and heroic from an epic film, but it didn't work. The movie was over.

The damage report. Both my shins were bruised blue and one was deeply gouged, a sticky black and red scab stretching across two inches. My knees and the backs of my thighs were worse. Later all these bruises would turn an ugly yellow.

Gently walking my fingers over my ribs I gauged where the worst pain was, which parts I'd have to be careful with when washing and dressing. It was academic, really: there were bruises almost everywhere and pain every time I moved. I jumped as a drop of red appeared on my stomach and banked a path down to my right thigh. Another drop followed it – the hot bath had set my buffeted nose bleeding. I stood watching it drip. The salty blood hurt my bruised lips. But my mouth was only a little mashed and my nose wasn't broken. My neck was okay for now, and there were only two bad lumps on my head, although between them they had a great sense of rhythm. But I was okay. At least I was home. If I could just keep panic at a safe distance, at least until all the other present shit was over. This wasn't the worst of what had to be sorted out in my head.

It was time to think about the boys. I could remember enough to know that Rich was in an even worse state than me. That's the way I had to function: stay focused, keep solving problems, don't stop to think. So, six aspirin and a change of clothes made me almost presentable. Think about the boys.

I knew where Rich would be. I phoned a minicab.

The minicab driver was mid-twenties, black, but I didn't get a good look at his face.

What was I thinking? Clear your head, Trash. Focus. People are depending on you.

The cab dropped me at Whittington Hospital; I paid with change I'd gathered from the pavement, spotted the Casualty sign, and limped inside.

At reception I was made to fill out two different forms and answer what seemed like a hundred questions. It wasn't easy proving we lived together. Maybe because I looked such a sorry mess the West Indian receptionist tipped me off that at some point the police would want to bend my ear. She wouldn't tell me if they'd already questioned Rich. I assumed they must have.

Where was Rich?

'Men's ward. First floor,' she said. Her accent was thick but not unpleasant. Nice on a woman. 'But him in a different room from his friend. You want to see the other boy you got to see him separate.' And then in a tone more warning than official: 'And I don't know if the police gonna like that either.'

The other boy? Rob? What had happened for him to end up in here? Well, at least I knew where he was. It was almost too much to take in. I didn't know hospitals. I certainly didn't know the police. I'd have to be careful. Before doing anything I'd have to talk to Rich.

I thanked the woman and she smiled. She signalled to an Asian male nurse to come over and lead the way. The first floor was up an escalator. I never knew they had escalators in hospitals.

The Asian guy was late twenties. Too old.

Get a grip, Trash.

Rich had a room to himself at the end of the ward. As soon as Asian nurse guy left me alone I broke down. I was trying to be brave and together, but it only worked at intervals. Periodic bouts of tears seemed the only way I was going to get through anything.

Rich's eyes were closed, he hadn't noticed me come in. Probably doped silly. I don't see how he could have slept otherwise. I moved a plastic chair up to his bed and sat down quietly. God, he must have hurt something evil. The cut below his right eye was stitched up ugly, and there were more stitches in his lips and chin. I tried counting the stitches. I tried to cry quietly. The rest of his face was bruises on top of more bruises. His unstitched eye was swollen shut.

Rich's hips and legs were covered by a sheet. Three fingers of his right hand were taped and his forearms were bruised blue and red. But worst was his ribs. I couldn't see them at all under the heavy strapping. I wondered how he could breathe.

I had to know something.

Slowly lifting the sheet I examined Rich's privates. I felt slightly queasy about doing it after what had almost happened to me the night before, but I knew it would be the thing that would concern him most, and I wanted to be prepared if he asked me. It all looked okay, but I wasn't satisfied: men's parts look tender and squashed at the best of times. So I scooped him up with my other hand, and felt around down there until I was convinced all was as it should be. Then I laughed at the picture I must have made and before I knew it I was sobbing out loud. Get a grip. The noise finally woke Rich. My face was on the sheet and I still had his johnson in my hand when he spoke.

'There's a time and a place, don't you think?'

Hearing his voice was too much. I dissolved into a gunk of indistinguishable noises and bodily fluids. My nose started again and within seconds a cocktail of blood, snot, and tears had spotted both of us. He directed me to a tall roll of blue tissue paper.

'Shh,' he was telling me. 'It's all right. It's all right,' over and over, which made me cry even more. His voice was no more than a strained hiss, and he could hardly move his lips at all. He didn't say anything about how I looked. I doubt he could even see me.

'They're not letting me stay long,' I managed. 'And the police want to talk to me.'

'I know. Don't worry. Just don't say anything. I know Rob won't say anything.' It took an age for him to get his words out.

'What should I tell them?'

'Nothing.'

'What about the money?'

'There was no money.'

'But they can find out.'

'Trash, there was no money. There was never any money. Keep thinking like that.'

'Okay.' (Sob.)

'They can't prove anything. We're the victims here.'

'Rich, they could prove everything.'

'Not unless we panic. There's no reason for them to make connections.' Out of necessity he kept his sentences short. 'Don't help them. Say nothing. Act traumatised. Give vague descriptions. You saw nothing. You remember nothing. There was never any money, just a fight, okay? Just a mugging. They'll never catch anyone.'

I realised what he was saying and sat up. 'Are you telling me we've got to cover up for the people who – who did this to you?'

247

'We don't want them caught, Trash. We want all the connections cut. Think about it.'

I thought about it and decided – for now – to give him the answer he wanted. 'Right.' I paused, then asked: 'Oh, Rich, are you all right?'

'Now that is a stupid question.'

'Sorry.' I laughed again and stopped myself. He didn't mind. 'I mean really. What have they done to you, darling?'

He sighed, then went through the grisly list. 'Broken fingers. Broken ribs. Many stitches, a wee bit pain.' He paused to let his breathing catch up. 'Nothing a good fuck and a cup of tea won't sort.' He tried to wink, which came off predictably badly. I winced.

'How are you feeling? I mean in your head?'

'Apart from the kettle drums you mean?' Rich looked down, then spoke, even more quietly. 'I'll tell you what I'm not thinking. Not thinking about myself much. I mean I think I'll be okay – I know I'll be okay. But I'm lying here and I don't feel too bad about all this, if you know what I mean.'

I tried to keep a handle on what he was saying, but his speech was fading and fragmented, and there were noises in the corridor, people talking, and things going by on wheels. As the gaps between groups of words lengthened it became harder to follow the flow.

'What do you mean, not thinking about yourself? I'd be thinking about myself.'

He paused. 'I feel relaxed.'

I nodded.

He went on. 'Been lying here actually thinking about other people. About you and Rob and, well, about what I've done. That's what I mean by not thinking about myself. Other things to understand now.' He looked up at me. 'Do you understand?'

'I understand.'

248

'Trash?'
'Mmm?'
'What happened to you?'

What happened to me? I've spent so much time going back over that one, that my version is probably just plain unreliable by now. I've got the facts straight; I know the physical events. But as to what actually happened to make me do the things I did – and then what happened to me in the sense Rich meant, I don't know. As I say, I've thought about it way too much, and it's all jumbled in with too much searching and invention. And anyway, I don't think that What Happened? is the question now. The question is: Something Happened, can you accept it?

What a question. I suppose that's what telling this story is about. Can I tell my story, even to myself? Well, it's been a few years. And I'll be honest, that intervening time has not been an uninterrupted libation of neat remorse. These feelings have often waned, often been dormant, often pushed away behind rage and resentment. But I knew they were there – and that's what I mean by real remorse, the anticipation of it, the knowledge that it is some day going to be solid. And I suppose that's as good a response as any. I know the stuff is there. But I don't have an answer yet as to what to do with it all. Maybe that's the problem. Coming from a culture which expects answers, I look for an answer when I should be learning to embrace the question. If I could keep a grip on thoughts like that.

The other thing Rich got in a nutshell. He said: There was never any money. And he was right. I don't know if we had hit on the way to win money through the board or if we had just been falling for a lot of teases and meaningless gibberish all along. But what I do know is that if, in that winning bet,

249

we really had cracked the formula, then it was information we did not want now.

Because the price was too high. And it was sure to get higher. That was the nature of whatever we had or had not tapped into. For this win we'd had to betray our families. What would the board require next time? And if we went on, and we got hooked, would we be able to stop before we lost ourselves in it all? Or before the price of winning was turning on each other? No. It wasn't worth it.

That's what happened to me. We might have found the answer and we might not. But I didn't care any more. I can't say for sure, but I suspect the boys reached something like the same conclusions on their own. Because none of us ever mentioned the bets again.

'How do you mean, what happened to me?'

'Last night.'

I shrugged, then regretted it. 'I got kicked around a bit. I ran when you told me. Do you remember telling me to run?'

'I remember. You were right to give up the money. Should have done it sooner.'

Quietly: 'There was never any money.'

'Clever girl.' Rich's one good eye looked down at himself and then up at my face. I think. 'Anything else happen?'

Jesus, what could he see? I decided he was in a bad enough way without hearing my whole story.

'You look different,' he went on.

'Not different. I'm still your piece of Trash.'

'Are you?'

'Dirty white Trash.'

'Who loves you?'

'You do.'

'Yeah? You think so?'

'Yeah.' I tugged his willy. 'And I'm okay. Nothing else happened.'

'Nothing?'

'Cuts and bruises.' My next words clawed against my saying them, but I got them out. 'Nothing a good fuck and a cup of tea won't sort,' I said.

Rich nodded, just barely. 'I was worried.'

'You had enough to think about. I got home. I slept – I had to sleep. My head hurt.'

'I know.'

'I should have come sooner. But I was – I was sleeping.'

'It's okay.'

'I was worried.'

'We're okay.'

We – Rob!

'Have you seen Rob?'

'For a second. He's cool.'

'Who loves you, Rich?'

'Me mam.'

'And?'

'Maybe you.'

'Fifty-fifty. Sometimes I pretend.'

'Trash?'

'Yes, my love?'

'Welcome back to the planet.'

I only got a quick look at Rich's expression, because the door opened and nurse guy walked in. But Rich looked sad, I remember that. I looked at nurse guy, waiting for him to gesture, or tell me time's up, or anything. But he stood frozen, framed in the doorway. I sat and watched nurse guy, and he stood watching me – sitting there holding Rich's willy.

I turned to see Rich's expression, hoping it would give him a laugh. But he was already fast asleep.

38

I found Rob in the open ward on the same floor.

Were he and Rich being deliberately kept apart? Did the police not want them talking to each other? Was it just that Rich was hurt worse? Anyway, after delivering me to Rob, nurse guy disappeared. No one checked on us again. I began to feel a little less on edge.

Robin looked pleased to see me. He also looked bloody ridiculous. What on earth had he done? Spread-eagled, stick-man drawing fashion, partly covered by a sheet, lay the *pendejo* formerly known as Robin. Besides a pitiful expression his only apparent injuries were to his hands and feet, which were heavily and comically bandaged, making him look like one of those sticky rubber ladybirds you throw at walls. Not sure whether he'd appreciate the resemblance, I didn't mention it. But I did a double-take when I noticed the drip in his arm. Jesus. Rob grinned and told me that he could explain everything. I shook my head, pulled up a chair, and settled in to listen. I might as well get comfortable. I sensed I wasn't in for the short version – Rob didn't know the short version.

'When I saw the money go I was off after the Paki. Did you see me run? I can't have been thinking straight. I didn't know at the time what kind of shape you and Rich were in. I was out of it from a sap on the head – I'm still concussed. High as

252

a kite. But not in a nice way. I've been sick with it. They tell me it could last for ten days or so. Shit. I hope that doesn't mean ten days of puking.'

Ten days. Erica was probably concussed.

I cleared my head and concentrated on Rob. 'Go on.'

'I couldn't let the money get away. No. I don't really think I was chasing the money any more. I think it was the man I wanted. The Paki. I just wanted to get that piece of shit and make him stand and fight.'

I heard the strain in Rob's voice and saw his hands move under the bandages. He winced and took several slow breaths, then began again quietly.

'That's what I wanted. He could have the money. I wanted someone to hurt.'

God help us. If my karma was looking shaky Rob's didn't bear thinking about.

'He was fast on his feet and I was groggy, and I lost him. That made me fucking furious. I've never felt rage like that. Just pure, animal rage. I'm glad I didn't catch him, because I tell you, for the first time in my life I wanted to kill. It scares me.' He wasn't looking at me. 'And I wouldn't give up. Something in my head stopped ticking and went off. I just kept running round and round the streets of Crouchy, then over the hill, down into Finsbury Park, hunting the Paki, and I don't know how long I'd been running, but my feet and legs were aching, and my head was all over the shop. That's when I was sick the first time.

'When I got my head together and looked up, shitloads of police had materialised from nowhere. Panicked old fogies had reported some mad guy running round in circles for hours, shouting. So out comes Plod. They'd been there ages before I noticed them. Just waiting for me to wear myself out, or come down off whatever they thought I was on. And then they moved in and surrounded me.'

Rob's eyes went dark and focused on something I couldn't see, before he quietly began speaking again.

'I was out of it. Cut loose from everything. I mean, I'd never felt so entirely fucked in my whole life. But it wasn't the being tired. I was beaten. I had nothing left. I felt utterly defeated. I've never been that low. I don't ever want to experience that again.'

He paused once more, his eyes returning to me, then laughed briefly.

'They were just about to move in for me when I got a surge of strength from somewhere, and I started to punch – not people, not the police. Just anything there was – walls, lampposts, billboards, traffic lights, windows.' Rob shook his head again. 'Plod fucked off back to a safe distance when I started in with the punching.' He laughed again. 'Plod thought I was on Angel Dust or something.'

He wasn't far wrong, I thought. I couldn't digest what he was saying. I just let most of it bounce off me.

'There were about a dozen of them. Dogs as well. They told me afterwards they wouldn't have let go of the dogs. They'd seen what people in my state could do to dogs.

'So they kept their distance and waited. Waited until I'd worn myself out and collapsed in a heap. I must have looked a picture. Then it wasn't so much a case of arresting me as scooping up the bits and delivering them here. They questioned me on the way, tied me in with Rich in two minutes flat.'

He motioned to one side with his head.

'The drip's for dehydration – all the running around. My legs are pretty well fucked up – muscles and ligaments. I'll be on crutches for a couple of weeks. I'll need physio. And –' with an amazed look – 'my feet were so swollen they had to cut my shoes off me. Good pair of Reeboks, gone.' He motioned with his right hand when he said 'gone', like something was disintegrating in the air beside him, like he'd have snapped his fingers had he been able to. I nodded and went on listening. He was right, he was out of it, almost cut loose from everything, in that it was an effort for him to keep telling the story, to keep from rambling.

'I'm pretty sore. But by some miracle my hands aren't too bad.' To prove it he raised his arms, oh, a good inch and a half. 'Cuts, only one broken finger. Not much skin left to speak of.' He paused, then sighed and said: 'I don't know what got into me.'

I couldn't help him there. He frowned and looked away again.

After a minute he said: 'I wanted to see things clearly. I wanted things to stand still and make perfect sense – that's what I imagined someone standing and fighting would mean. I wanted to know and see my enemy.' He shook his head slowly. 'But the guy with the money got away, and who knows. Well, who knows.' Who knows exactly. It wasn't a question. His voice had tailed off. I didn't think he was going to make any more sense, and I was glad he seemed to be finished talking.

'What happened to you?' he asked. Finally.

I paused and sighed. And I suddenly knew I was going to tell him everything I hadn't told Rich. Damn it, someone was going to know. And it occurred to me that, throughout this whole thing, me and Rob had been straighter with each other than me and Rich had. Not that it had always been the most cordial or intentional of arrangements. But we hadn't kept some feelings from each other in the way lovers always will. So much for love. Anyway, I felt I could talk to Rob now. After some of the things we'd been through I felt like he damn well owed it to me. So I talked. At the very least, I figured, I'd listened to him and so someone could listen to me.

'Several things happened,' I started, not sure how to actually say it. 'Not much when you and Rich were there – cuts and bruises.' I looked him in the eye.

255

He took the bait. 'But?'

'There's a bit more.'

He hesitated. 'You sound as though you haven't told anyone. Meaning Rich.'

'That's right.'

'You going to?'

'Not for now. He's in a bad enough way.'

'And I'm not?'

'Rich would worry.'

'I worry about you, too, Trash.'

I looked at him. He really didn't know what had been happening to him the past few weeks. 'I'll tell him in my own time.'

'What happened?'

'Oh, after they left Rich they got me on my own.'

'All of them?'

'Two.' I had started to cry, which hurt my ribs and my face.

'You want to tell me?'

I shook my head, which hurt. But I said: 'They hit me. And they were going to rape me. But something panicked them and they ran off.' More tears. 'I was so scared, Rob. It was fucking horrible. I'll never forget it.'

'You have to tell Rich. Or someone. You might need help.'

I shook my head again. 'I don't want to tell Rich. It would eat him up, and he's hurt enough. You've seen him. He can't cope with anything else at the moment.'

'Then you have to tell the police.'

'No, Rob.'

I was about to go on when I saw something change in Rob's face. I didn't know what was up, but I instinctively froze and waited for what he would do next. How very professional; the boys had trained me well.

Rob's eyes had flicked onto the alert and he smiled away to my left. I turned to see a pretty blonde nurse pretending to read the chart at the end of his bed. It was a few minutes before she left us alone and walked off to an office at the far end of the ward. We talked in whispers after that.

'You have to do something,' Rob went on. 'Those cunts are still out there. They could do it to someone else.'

I sighed and looked at the floor. 'They probably will,' I admitted. 'But knowing that is something else we'll have to live with. One more thing we've brought on ourselves.' I could see Rob didn't like that. I continued: 'Yes, on ourselves. And I can't tell the police. We're on the wrong side, remember? We can't just run back to them now it suits us. Besides which Rich says we should be cutting all the connections, covering ourselves. If they get caught and talk up the money then it's back to us. It won't look good.'

Rob's face twisted. 'Fuck, he's right.'

'It's all right, Rob. What happened happened.' I rested a hand on his arm. 'It's like you with the running and the punching out traffic lights or whatever you were doing. It's the same thing. We made it all happen, Rob.'

'No! Not what nearly happened to you.'

'Yes. Look at you. Did you want your hands and feet full of holes? Did you ask for that? Well, you did. We made it all happen. That's what the board gave us.'

'That's a lot of weird shit to take in.'

'But do you understand why I don't want to lay anything else on Rich? At least not yet. His head isn't right.'

'No, I don't understand. I think there've been enough secrets.'

'You'd like it all to be easy answers, wouldn't you? Everything on the table. But it isn't like that. You're my friend. You and Rich are my best friends. I expect you to help me keep this secret. That means I want you to lie for me. It's our secret, our lie. And it's not as if it's the first thing we've kept quiet about.'

He tried briefly to disguise a look, then turned his head to one side and nodded slowly.

'One more secret is nothing, Rob.'

'I don't think this particular secret is nothing, Trash.'

I leaned over and spoke, gently. 'Rob,' I said. 'Stop punching walls. It's all over.'

He sniffed and closed his eyes, but I saw the tears. 'Thanks,' I told him. 'I know you'll do this for me.'

39

The police business turned out to be just routine suspicion. Maybe it had been a quiet week for Plod. Maybe during quiet weeks they grilled victims. They could catch victims.

We were all interviewed and re-interviewed separately by the same two CID men, and with an extra WPC for me. And although they had nothing to push us with I'm sure we came close to fucking up. I think they were taken aback by how tough we came on, how un-victimlike we insisted on being. In particular I was way too defensive. In hindsight maybe I should have cried on the WPC's shoulder and screamed black bastards, or feigned interest in the Islington Victim Support Group. Because they just kept looking at me. This one CID guy, the one that looked like a corn-fed Bill Wyman. I could smell his thoughts. He's thinking: if this bitch isn't guilty of something then she bloody well should be. Bright lad. Tough luck. We kept schtum.

Thing is, though, he was right; we were guilty of the odd crime or two. And it's his job to smell that on people. We were now recognisable as people capable of crossing the line, of doing something they shouldn't, and knowing it. And *liking* it. We were Bill Wyman's new nemesis: one-time model citizens newly capable, through a combination of frustration and choice, of ceasing to behave in the prescribed way, and proceeding in a direction the law couldn't control with threats or logic. Society fears people like us more than anything else, because we came to be what we were by reasoned thought. We were not born into it; we don't come from the underprivileged estates and broken homes that breed the career hoodlums. No, we are informed converts, and we are our own breeding ground.

And we are only the first. if I can predict anything at all of the future, it is more people making that choice, and for better – or worse – reasons than ours. As a generation we have the facts, we have the want, and we don't have any alternative. We can see things getting worse, feel the slide. In all classes, at all levels, the gap between what our parents wanted for us, and what is really available, is widening. And growing with it is a ravenous collective bitterness. Okay, me and the boys were soft enough, conscientious enough, not to keep taking the next step. But there will be others who won't find it so hard. Pondering at these things, I remember thinking, Bill Wyman man has his work cut out. How will he deal with that? Well, we've seen the beginnings of it already. It's simply this: he will be given more freedom to do his job, at the expense of everyone else's freedom. His new enemies will choose to exist and operate outside of society. And outside of society there are no citizens, no laws, no right of reply. From there you can follow the thought process virtually anywhere you like. Boy, but thinking can make you tired.

Well, for all their Mutt & Jeff questioning Plod had nothing on us and, as they say in the movies, we walked. Or rather, I walked. Rich got to suck Health Service soup for three more days, poor crippled Rob for ten. I phoned their families. Rob's mum gave me the third-degree then hopped the next Intercity south. I don't know what passed between mother and son but I do know Rob was ready to face up to things. Rich's lot seemed less concerned. I spoke to his dad, who just sounded empty and worn out. In the end Rich heard a big *nada* back from anyone. So, as far as his family went, he really had risked everything. And I suspect that, had we not ended up beaten into cake mix, the same would have been the case for Rob and me. But even knowing he was in hospital didn't sway Rich's family. On being discharged he went back to blond Bob's alone.

I, meantime, did what I did best, and ran home. Only this time, home as I'd always known it wasn't there. The long suffering diplomat – my dad – had left. He was renting a small flat a couple of miles away. No one would tell me why. He had been quarrelling with my mum for a few months, was all I could pick up. There was no other woman, I was sure of that. He kept in touch by letters which contained generous cheques, and instructions for the garden. I suspected and hoped it was just a temporary thing, a mid-life re-evaluation they were going through. It couldn't be permanent – I didn't come from a broken home. I kept thinking this and told myself they'd be all right.

Nicola hadn't told mum about the money I'd stolen. She hadn't had to. They all knew something had been very wrong. I never told them exactly what, but hinted at something about college debts and drugs, just to throw them a bone. I felt lousy. Of course they asked me how much money, if any, I needed to get out of the brown, which made me feel worse. And I cried in front of mum and Nicola, and I think that's when they began to feel I was theirs again. My mum cried, too, although I don't think I'd ever seen her look so happy. My dad was quiet when I phoned him. He sounded very tired, but he promised me he was okay. It was only when I asked when he was coming home that I was sure I could hear him crying.

Nicola was perfect. I admire her so much. She ferried me to outpatient appointments and made sure I followed the nurse's instructions to the letter. My bruises were hurting as they healed deep down, and the blows to my head had caused the muscles in my neck and arms to seize right up, so that I needed her to help me wash and dress. It's not something you want to have to do for a sibling, but my baby sister's selfless love in those weeks humbled me. She attended to everything with grace and care, and each little favour and attention made me think of the person I'd been, and was now ashamed of. At times I was amazed at myself. I couldn't imagine how I'd got to where I had. Just couldn't picture the chain of events. But then I'd see the glow from the spark, and I'd know there had to be a reason. And I'd stop and close my eyes, and think, and for a few moments, sometimes long lucid moments, I'd see clearly the how and the why of everything.

When my limbs stiffened I was often incapacitated for hours at a time. I couldn't lay in bed in one position for long, and had to be helped to move every couple of hours. There was still sometimes a little blood in my urine. Nights were fitful, but more and more I was sleeping real sleep. That felt good, but somehow sad, as if in those hours of sleep something was gradually dying. Proper rest was affecting my mind as much as the loss of it had in reverse. I suppose I was returning to normal. And I know I was resisting it just a little.

Nurse Nicola insisted I move in with her so she could help turn me during the night, and we slept and snored together as we had as kids, breathing in unison, smelling and warming each other.

I phoned Richard a couple of times, but didn't see him again until we met to collect Rob from Whittington. The phone calls were short and unspecific. Our visits to Rob never coincided. Rob had a surprise for us, he said. He was heading back up north. Maybe for good, maybe not. He had some plans he had to follow up quickly, before he was too old.

We couldn't think what he meant by that, although in hindsight I should have been able to guess pretty close. But there was no time to question him. He wasn't even coming back to blond Bob's. His mum was there at Whittington with a taxi to take him to Euston. As it swallowed up him and his crutches I couldn't help thinking what a shitty ending to everything this was. Going home to your mum. No proper goodbye. Not even a night on the drink. The Rob of our college days would never have let the moment pass like this. Poor Rich was devastated. They'd lived in each other's pockets for ten years. Rob had been his mate, his confidant, his rival, his hero. And in the closing of a door he was gone, limping out of his life and home to mother. Rich wept, and I took him back to the flat.

We managed to make love that night, gently, me on top. But it wasn't worth the pain when it was over. I did it for Rich but I still wasn't comfortable with the idea of sex. Rich cried again, but not from his injuries. I hated seeing him like that.

He was taking strong dope to make him sleep – legit prescription stuff – and was okay once he got off. But sleeping next to him reminded me of too much. It was like being tempted back onto a drug. I wanted to be home. For the next few weeks I shuttled between my folks' place and the flat, rarely staying the night with Rich. Then one day I informed him I'd applied for teacher training the following autumn, and he told me, yes, he was up for a job as well, that my dad was pulling strings at the Foreign Office. Exams and vetting would take time, he said, but it might be worth it if my dad could get him on the fast track. My dad had asked him a lot of questions about us, he said. Then I told Rich I'd got a part-time job at the 3-screen cineplex near home, and I might as well be living there most of the time. And he said that sounded sensible. When his ribs were properly healed he was going to do some voluntary work of some kind, impress his future employers, he said. Pad out his CV. Sounds good, I told him. My teacher training would take me to Middlesex, I said.

The autumn was settling in. My dad still had not come home. One day I sat in my room and cried for him. As a little girl, crying had always made him do what I wanted.

I saw Rich at weekends. Gradually the patter and the companionship and everything else came back, and Rich stopped missing Rob so much. I thought about him sometimes too, about different things. At home I still slept with my sister, although I was pretty well recovered. She liked it, and she liked to sit with me when I took my bath, to tell me the last of my bruises were yellowing out, or to read aloud from magazine articles, or shampoo my hair and pour on the clean water. She liked to soap me under the water and dry me with the towel, and I let her. She was always too gentle and I'd have to do the drying over. But I never said no to anything Nicola asked. I never stopped her seeing and feeling for herself that her only sister was there and was not going to go away again.

In March of the following year, roughly six months after we placed our last bet, Richard began working at the Foreign Office in Whitehall. My dad was still not home, and I had stopped believing he was coming home. Five years later Richard is a respected civil servant. Like my dad, his accent and not having been to Cambridge means that he will only get so high on the ladder. But he gets to dress well and meet important people, and he has seen many parts of the world. His pay is lousy but he claims to enjoy his job, and I believe him. In the five years he has not heard from his sister or his parents, despite regular attempts at reconciliation from his end.

In the same month as Richard joined the government, Robin joined the army – this was the plan he had to carry out before he got too old. And he was pushing thirty when he started. Royal Engineers. He remembers how everyone ribbed him throughout basic training, and for months after, calling him grandad, and professor because of his university degree. But he has fitted in and become well liked, which doesn't surprise me. Within a year he made the boxing team and then into 59 commando, the Engineers' elite. His pride in the achievement is obvious.

He's an old, old man by army boxing standards, and his

letters agonise on the hell of keeping his weight down below eleven seven. He's never lost a fight, he says. A few split decisions and the odd ticking off for rough stuff. I'm constantly surprised at how interesting I find hearing about all this, and the virtual blow by blow accounts of fights in his letters never bore me. He describes his style as more thoughtful than most. Not too dramatic to watch, but effective. Deceptive, is the word he uses. He is particularly proud of having perfected a right-hand lead. He says his opponents are always fooled by that, because they don't expect it from an old guy, and they never see it coming. A right-hand lead, he says, is a risky punch requiring great speed and, above all, confidence. Throwing one of those means dropping your guard and leaving your head and torso wide open for your opponent to attack – I suppose that's where the deception comes in. But when they connect they sting an opponent like nothing else. He sounds happy enough, does old Rob. He likes most things about army life: the travel, the close friendships, the simplicity of many aspects of the job; but he loves boxing more than any of it. He says he hopes he can keep doing it for a few more years, and doesn't know what he'll do when he has to give it up, which will, he concedes, be sooner rather than later.

I trained, but never worked as, a teacher. I decided telling people things wasn't my job. I just couldn't master feeling that much certainty about anything. Not like Rob. Although where will his certainty leave him in a few more years? I work in an employment agency in Kent, which I think is a bit of a disappointment to my mum. Sign of the times, I'm afraid, one families like mine will have to get used to. I don't earn much, and I still live at home – another sign of the times. Nicola moved away to college, then to live with her latest boyfriend, whom she keeps on a short lead. She is the organised one, and she makes sure we are always in touch. She deserves a good future, but I don't want to think about that. She was born with love and sense for two, that one. I do not know what I would do without her. We still share a bed whenever she visits without Philip.

I like my job and really throw myself into it, although I know I'm capable of more. But I'm too tired. For now, though, I love thinking I can help find someone some good solid work, something that will take their mind away from panic, and worry, and help them. The problem is – and I've been told this, and told I have to think about it and put it into perspective along with my other goals – the problem is that I take it way too personally when some stuck-up fucking bitch or twat doesn't appreciate the effort I've made to fix them up with something that I think really suits them – often something I'd be glad to have myself. You work fucking hard and you think about them as people and they just don't see it. They see themselves and only themselves and not the effort you have made. When they come on ungrateful I see red. Bright fucking red. I mean it, there are colours in front of my eyes I don't want to be there. Maybe I've dreamt it, but sometimes I find myself knowing I have seen fires in the corners of rooms, not then, but days before when I was angry. I could tell you some things about anger and black lights and fires. And I remember the fires and that's when I wonder if I'm really remembering them or if I dreamed them. It is at those times I can understand a lot of things you are not supposed to understand. Like things Rob once said.

Sometimes when I have bad days I daydream about finding work for everyone who comes into the agency, and making them happy, and that calms me down. I try to see the good colours. When that doesn't work I have to have other daydreams in which things happen to the people who are ungrateful to me – I know their faces and their voices and their histories and strengths and weaknesses, I know what will hurt them, I remember the facts in their files – and that makes the red in

266

front of my eyes go away as well, but I'm not sure why. In these daydreams they get beaten and robbed and hit hard. I see men and women I am angry with getting hurt and I don't feel what is happening to them. And I'm responsible for meting out this justice. And after they've been punished and they're still in pain they realise it's me in control and they know they should have been grateful for my help because it isn't easy matching people up with the right job for not much money or even thanks and then getting told you have to reevaluate your goals, because good jobs don't grow on fucking trees these fucking days. That people can make me feel this way about them makes me even angrier, and it takes more time for the colours to go away. Maybe if they knew what it was like to have someone hurt them, they'd be grateful and better people for it. Some pain would do some people some good, hack some of the scum down off their fucking HIGH HORSES. That's why I dream the daydreams. Well, sometimes I feel better for these daydreams, but usually I forget my anger very quickly and just get on with enjoying my job.

But most of the time I still feel like I did then, six years ago. I still have the fear that things will not hold together, that the things which are putting a roof over my head and the groceries on the table now will not always be there. Something will make things change in a way I can't control and the things I need will be taken away. And now I know, I look back and I under-stand that I must have always been this way. That it is not just the way I lived at a certain time, and the things I did with the boys, which made me have this fear. Look at the boys, they are not like me. They are tougher and wiser, but they do not understand the things I understand, nor would they want to. I don't know whether I envy them that, or whether I think they are being blind. Should I shout out to them? There must have been something in me that was afraid to start with. A seed of fear must always have been in me. That is my personality

– you don't just panic, you have to feel things first. And that fear made me desperate enough to do desperate things. Well, I have done desperate things and I am still afraid. But now I often don't care, which is both bad and a relief. Not caring is a sad and numb feeling, but it is a respite. You are the roomful of drunks, and I am talking, and that's supposed to help. It is all going to get better from here, supposedly.

Anyway, I carried on seeing Rich for the first six months he was in Whitehall, but when I moved away for teacher training – not very far, I admit – that was that. There was no big scene when I went. It was no big deal.

The other diplomat – my dad – stayed in Whitehall long enough to see Rich well established, before taking a permanent posting in Malaysia. Six months into his stay there he died in his sleep of a heart attack. Nobody was with him at the end. No one who knew him suspected anything. He had never complained of any pain.

40

And that, I suppose was the unexpected consequence of what I did, six years ago, in that borrowed flat. Everything else you can look at and say: you deserved that, or: that has balanced out. But my dad's death was an extra punishment thrown in from somewhere I couldn't reach. I took it terrifically hard. It came at a time when what was left of the family was just starting to do okay again; when having dad abroad for a while was helping us focus on being good to each other, in preparation, we hoped, for welcoming him back. My parents had spoken on the phone a few times, and I once overheard mum telling Nic: 'He just needs time.'

And then he was gone.

No one ever said it was my fault, and it would have been selfish and cowardly of me to come out and say it myself, and to take comfort from the reassurances to the contrary that would have resulted. But the possibility was there in front of my eyes. I didn't know what to do. It even drove me back to mass for a while. We went as a family, a few times a week. But something jarred in me every time I entered the building. It got steadily worse until I believed I was bringing something malevolent with me into the service, smuggling in a presence under my coat that I would then let out and the whole thing would end like a horror film, with bodies and crosses and blood on the six o'clock news, all because of me. After I stopped going to mass I was a little unhinged for a while. That part I don't remember too well.

But there was a night in hospital, and then a good deal of time off teacher training while I saw counsellors and a stress specialist. Everyone I saw wanted me to talk. And I sat there thinking: Yeah, right, not in a thousand years.

But I have talked, I've told it all, and part of it is the possibility that my dad worried himself to death over what his daughter was doing to herself. I live with that, but I also live with the possibility that thoughts like that are the worst kind of self-pity: that my dad simply had a heart attack, and that's it.

But he did leave home because of me. No one ever suggested as much, and I'm grateful to mum and Nic for that. But it all fits into place: the letters, phone calls, quizzing about drugs. I think my dad must have despaired when I rejected his help. What father wouldn't? Perhaps he took it out on mum. Perhaps she made him go. I'll never know, because I'm never going to ask. Because I don't deserve to know. I wasn't there when it mattered, and I can't backtrack now.

But if you really understand anything about my story I think that you have to forgive me. There is no telling what situations you will find yourself in. All that is certain is that they will come thick and fast, and that the challenges they'll present will be dressed up differently from the ones my parents' generation once faced with relative assurance. Rich once said something to me about mythology, and he was right. There are dragons in the world, and the most dangerous are the ones we have created ourselves and then let loose, not knowing what to do with them.

I mean that the world is changing too quickly for some of us. It certainly changed too quickly for my dad. It is like a bad dream; we turn around and something else, one more thing that we loved or hated, but that we at least recognised, is gone. And in its place is another dragon.

I have cried my tears for my father. He would want me to forgive myself, and one day I will. I was after all, part of the family he chose to have, the gamble he chose to take. And maybe one day I'll start to forgive myself for what I did one late summer day to two people on their way to a bank, as a part of their job. But I think that's unlikely.

Yes, I know you could say I have suffered retribution. But retribution doesn't reverse what I did. I changed their lives that day.

I turned them into victims. I forced on them a process of reconstruction. I made them repair and rethink themselves. They had no more in the world than I did. Thinking about it makes me want to reach out to them, to know where and how they are now. And that is my punishment, not being able to atone, the one thing I want to do. Yes, I will forgive myself over my dad. But how will I ever stop seeing the shocked white head of a girl called Erica as her thin skull struck the ground and her hair went from blonde to bronze and put the red in front of my eyes. How will I stop seeing her gagging when I forced the gas weapon into her mouth and cut off her air and made her scream that scream of irreparable hurt.

Has this helped? Have you been a roomful of good drunks? I don't know yet. And in fairness to the process it's not something you should know. You should be left with the impression of my failure and my suffering as a warning to yourselves and others.

And fuck that as well.

This is not a morality tale. There are no warnings here, no cautionary lessons. Because the new rules have wiped them out. There are no rewards for good behaviour, no halos for obeying the good angel. Time's on speed, you're dead before it matters.

That's all the answers I have. But I didn't start this to provide answers, only to talk at someone. And I have talked. Thank you for your accelerated time.

PART THREE

41

We don't place bets ourselves any more. We have people to do that for us. We employ other people, too: I have a housekeeper, Richard has a driver; Robin has a 'companion'. My housekeeper calls me Natasha, as does everyone these days.

My husband and I own a town house in Marylebone High Street, which is convenient at weekends. During the week we stay at the flat in Highgate village. Both properties cost a small fortune, I believe. Choosing the furniture and colours for both took a year. Next year we will leave the flat and move into a bigger house closer to Hampstead Heath. We might sell the flat or we might not. Richard knows. Dealing with money is so tedious. Richard does all that. I choose things, and entertain.

We entertain Robin a great deal. We eat and drink and talk and then we have our little ceremony. Richard says we won't have to do the little ceremony for much longer because soon the money will start working for us by itself. He's talking about us living off investments, something like that. I don't mind. I don't mind the ceremony. But it would be nice having one less thing to worry about. Life is such a worry.

Robin is due for dinner any time. I look out the window and here he comes. He is parking his big silver motorbike. I don't need to know about things like motorbikes. Revving its engine, enjoying it a few more seconds before getting off. He has two more motorbikes and two flats of his own, one flat each for him and his companion. I've met her and I suppose she's very beautiful. Certainly better looking than the last one.

The housekeeper has been helping me cook the dinner. We are having three courses. That's another thing I choose, menus. I choose the wine and the cookbooks and the plates and cutlery. I change a lot of these things quite often, but Richard says I will have to stop buying nice things for a while when we sell this flat and convert some of our money into shares. (I really don't follow a lot of this. I just let him and Robin get on with it. There's no need for me to follow it.) That's fine. I don't mind tightening my belt if it will help us in the long run. It will, Richard says. The money is doing no good lying under the floorboards in duffel bags. It's just rotting away, losing its value, he says. Best to make it work for us. But I'm not sure. I'm not sure what happens to money when they take it out of your house and you can't see it. It doesn't seem yours any more.

Here's Robin coming up the stairs and using his key to our flat. Of course, flat isn't really the right word – the housekeeper has two rooms to herself, that's how big it is. Richard is at the house in Marylebone High Street, going through the books, planning our big move into investments. He's had a lot of advice and is very excited. I am worried about the dessert. I'm not sure the housekeeper has grasped the recipe.

Robin is changing out of his leathers and into something nice. He has a room in our flat as well – flat, it's more like a castle! He is with us a lot, like old times but not like old times. No, flat is definitely not the right word. He is looking forward to dinner. Richard should be here any minute. The driver is with him. We pay these people with some of our money. They like working for us because we pay them well. If they work hard for us they can have a job for life. We understand their problems. No one wants to leave us.

I make Robin a Jack Daniel's and tap water, the way he likes, and ask him what he's done with his day. He has spent the morning with his companion and the afternoon in the gym. He talks about moving into a house big enough for a private cinema. He says it may have to wait a year and shakes his head.

276

The doorbell rings. Four rings. That is the code for our Chief Runner. The Chief Runner is the man who oversees the team who place all our bets. He is the most well paid of all our staff, because we have to keep him loyal and honest. Last year we paid him £60,000 in cash, which is nothing to us. Under him are five other runners, two women and three men. They all deliver money to him and he brings it here. Today he hands us a small parcel. Six thousand pounds. An exceptionally slow day. All winners, but poor odds. Robin takes charge of the money. The Chief Runner declines a Jack Daniel's and tap water but takes a cup of Earl Grey tea. He is a black man. He works for me, and I bring him his tea and smile and he smiles.

We are waiting for Richard to come home, and then we can eat. I invited my mum and dad, but they couldn't make it this time. Perhaps I'll go and see them this weekend and take them some presents. Richard is very tanned just now, because we have just been away skiing. We are good skiers, although I like to go slowly. He looks good tanned, and he managed to lose a few pounds on the slopes as well. I am thin and fit. They keep me that way at the health club, because I pay them to.

I am looking forward to seeing Richard walk in the door in his good clothes and his tan. And I am looking forward to the house-keeper and the Chief Runner and Robin seeing him walk through the door and come to me and kiss me. I will look at them looking at me, and at all I have, and at all we have, and we will all feel happiness before sitting down to eat the food I worried so long over.